Scattering Like Light

S.C. Ransom

nosy crow

"Small Blue Thing"

Today I am
A small blue thing
Like a marble
Or an eye

With my knees against my mouth
I am perfectly round
I am watching you

I am cold against your skin
You are perfectly reflected
I am lost inside your pocket
I am lost against
Your fingers
I am falling down the stairs
I am skipping on the sidewalk
I am thrown against the sky
I am raining down in pieces

I am scattering like light
Scattering like light
Scattering like light

Today I am
A small blue thing
Made of china
Made of glass

I am cool and smooth and curious
I never blink
I am turning in your hand
Turning in your hand
Small blue thing

For Pete, with all my love

First published in the UK in 2012 by Nosy Crow Ltd
The Crow's Nest, 10a Lant Street
London, SE1 1QR, UK

Nosy Crow and associated logos are trademarks and/or registered trademarks of
Nosy Crow Ltd

A CIP catalogue record for this book is available from the British Library.

Printed and bound in the UK by Clays Ltd, St. Ives Plc
Typeset by Tiger Media Ltd, Bishops Stortford, Hertfordshire

Papers used by Nosy Crow are made from wood grown in sustainable forests.

3 5 7 9 10 8 6 4 2

ISBN: 978 0 85763 013 1

www.nosycrow.com

www.smallbluething.com

Airport

I could feel the sweat prickle on my forehead as the man in uniform glared at me. "Miss, just go back through and put all the jewellery in there, please," he repeated, nodding towards the small plastic tray. "*All of it*, like it says on the notice," he stressed, as my hand hesitated over my wrist.

"I . . . I . . . I'll just be a minute," I stuttered. Then, under my breath, I hissed, "Callum! I need you now, *quickly!*"

"Come on, please. You're holding up the line." The security guard was getting annoyed. Ahead I could see my parents picking up their belongings from the other side of the X-ray. They hadn't noticed that I'd stopped. I couldn't believe that I hadn't thought this through, that I hadn't realised that the amulet would set off the alarms on the metal detector. Where *was* Callum?

The security guard picked up the tray and thrust it towards me. I couldn't help looking around me, knowing full well that I wouldn't be able to see Callum, but searching for inspiration to explain my odd behaviour. I was clammy with fear. "Callum!" I hissed again, as loudly as I dared.

"What's the hold-up here?" An officious-looking man in a suit was pushing up behind me, desperate to get through and on to his flight. I looked wildly between the two angry men, and swallowed hard.

"There's something not right here. I'm calling for the police," announced the guard, taking in my obvious discomfort. He pressed a red button on the side of the metal detector. Within seconds armed policemen converged on the spot, their guns conspicuously at the ready.

"Really, there's no need for that," I said as calmly as I could. "It's just that my bracelet is very tight and it hurts to take it off, that's all." I smiled at him as sweetly as I could, trying not to look at the machine guns. They hadn't pointed them at me yet, and I really didn't want them to. In the meantime, my parents had noticed the commotion and were heading back towards me.

"Can't you just examine it where it is?" I asked, trying not to sound too desperate, hoping that I could avoid a confrontation between Mum and the guard.

"That's not the procedure. All jewellery has to be removed until you can go through the scanner without setting it off."

"Alex? What's going on?" called my mum. "What's happening?" she asked the guard pointedly. "Why won't you let my daughter through?"

"Stand back, please," said one of the policemen, stepping in front of her.

"Look, I'm just taking it off now, OK? Then I'll come through the machine." I put my finger under the bracelet and eased it off my wrist, making sure that I kept my finger inside for as long as possible. "Come on, Callum, get here now!" I muttered again. I was just about to drop it into the tray when there was a welcome tingle in my hand and a familiar voice in my head. "Go, I've got everything covered here. You'll be fine."

Heaving a sigh of relief I slipped the amulet into the little tray along with my watch and necklace. "OK, shall I come through now?" I asked the guard hopefully. His colleague at the X-ray machine picked up the tray and lifted the amulet out with the end of a pen. Trying not to look at what they were doing, I took a tentative step towards the metal detector. "Is it OK to go ahead?" I asked, catching the eye of one of the policemen, not daring to take another step until he had finally nodded. Mum had wisely kept silent as soon as she had seen the guns, but one glimpse of her tight-lipped expression told me that she wasn't finished.

I stepped carefully through the threshold of the detector, which remained mercifully silent. They weren't done with me though. A female guard stepped forward and gave me a thorough pat-down, and all the while I was trying not to look at what the guys by the machine were doing with the amulet. Finally the female guard declared me safe, and I turned towards the conveyor to retrieve my belongings. Dad had picked up most of the stuff, but the guard holding my amulet was clearly waiting for me.

"This yours?" he asked, dropping the amulet from his pen into a separate tray.

"Yes." I nodded. "Can I have it back, please?"

"It's been randomly selected for further testing," he announced in a bored tone.

I tried not to panic as I thought about what Callum might be doing to keep me safe, and how much longer he could keep it up. Desperately trying to keep my fear contained, I smiled at the guard. "Oh, I see. What does that mean?"

I was trying to talk to him as the luggage from the impatient queue behind me started to pour through the X-ray machine and down the conveyor. The man in the suit brushed me aside so that he could retrieve his laptop case, and I felt his radiating disapproval.

The guard continued indifferently, "It's got to be tested for traces of explosives." He placed a small cloth in some special tongs and started to wipe the bracelet with it, being careful not to actually touch it himself. I bit my lip.

"What are they doing now, Alex? What's the hold-up?" Mum was at my side, bristling with indignation.

"They seem to think that my bracelet might be dangerous, that's all," I answered as calmly as I could, wondering if at any second Callum might lose the fight that was no doubt raging around us. If he was beaten I would be as good as dead within moments. I knew that he would give everything he possibly could to keep me safe, but I had to do my bit and get the amulet back on my wrist as quickly as possible.

I forced myself to relax as the guard put the small cloth into some sort of detector, then pressed a few buttons. The wait seemed interminable but was probably no more than a minute. Finally a little green light popped up on the detector. The guard's shoulders slumped slightly. He had obviously hoped for a more interesting result. Really bored now, he picked up the tray with the amulet in it and tossed it on the table in front of me, already looking around for his next victim. "All clear. Next!" he shouted as the tray rattled to a stop. I reached for the amulet gratefully, desperate to have the comforting silver band back on my wrist. But as I lifted it my eye was drawn by some engraving on the inside. Puzzled, I looked closer. There were definitely words there, words I had never seen before. But I didn't have time to examine it further. Sliding it back into place on my right wrist, I heaved a great sigh of relief as the familiar tingle washed through my arm.

"Honestly, it was OK, there's no one around," said Callum. "You didn't need to panic."

"How was I supposed to know that?" I muttered under my breath.

"What was that, Alex? Did you say something?"

"No, Mum, nothing. Just thanking the security for being so vigilant." I smiled at her as convincingly as I could manage. I felt cold and clammy as my breathing and heart rate returned to normal. We walked swiftly through to the departure lounge.

"I'm just going to find the loos; I won't be a minute," I announced as my parents looked about for somewhere to sit.

"Don't be too long, Alex," Dad called after me. "They'll be calling our flight soon."

I waved to show him that I'd heard, then quickly put on my mobile phone earphones. As soon as I was out of sight I found a quiet spot and leaned against the wall. "Don't do that to me – I was really worried!" I hissed to Callum. "What took you so long, anyway?"

The voice in my head was as rich as chocolate, and I could picture his gorgeous features as he spoke. His tousled, dark-blond hair, his perfect skin, his slightly crooked nose and, of course, his mesmerising blue eyes. I couldn't help stealing a glance at the amulet, where the stone was dancing in the bright airport lights: the stone that looked exactly like those eyes. . .

Callum sounded a bit bashful. "I went off to see if I could travel on planes. I've never tried before, but they left me on the runway. I know, I know," he said as I snorted with relieved laughter, "but it was worth a pop. I could have come with you if it'd worked!"

"I couldn't believe that you weren't right there."

"I know you don't like me talking to you when you're with your family, and anyway who knew the queue was going to move that quickly?"

"It's not that I don't like it," I corrected him. "It's just that it makes life extra difficult, that's all. I always want you around, you know that."

"I do know that," he replied. I didn't have my mirror out, but I heard the smile in his voice. I could see Callum only in reflections. He was a Dirge, someone trapped in a half-life of misery after drowning in the River Fleet in London. My bracelet, or amulet, matched the ones that Callum and his friends wore, and when I had found it in the mud of the Thames it connected me irrevocably to him. I had given Callum my heart, and I was determined to find some way to make a future together possible. And I was working on a plan that I was feeling pretty confident about. But my amulet was the only escape route for the other Dirges, and I had to be really careful to keep it on at all times: it was the only way to be safe.

"Well, panic over anyway," I said. "It's just I still remember that horrible fight with Lucas." I tried not to shudder as I thought about it. Lucas had very nearly compelled me to remove the amulet, and I never wanted to go through that again.

I could feel Callum's featherlight touch on my cheek. "He's gone, I promise, and none of the others will do that to you, not while I'm around."

I couldn't resist it any longer; I pulled a little mirror out of my pocket and pretended to check my hair. Callum's glorious face appeared behind my shoulder in its usual spot. It was even better than my memory, and I just had to smile at him. I reached up towards my shoulder and gently stroked his cheek, trying to be an unobtrusive as possible. It felt as if I were trying to stroke a thin gossamer film. "Thank you for keeping me safe," I breathed, staring into those deep-blue eyes.

"I love you, Alex, and I'm going to look after you in whatever way I can."

"I'm going to miss you so much while we're away," I sighed, glancing at my watch. "Oh! I've got to get back to the others, Mum'll be having kittens if I'm much longer. Will you stay with me until we get to the gate, even if I can't speak to you?"

"Of course," said Callum. "I just wish I could come with you."

I stashed the mirror back in my pocket after one last glimpse of his face, then walked quickly back towards my family.

"Oh, Alex, there you are! I was just going to send out a search party," scolded my mum as I threw myself down into one of the empty chairs.

"I don't know why you get so het up," drawled my brother, Josh. "We'll be ages here, and then even longer at the gate. It's all a ploy to get us to go shopping." He paused, then smirked at me. "Time for you to go and get some overpriced perfume to make you irresistible to Max."

I laughed. We were going to meet some old friends of our parents' in Spain, who had two kids, Max and Sabrina. We hadn't seen them for a few years and we were all looking forward to meeting up again at the hotel. But the last time I'd seen Max he was short for his age with huge braces on his teeth, lank, greasy hair and an obsessive interest in sports cars.

"Max!" I snorted. "Oh sure, he's just my type. More likely that you'll need something to win Sabrina over – perhaps a paper bag to put over your head?"

I could tell that Josh was about to come up with some pithy put-down when Mum butted in. "I told you we didn't have much time. Our flight has just been called." She didn't even try to keep the smugness out of her voice. "Come on, let's go."

I could see Dad smiling as he turned to pick up the bags.

"You played right into your mum's hands. She'll have us here at the crack of dawn next time!"

"Oh don't," groaned Josh. "I might refuse to come with you if she gets me out of bed any earlier."

"And turn down a free beach holiday in Spain?" I laughed. "Yeah, right!"

We gathered all our hand luggage and started the long walk to the gate. All the time I was conscious of the familiar tingle in my wrist that told me Callum was next to me. He was mostly quiet but I loved knowing he was there, only occasionally asking questions, which I could answer with a nod or shake of the head. I tried hard not to think about the fact that I was going to have to say goodbye very soon.

At the gate the plane didn't seem to be ready, so we settled ourselves down into another set of chairs to wait again. Callum continued to talk to me about the things he was seeing, what he had been doing and generally anything that would stop both of us dwelling on our impending separation. He was talking about the security guard at the scanner, when I suddenly remembered the inscription on the amulet.

"I just need to tell Grace something," I announced as I leapt up from my chair. "I'm going to ring her quickly."

"I do wish you'd thought of that earlier. Don't go far," said Mum, exasperated.

"I won't," I muttered, reaching for my earphones. I walked towards one of the windows and looked out at the plane that was waiting to take us to Spain. There was a frenzy of activity going on underneath, with hordes of people getting it ready to leave.

"What's up, Alex?" Callum's voice was crystal clear in my head.

"Earlier, when I took off the amulet I saw something inside, some engraving. Did you see it?"

"Nope, don't think so. What was it?"

"Well, words, I guess. Not a picture anyway."

"So it has engraving – what's the big deal?"

"It didn't used to, that's what. When I first got it I examined it pretty closely, and there was nothing there. I did think at one point I had seen something, but when I looked again it was just the beaten silverwork. But today it was really clear."

"That's weird. What did it say?"

"I didn't have the chance to read it. Is it safe to have another look now?"

I could sense Callum's hesitation, but he finally spoke. "There doesn't seem to be anyone about. Keep your finger in it while it's off your wrist; that should give you some extra protection, and we'll still be able to talk. I'll let you know immediately if I see anyone."

"OK, let's have a look." I gently prised the C-shaped bracelet off my wrist, keeping my index finger firmly inside the band as instructed, and the comforting tingle told me that I still had my connection with Callum. I quickly turned it over, peering into the inside. There, engraved along the underside of the silver band, were some ornate letters.

mor memoriae

"Can you see that?" I breathed. "That *so* wasn't there before!"

"Spooky. What does it mean?"

"I don't know. I think it's Latin, but I'm not sure. And is that scratch between the words an 's', do you think?"

"Let me look. I don't even know if I know any Latin." We both peered at it silently for a minute, then he sighed. "Nope, not a clue. Can't have been one of my subjects."

"But it's so weird! How come I can suddenly see it when it wasn't there when I first found it?"

He considered that silently for a moment. "Hmm. Have you looked at the inside since we got it back on your wrist in the hospital?"

I thought back. So much had happened in the few short weeks since my brush with death at the hands of Callum's sister, Catherine. She had stolen the amulet and then persuaded me that she had destroyed it. The second I finally got it back from her accomplice, my ex-boyfriend Rob, I had stuck it back on my wrist and refused to take it off. The danger was one thing, but the thought of not being able to talk to Callum was far worse. Without it I couldn't call him to my side, see him in the mirror, feel his featherlight touch. I'd never felt so lonely in all my life.

When Catherine had stolen all my memories in order to escape life as a Dirge, Callum had been able to take a copy and had saved my life by putting them back. Now, with my amulet on, I was able to see the emotion in people's thoughts. When people were happy or thinking of good memories, their auras were shades of yellow, bright sparks of happiness that flicked above their heads like fireflies. Angry thoughts showed up as red clouds, while unhappy, miserable people had purple mist around their heads. Glancing at a crowd of passengers whose flight had been delayed I could see mostly red clouds above the adults and flecks of yellow bouncing around above the heads of the children.

Something in the transfer of memories back to me had given me this unexpected ability, and I loved it. I could tell when my friends were down and needed cheering up, or if Mum was cross about something. Maybe the amulet had given me the ability to see the mysterious lettering too.

"Apart from when it was stolen, it's not left my wrist for a second, so I haven't looked," I admitted. "But it could make sense that I got this talent from you too." In the faint reflection in the large plate-glass window I could see him behind me, looking at the amulets that were on our superimposed wrists. The strange blue opal-like stone glinted in the bright light, the flecks of gold flashing briefly whenever I moved.

"What else is it going to reveal, I wonder?" he murmured. "What other strange things will you find that you can do?"

"Who knows?" I replied as casually as possible, not wanting to discuss those possibilities. Not in the middle of the airport, and not before I had done some investigating. "I'll ask Josh about the inscription; I think he did some Latin at school. Or google it when I get to the hotel."

"Look – your mum's waving at you. I think you're all about to go through the gate. Do you want to say goodbye now, rather than on the plane?"

"I wish you could come with me," I grumbled.

"I know, it sounds like fun. Two weeks of eating, sleeping and surfing – what more could you possibly want?"

"You, silly. That's what I want, and don't pretend you don't know."

"I'll be here when you get back, I promise."

"I love you, Callum, more than anything else in the world."

"Me, too. Look, your mum's coming over; you should go. I'll see you back here really soon." I felt his lips brush my cheek with the softest of touches.

"Bye," I sighed. "I just wish I could give you a hug and say goodbye properly."

"Have a good time, gorgeous. I love you." His beautiful voice echoed in my head, and then abruptly the tingle was gone.

The trip to our favourite holiday destination was uneventful but slow, and it gave me time to think about my plan. I knew that I had been responsible for releasing the Dirge called Lucas from his life of misery. What I didn't yet know was what had happened to him: if, as I hoped, he was alive somewhere, that meant I could rescue Callum too. But if I had allowed him to die . . . I had to find out, to be sure. I had spent the last few weeks scouring the Internet for information, but there had been nothing about him appearing in the river as Catherine had done. So my plan to be united with Callum in the real world was on hold until I knew that he would be safe. And then I would also be sure that I would never again have to speak with Catherine. She seemed to know about how to release the Dirges, and thought that I needed her. It made me feel pretty smug to know that I didn't. Thinking about Callum kept me occupied for most of the rest of the flight, imagining how brilliant it would be to have him with me; the fun we would have in Spain.

It was late afternoon before we finally reached the hotel, and Josh and I had the opportunity to go down to the beach. The weather was perfect, still warm but with a light wind to cool us down. The beach was long and wide, and out on the water huge numbers of bright sails whipped back and forth as the expert kite-surfers took advantage of the constant breeze and jumped and twisted above the waves. As usual I was amazed that none of them got tangled up, but they were all too good. Every few minutes one of them glided effortlessly to the shore, and in a single motion scooped up their boards and guided their huge kites up the beach where teams of beautiful people were ready to anchor them to the ground. As an advert for a healthy, athletic lifestyle it was hard to beat.

Josh and I walked further along the sand towards the area where the new surfers were learning to control their slightly smaller kites. As we walked I couldn't help relive one of my favourite fantasies: walking along the beach hand in hand with Callum, watching the sun glint off his golden hair, feeling his strong fingers intertwined with mine. He was gorgeous and fit enough to blend seamlessly into the picture, I thought, looking at all the toned bodies lying around. I wondered again how long it would be before I could put my plan into action, a plan that would rescue him from his hideous existence and allow us to be together.

"Max should be here somewhere," said Josh, interrupting my happy thoughts. "He said that his lesson should be finishing around now. Can you see him anywhere?"

"No," I replied, squinting into the sun, which although low in the sky was still bright.

A deep voice cut across our conversation. "Alex and Josh! Long time no see!"

I looked round in surprise at the stranger standing behind us. With his wetsuit rolled down to his hips, revealing a perfect six-pack, he towered above me, his wet dark hair pushed casually off his forehead.

"Max?" I gasped, as he and Josh hugged briefly.

"Hi, Alex." He turned towards me, flashing the most perfect smile. I felt my jaw drop: the geeky teenager was long gone. Max could have been modelling the surf gear. He was absolutely stunning.

Surfing

"Honestly, Max, I would totally have passed you in the street, you've changed so much since I last saw you." We were lounging around one of the low tables in our favourite beach bar, keeping a wary eye out for stray volleyballs from the match going on in front of us.

"How many years has it been since we were all last here?" asked Max, looking at his sister, Sabrina. "I can never remember that sort of stuff."

Sabrina pursed her lips and folded her arms. "Oh, ages. I mean, we were both pretty young then, weren't we, Alex?"

"Young enough that we weren't allowed out alone in the evening, any of us!"

"However hard we begged, I remember that!" laughed Josh.

Although we were old family friends, Max and Sabrina had been living in Hong Kong for a few years. They'd recently moved back to England, to a house not far from ours, and I was looking forward to catching up with Sabrina during the holiday.

We were all staying at the same hotel. It was really cool, and Josh and I loved it. Breakfast was served until late, there was a great pool, and then there was the beach: miles and miles of uninterrupted golden sand that wasn't stuffed full of loud tourists and toddlers. It was perfect for surfing and was studded with beach bars: every day all the kite-surfers descended on the various bars, each with its own unique appeal. One had huge beanbags on terraces overlooking the sea where you could watch the sun set, another had a huge selection of frozen fruit that they would juice into drinks, and our favourite had the beach volleyball court.

We were settled in one of the best seating areas, having kicked off our flip-flops and stretched out. On the other side of the table the boys were intently watching the action on the court.

Sabrina leaned over, checking that the boys weren't listening. "So, Alex, come on, who is this mystery boyfriend?"

"Oh, he's more of a penfriend really, I suppose. What's Josh told you about him?"

"Not much at all, despite my prodding him. So what's his name?"

"Callum," I admitted.

"And where does he live?"

"Venezuela. We don't get to see each other much."

"Wow, that is a long way. How did you meet him?"

Although he was facing away from us I could see that Max was suddenly still, and I just knew he was listening. "Ah, well, sort of via a friend. It's not been going on long so we haven't, I mean, I've not travelled there, not yet." I tried to sound as uninterested as possible, not wanting to get into a lengthy conversation about Callum. Keeping track of the lies was just too difficult. "So what about you? How's your love life? Busy?"

"Ha! I wish. There's no one right now," she replied, giving me a knowing grin as the match finished and the boys turned back to face us. "But give me time!"

She picked up her freshly squeezed orange juice and sipped it through the straw as she looked at some of the other people sitting around. "This place doesn't change, does it?"

There were some seriously beautiful people there: kite-surfers who were tall, bronzed and fit, girls with tiny shorts and legs that seemed to go on forever, and everyone had tousled, sun-kissed hair. I felt very pale and uninteresting in comparison, and looking around our little group it was obvious Sabrina felt the same. Neither of us had much of a tan and we were never going to be as cool as some of the others who looked like they spent their entire summers there. The boys looked rather more as if they fitted in.

"Do you think any of these guys ever go home?"

"Nah," drawled Max. "I reckon they move from here to the ski slopes and back again. It's a lifestyle I think I could get used to."

"So how's the kite-surfing?" Josh asked him. I knew he was keen to try it, as he had been a bit young the last time we had been to the beach, but he was worried about humiliating himself in front of a crowd of semi-professionals.

Max nodded enthusiastically. "Yeah, it's been good."

"Have you been having lessons?"

"I've had a few," he said. "I think it's going quite well. I'm not sure how many more I'll take though. Hiring those kites is expensive and you don't get very long."

Josh rubbed his hands together. "Oh, great, you can give me some tips. I've been dying to have a go at it, and it would be great to have someone I know teach me rather than one of those condescending instructors!"

"Ah, well, I'm not sure I'm good enough to do that." Max coughed a little nervously. "You'd be far better getting a pro to teach you."

Sabrina laughed. "Come on, Max, don't be so modest! Why don't you just tell them?"

Josh and I turned to look at Max, who was going a deep shade of red. "OK, OK, I suppose," he mumbled. "I seem to be quite good at it, and the instructor has been great. He's asked if I want to enter into some sort of competition for beginners next week, but I'm not sure. I just want to have some fun."

"Really?" asked Josh, looking impressed. "That's excellent. Do you think we could join your lesson? I'm going to need a really good instructor."

"Do you fancy having a go, Alex?" asked Sabrina. "I'm thinking about trying it."

"You must be mad!" I said. "There's no way I'm going to do that; I'd maim someone. I'm going to work my way through the pile of books I've brought while I get a tan!"

"That's very lazy of you," laughed Max. "Aren't you going to get any exercise at all?"

"I might take the odd stroll up the beach, but I'm on holiday." I stretched out and dug my toes into the sand. "Eating and lounging around here is about as much exercise as I intend to take."

"We'll have to roll you back on the plane then," teased Josh. "Maybe we should think about booking you an extra seat... Look out!"

We all made a quick grab for our drinks as a volleyball landed squarely on our table, but Max was too late. His glass went flying into his lap, the remains of the beer soaking his shorts. The player responsible came running over, apologising profusely in Spanish.

"No worries, mate," said Max, smiling tightly as he handed back the ball. "It was nearly finished." He sat back down, wincing as the cold cloth stuck to his skin.

"You need to change; that's not a good look. You'll never

pull like that."

Max shot his sister a venomous glance. "Thanks for the advice, Sabrina."

"You on the pull then, mate?" asked Josh. "What happened to the lovely Kate?"

"Ah, you know how it is," replied Max. "We wanted different things. She's history now."

"Really? I thought you two were pretty serious."

"Yeah, that was the problem. So did she. I just wanted a bit of a laugh."

"Ah," said Josh knowingly.

"Poor girl, she was gutted," said Sabrina to me in an undertone. "She thought she had him nicely tucked up."

I tried to make an appropriate noise, but as I didn't know Kate it was difficult to get too worked up either way. "Obviously never heard of the 'treat them mean, keep them keen' rule," I muttered back.

"What are you two whispering about over there?" asked Max, standing up and pulling uncomfortably at his soggy shorts.

"Nothing," I laughed. "Max, you *really* need to go and change. Maybe we should all head back now? Mum and Dad want to take me and Josh out for an early dinner tonight."

"Yeah, OK," Max agreed. "Let's all meet up on the beach tomorrow, then." He looked at me and smiled. "Are you sure we can't persuade you to give the kite-surfing a crack, Alex?"

"Not a chance," I laughed, caught off guard for a second by the way his eyes crinkled up. I was still stunned by the change in him. His dark hair had dried into a perfectly dishevelled look, and in the last of the afternoon sun his eyes were glinting with amusement. I could see why the luckless Kate had been keen to keep hold of him. Suddenly feeling a bit flustered, I fished under the low table for my flip-flops. "Come on, time to get back to the hotel."

It wasn't until much later that I realised I hadn't given Callum a thought all afternoon. Not, in fact, since I had met Max on the beach. "It's only because he's an old friend, that's all," I muttered crossly to myself as I looked at the amulet. The stone flashed in the dim light, but its depths didn't move or swirl. It looked like a perfectly ordinary stone and not a bit like the mysterious, powerful thing that I knew it was. Even the auras above people's heads didn't seem as vibrant this far from London. Callum seemed an impossibly long way away from me and I found myself clenching my fists and screwing my eyes tightly shut, recalling every detail I could of his exquisite features. But the details blurred in my mind. "I still love you, Callum, no matter how far away I am, remember that," I whispered, and I wondered for a moment who I was trying to convince.

The next morning I found a quiet area on the beach where I could sunbathe and read while the others went off to surf. I still felt really guilty about forgetting Callum quite so quickly. As I settled down on my towel with my book, the sun caught on the golden flecks in the depths of the stone in the amulet and I wondered what he was doing at that exact moment. Was he stalking the cinemas, looking for happy people watching comedy films, gathering the sustenance he needed for the day? Or was he in the Whispering Gallery of St Paul's Cathedral, where he and the others lived? But as I had those thoughts I knew exactly where he would be; up at the Golden Gallery above the top of the St Paul's dome. It was our special place; the only place where he appeared to me to be real and solid and – well, properly human. Over the last couple of months we had spent as much time as possible up there. And I would bet all the money in my savings account that he was leaning on the railings, looking at the view, thinking of me.

"I miss you, Callum. I'm not sure if you can hear me but, in case you can, I wanted to tell you again. I miss you horribly."

I picked up my book and considered it, but the trials of Jo, Meg, Beth and Amy were not going to distract me. As I put it back down with a sigh the amulet glinted on my wrist, reminding me of the inscription on its underside. How weird that it should suddenly appear like that. Once I translated it, would it give me any clues? Would it confirm what I hoped about how Callum and I could be together forever?

I pulled my little rucksack towards me and rummaged around in it for my notebook. I had written the words there after Callum and I had looked at them in the airport. Flicking through the pages I came to where I had scribbled them down.

mor memoriae

Resolving to ask Josh about it as soon as I could, I picked up my book again and settled back on to the warm sand.

Later on I caught up with the others. The three of them were lounging by the pool looking completely exhausted.

"Honestly, Alex, you should come tomorrow; it's really great fun," said Sabrina, wincing as she reached to pick up her juice from the table.

"It looks like it! All three of you seem ready to expire! So, anyone but Max actually get on to the water today?" They all looked shiftily at each other. Finally both Sabrina and Josh spoke at once.

"It wasn't really about that today. . ."

"You have to learn to control the kite first, you know, otherwise. . ."

I held up my hand. "It's OK, I get the picture. No racing through the waves, clearly. I'm glad that I didn't waste my time coming to watch you. How about tomorrow? Did the instructor say you could go in the sea then?" I tried not to smirk at Josh but failed utterly.

"Actually, he did say that they did really well and showed promise," said Max.

I glanced over at him. He was sitting on the edge of his sunlounger, elbows on knees with his head dipped. His thick dark hair obscured his face. "Are you OK, Max?" I asked gently, touching him briefly on the shoulder. He flinched and glanced up at me, brushing the hair out of his face with his long fingers. I couldn't help noticing how brown he had gone already, and the healthy pink glow to his cheeks.

"Uh, sorry. I'm just a bit wiped out. The instructor was keen to find out how much he could get me to do, and it was all a bit more energetic than yesterday. I'm not sure I can move." He smiled briefly.

"Well, how about we give the bar a miss tonight, but meet here later and then go into town for a pizza?" asked Sabrina, wincing again. Max glanced over at his sister and a look that I didn't understand passed between them.

"Perfect," agreed Josh, stretching out. "In that case, I'm going to get some rest right here. Wake me twenty minutes before you want to leave, will you?"

As good as his word, Josh stayed on the sun lounger while the pool closed around him, and gave himself the briefest of time to get ready before we met up at the bar. Tarifa town wasn't too far away and the hotel had a minibus that ferried the guests to and fro in the evening. Our favourite pizza restaurant was the one we always described as being in a cave. We'd been there frequently as children, and the low arched ceiling in the old Spanish building along with the dim lighting, no windows and lots of dark wood made it feel very much as if you were underground. They also produced pizzas the size of wagon wheels, and I only ever ordered half a one. Josh, though, had a huge appetite and had been getting through a whole one for years.

We waited in a queue for a while before getting a table, and were soon tucking into the enormous platefuls of food. The others had worked up a considerable appetite and they attacked their pizzas with enthusiasm. Eventually, though, even Josh slowed down and we looked at the carnage on the table. My brother leaned back, fingers linked behind his head.

"Oh, I needed that. Do you think we'll be as hungry after every lesson?"

Max was chasing his last piece of pizza around the vast plate. "I always am." He chewed for a second then pushed the plate to one side. "You going to finish that, sis?"

"Help yourself." Sabrina slid the plate towards him. "You need to start training yourself to eat less before you go to university or you'll be broke within a week."

"Very true," mumbled Max through a large mouthful of pepperoni.

"Which ones have you applied to?" I asked.

"First choice Leeds, insurance Exeter."

"I've got Leeds down too," said Josh. "I didn't know you

might be going there as well. That'd be good."

"Depends on my grades," Max replied gloomily. "The exams were harder than I expected. I'm not sure that I'll get into either."

"What subjects did you take?" I asked.

"History, English and Latin."

Latin! Perfect. I could get Max to translate the inscription for me. He would know much more than Josh. I turned to him and smiled. "All of the subjects I gave up as soon as possible! I don't know how you write all those dull essays."

"You do sciences, don't you?" he asked. I nodded. "Well, I'm clueless about any of that. So we make a good pair, don't we?"

At this, a look passed between Max and Sabrina and, much to my annoyance, I found myself blushing.

"So what are your plans then, Alex?" Sabrina cupped her chin in her hand and leaned forward, a friendly, interested smile on her face. "Which universities are you going to apply for?"

Despite the warm Spanish night, her question made me shudder and I felt a cold clammy feeling creeping down my back.

"Alex is still thinking about that, aren't you, sis?" said Josh kindly. "Her work experience at the vet's wasn't exactly a barrel of laughs."

"No, you could say that," I said, sighing. "It was a complete nightmare, in fact, and now my plans for university are shot to pieces. Ever since I was small, all I've want to be is a vet, but the grim reality is that it's actually a mostly dull job with the occasional killing spree to liven things up."

The others laughed awkwardly, not sure how serious I was being. I carried on:

"One day, they brought in a little dog. It was a stray that had been hit by a car." The memory was fresh and clear in my mind; I could almost feel the matted white fur, smell the sharp antiseptic, see the trust in the dog's eyes. "He was horribly injured and was facing a life of abject misery. So I got the job of holding him, to keep him calm and talk to him while Mr Henderson gave him a fatal injection."

I tried not to think about the details, holding the little dog as the anaesthetic did its work, watching as his tail, wagging throughout despite the horrific injuries, finally slowed, and as his eyes turned from soft and warm and welcoming to cold and glassy as the spark in them faded.

Not daring to raise my head I carried on. "It was hideous. And it's made me realise I'm just not cut out to be a vet. The trouble is it's left me with no idea what I'm going to do now."

I glanced up and saw that Max was watching me intently, a look of understanding and compassion in his eyes. His hand reached across the table and gave mine a gentle squeeze, holding on to my fingers for just that fraction of a second longer than he should. I suddenly found that I couldn't hold his gaze and looked down quickly at the tabletop again. He let go and the conversation moved on around me, and I smiled and laughed in all the right places, but something wasn't right. I couldn't work out if it was the memory of the death of the little dog that was unsettling me, or the memory of Max's touch. My fingers felt as if they were burning where his had held mine.

Rescue

Although it seemed to be asking for trouble, I started watching Max and the others kite-surf every day. Max was getting seriously good and was looking more and more as if he was one of the locals. Every afternoon we went to the beach bar and most nights the four of us ended up in the town. Both sets of parents had insisted that we got back to the hotel at a reasonable hour, but we still had time to dance and talk and laugh, and every night I tried to ignore the growing interest in Max's glances. And each day I tried to pretend that I wasn't intrigued by him, and flattered by his interest.

On the Saturday night we negotiated that we could stay out a bit later and managed to get into a party on the beach. It was held at one of the bars along from the hotel. There was no moon, and away from the road the only lights were from the fantastic array of stars and the twinkling lights on the horizon. I couldn't quite believe that I was looking at Africa: the lights were in Morocco, just a few miles away over the Strait of Gibraltar. The wind had dropped and as we approached the party the music thudded out into the dark. It seemed really bright after the darkness of the beach, and I could feel myself blinking as we looked around. All the cool and beautiful people were there, lounging about or dancing in the small area where the tables had been pushed aside.

Max's kite-surfing instructor was with some friends and we were immediately invited to join his group. The friends were all fantastically fit and I could tell that Josh felt slightly intimidated. Max, though, was looking perfectly at home, flirting with the girls. I spent hours dancing with Sabrina and the others from her surf class, but I couldn't help stealing the odd glance in his direction. After a while he disappeared from view, and it wasn't until I went to the loo a bit later that I saw him, deep in conversation with a gorgeous brunette. She was obviously a kite-surfer, tanned and athletic, with a sleek short crop that showed her long and elegant neck to full effect. I couldn't hear what they were saying but she was using her hands to describe something to him. He was smiling and nodding, and as I watched he leaned towards her and. . .

"Alex, are you OK?" Josh had appeared and was standing right in the way.

"Yes, I'm fine. It's a great party, isn't it?" I moved to one side so that I could see behind him. Max and the girl had gone. I quickly scanned around, and finally saw him. Max was leaving the party, following her away from the lights and into the gloom beyond. For some reason that really annoyed me and I couldn't work out why. What Max did was really none of my business, and there was no reason why he shouldn't pick up a girl at a party. I just didn't want him to, I realised. I wanted him to be there so that I could talk with him and laugh about the music and the terrible dancing of the guy in the fluorescent shirt.

Josh had followed my gaze. "He fancies you, you know."

"Really? I'd not noticed. Anyway, it looks as if he's got over it." I tried to cover up the slightly regretful tone in my voice.

"Come on, it's your turn to get me a drink." Josh slung his arm around my shoulders as he manoeuvred me to the bar, giving me a quick squeeze as we walked. "Don't be so hard on yourself, Alex. I mean, who's to know?"

"What are you talking about?"

"Oh, nothing. Just enjoy yourself, that's all I'm saying. You're on holiday, after all."

I carried on dancing with Sabrina but I wasn't as enthusiastic about it as before. I couldn't get the picture of Max smiling at that girl out of my head. Eventually I forced it away by wondering what Callum was doing, and the more I thought about him, the less I wanted to be at the party.

After a while I noticed that Max had reappeared, joking and laughing with Josh. He was looking slightly dishevelled and was clearly in a very good mood. There was no sign of the brunette. I tried to ignore him but at one point I couldn't resist looking over to where they were standing. Max was staring straight at me, a half-smile on his lips, and when he saw me looking back he quickly turned away.

Moments later he was at my shoulder. "Fancy a dance?" He was holding out his hand, waiting to lead me across to the tiny dance floor. The candles and fairy lights made his dark hair shine, his eyes unreadable. Callum would understand that there was no harm in a dance, wouldn't he? I was about to take Max's hand when I remembered the brunette: not an hour before he had left the party with her, and a desire not to be his second conquest of the night washed over me.

"I'm a bit bored with dancing now." I shrugged as nonchalantly as possible, determined to make a point. His smile faded and he turned away.

I didn't sleep well and the next morning I woke up ridiculously early. Sabrina was snoring gently in the other bed so I couldn't turn on the light to read. Finally I gave in and got up, hoping to clear my headache by heading for the beach. Leaving a note I eased the door open silently and escaped into the cool morning air.

I enjoyed the early morning and had done this before: walking along the huge beach pretty much on my own, watching the little birds race around on the sand between the waves, listening to the silence. I could go for miles without seeing more than a handful of people.

As I walked I tried to put Max out of my mind and focus on what was important: working out how to bring Callum over so we could be together. First, I *had* to find out what had happened to Lucas after he'd attacked Rob. I knew that he hadn't taken all of Rob's memories, because when Rob came round he could remember everything apart from the last five weeks, everything since I'd found the amulet, in fact. I'd fought Lucas using the power in my amulet and he'd dissolved into a puddle of sparks. Without a complete set of memories, it didn't seem possible that he could have done the same as Catherine and come back to life. Or *was* it the same? Was Lucas sitting in a London hospital somewhere with only five weeks of Rob Underwood's memories in his mind? Or was he dead? Drowned in the river as he rematerialised? Or had I sent him on somewhere else? Somewhere he could be properly dead as all the Dirges hoped they could be?

I had no answers. The same questions continued to circle my brain as I walked. If I *knew* that Lucas was OK, then I could risk seeing if the same thing would work with Callum. All I had to do was stand in front of him, our amulets together, and *push* hard with my mind. The only thing I was sure about was that I didn't need Catherine. She said that she knew how to rescue them all and that she would never tell me, but she didn't know what I had done to Lucas. I could feel the power in the bracelet, just waiting to be used. I looked down at the silver on my wrist, glinting in the low, early morning sunshine, and wondered yet again how it did what it did.

Looking up I realised that I had walked further than usual. I was approaching the part of the beach where the kite-surfers practised later in the day, but this early it was still mostly deserted. One lone surfer was out on the water, and I stopped to watch for a moment. The bright red and yellow of the kite was easy to see against the dark turquoise of the waves.

The beach was long and curved with a headland at one end and the town and port at the other. I was much nearer the headland end, where over the years the incessant wind had blown half the beach on to the land to make huge, towering sand dunes. The kite-surfer was tacking away from the beach, towards the dunes. I loved the way the kites moved, and good surfers were incredible to watch: they could catch a wave just right and have the wind lift them in their harnesses and take them ten or more metres up into the air before they landed at high speed to chase the next one. With the boards attached to their feet they could go astonishingly fast. I sat for a moment to watch the kite's progress, just as it caught the wind and the surfer leapt into the air.

He arced gracefully around to land at high speed on the next wave. With the wind behind him he was flying towards me. As I watched he got closer to the shallows and I heard his board hiss on the water as he drew level with where I was standing. He was so close to the shore that I thought he was about to jump off his board and run up the beach, but he was going too fast for that. He whipped past me, the bright kite almost glowing in the early morning sunshine. Smiling at such an obviously showy manoeuvre, I turned away to continue my walk but I hadn't gone more than a couple of paces when there was a horrible cracking noise. Spinning round I could see the kite collapsing about fifty metres further down the beach. There was no sign of the surfer. I watched for a moment, wanting to check that he was OK when he surfaced, but nothing happened. All I could see were the ropes from the kite disappearing under the water.

I quickly scanned up and down the long beach, but it was still deserted. Long seconds passed and there was still no movement from under the waves. "Oh, please, no!" I exclaimed under my breath as I realised something was badly wrong. I ran as quickly as I could through the soft sand until I was as close as possible. Dumping my shoes and my phone I splashed into the water. It was cold at that time of the morning, and I gasped as the waves soaked me. I was soon wading waist deep to reach the nearest part of the kite. The leading edge was still inflated, and the whole thing looked as if it could take off again at any moment. There was still no sign of the surfer. He had to be trapped or unconscious or something, but he would still be attached to the end of the ropes. I needed to find him quickly. Praying that the kite stayed on the water, I grabbed handfuls of it, pulling it towards me as I half waded, half swam through the surf. How long had he been under? Was it too long?

"Where are you?" I started screaming. "Help me!" I bellowed, wasting precious seconds to look up and down the beach again. There was still no one around, and the ropes seemed endless as I pulled and tried hopelessly to run through the dragging surf.

Finally I realised I was pulling against a dead weight, and as the water reached my chest I gave a last heave and dragged the surfer back into the air. The tension in the ropes loosened for a moment and I grabbed him by the shoulder. "Come on!" I shouted at the motionless body, trying to get a grip on the slippery wetsuit. Finally I got hold of his arm and with a superhuman effort lifted him up and over so that his face was out of the water. I was just reaching over to cup him by the chin and drag him towards the shore when he suddenly started thrashing wildly, coughing a great plume of water up into the air. Gasping for breath he finally found his feet, looking around wildly and pushing his wet hair off his face so that he could see. It was Max.

"Max!" I screeched. "Max, are you OK? What on earth are—"

"Quick, get to the top of the kite!" he interrupted me, spluttering. "We have to stop it flying again." His voice was rough and hoarse, but still recognisable.

"But how did you—"

"No time," he shouted. "I'm hurt. Quickly, keep it in the water." There was no doubting the urgency in his voice so I turned and thrashed my way as quickly as I could through the waves to the great folds of material that were now billowing ominously on the surface of the water. Praying that it wouldn't lift off with me hanging on to it, I grabbed the inflatable section of the kite and held it down.

Still coughing and spluttering, Max tried to drag the kite, but wasn't able to help much. I was going to have to do it alone. I dug my heels into the sand and gathered up as much of the fabric as I could, slowly getting it moving towards the safety of the shore. I knew we were in trouble when a gust of wind lifted a large section. I could feel the power as it lifted me effortlessly up through the water, the folds of fabric coming alive as the air surged under it. If it took off with me hanging on I would be in real danger, but I couldn't let it go as it was still tied to Max's harness.

"I can't hold it!" I gasped, realising that I was losing the battle. The kite was like a living thing, growing stronger as more air got underneath it. "I've got to let it go. Hit the release now!" I caught a brief glimpse of Max behind the billowing clouds of fabric, struggling with the mechanism. If I let go too soon he'd be dragged off, injured and unable to fly it. The slippery fabric started sliding through my hands. But if I tried to keep hold of it I would be dragged up and out of the water, dangling until I couldn't hold on any more. Then I would fall. . .

With one last effort I tried to bring the kite under control, but I was in the wrong place and the wind was picking up. I couldn't see Max.

"I have to let go NOW!" I bellowed. "Are you clear?"

The wet fabric made a loud cracking noise as the wind finally claimed it. The kite was suddenly pumped full of air and it rose up and off the water. I could see Max behind it, still wrestling with his harness. The ropes started to speed up through my hands.

"Cut it free!"

At last I saw the sunlight glint off a blade, and within seconds the tension holding the kite was gone. I let go just too late as the ropes ripped through the skin on my palms. The kite rose up and disappeared over the headland as I staggered backwards in the water. It was suddenly very quiet.

"Alex! Are you OK?" This time the panic was in Max's voice.

I turned towards him, weak with relief. "That was way too close. What on earth were you doing out here on your own?"

He ignored my question and started making his way towards me, clearly in some pain. "Where did it get you?"

I brushed the wet hair out of my eyes and noticed my hand. "What on earth. . . ?" I lifted the other: both palms were bleeding profusely where the nylon cord had flayed them. I was covered in blood.

"It's OK, just my hands. Come on, let's get to the shore."

I let him rest his weight on me as we staggered up on to the beach. As soon as we were clear of the waves we flopped down, exhausted.

Max was coughing as he struggled to get the clips of the harness undone. "How much of the sea did you try to inhale?" I asked, stopping briefly in my examination of my hands to thump him on the back.

He lifted his head and gave me a wan smile. "Ha ha. It feels like about half an ocean." Finally he was free of the straps and he dropped back on the sand, wincing and holding his leg, which seemed to be causing him some pain.

"Are you all right, Max? What on earth were you doing?"

Max coughed again before answering. "I didn't intend to go out. I was practising just flying the kite on the land and it was going well, so I thought that a little scoot up and down the beach in the shallows wouldn't do any harm." He paused for a second and looked at the water. "I guess I don't know the beach as well as I thought."

"What did you hit?"

"It was something hard under the waves – a rock, I guess. I saw it too late and was going too fast to jump over it. I managed to get the board up a bit, but not enough." He looked around. "I should have looked at the flags. This bit of the beach isn't safe for kites when the tide is out – too many rocks." He turned and pointed at sign further up the beach.

A shiver ran down my spine. "I can't believe that you came so close to killing yourself."

Max didn't turn, but just shrugged a little.

"You were very lucky. Where did you get the kite from?"

"It's mine, or it was," he said, looking miserably over towards the headland. "I bought it last night." I looked at him in surprise. "Yes, really," he continued before I could say anything, but he was starting to go pink under his tan. "It was going cheap, and I thought – why not? It would save spending all the money on lessons, and I could spend more time practising. . ." His voice petered out as he looked at my furious face.

"That's ridiculous!" I exploded at him without thinking. "It's far too dangerous and anyway, we're only here for another week."

A small smile appeared on Max's salt-covered lips. "I didn't know you cared."

I could feel myself blushing to my roots. "Who – who was it who sold it to you, anyway?" I stammered quickly.

"It was a girl down at the beach party, last night. And as it was the first time I had used it, I hadn't realised quite how fast it could go."

"Oh, Max, that was dumb." I couldn't help butting in.

"I know," he sighed. "I know it was stupid, dangerous and probably a complete waste of money if I've already trashed it." He paused, brushing the unruly mop of dark hair out of his eyes, eyes that suddenly started to twinkle at me. "But before it went wrong it was really good fun!"

"Well, if it's yours we're going to have to arrange a search party for it. It will have landed somewhere. But, Max, your leg! We should get you to hospital."

We both looked down at Max's leg, where a huge bruise was visible around his knee. He had rather nice legs, I found myself thinking absently before I stopped myself. Max stood up and put some weight on it experimentally, then took a few steps forward. I could see from his face as he turned that he was in some pain, but he covered it up before he turned back.

"Nah, I reckon I'll be OK. I don't think anything is broken, just a bit bruised." He lowered himself carefully back down on to the sand. "I could do with just sitting for a bit though, before we start walking. It's a long way back. Anyway, never mind my knee; how are your hands?"

I looked at my palms: both had raw streaks across them where the top layer of skin had been torn off, but the bleeding had mostly stopped. "I'll live. They'll smart for a while but no lasting damage, I reckon. They'll just need a bit of time." I glanced at my watch, then sat up with a start. "Crap! I've missed breakfast! We've been out here for ages. I'd better send Mum a text and let her know what we're doing."

Max looked uncomfortable for a moment. "What are you going to tell them?"

"What do you want me to say? That there was a problem with the kite?" I guessed.

He nodded, going pink again. "Nearly killing myself because I was showing off doesn't sound too smart, does it?"

I laughed. "Fine, but I do need to explain where I've been all this time." Then I glanced down, looking at the state I was in. "Especially given that I'm soaking wet and wounded. Any ideas?"

Max turned to face me, looking me up and down with pursed lips and a frown. He had rolled down the wetsuit and it was really hard not to let my gaze wander away from his face. "We could say that the kite escaped when I was checking it and you tried to help me save it. Would that work?"

"I suppose. Or you could just tell them the truth, that you

were testing the kite, hit something, twisted your knee and had to let the kite go. There's nothing wrong with that, is there?"

"No, I guess not." He was twiddling a piece of the severed rope through his long fingers and didn't look up. I quickly sent my text and waited for him to speak. We both sat watching the sea for a while. It was still too early for most of the kite-surfers, but a couple were now out on the water and we watched in silence as one raced past us, leaping into the air as he turned his board into the waves.

"I was watching you," I said eventually. "That jump you made just before you fell was awesome!"

"I know," he said ruefully. "I was so pleased with myself. It felt as if I was really flying."

"It was very high," I agreed. "What happened?"

"I dunno really. I was going really well then I glimpsed you on the beach and I couldn't resist showing off a bit. Then there was a huge crash and I was underwater."

I sneaked a look at him: he was sitting with his head bowed, his long dark hair flopping over his face and obscuring his features. The long fingers were still playing nervously with the rope.

"I thought I was going to die, Alex, I really did. The fall winded me and I ended up with a couple of lungfuls of water. I didn't know which way was up and I was panicking badly. I couldn't believe it when I saw you turning me over." He was silent for a moment. "Without you I'd be dead."

What he was describing seemed oddly familiar, and as he finished talking I remembered why – Callum had described drowning to me, that feeling of your lungs burning, having no choice but to suck in the deadly water, losing all hope...

"You're such a drama queen!" The last thing I wanted was

for him to feel that he owed me for something like that. "There were people around, just up here in the trees and not down on the beach. Don't go giving yourself a funeral just yet." I gave him a playful punch of the arm but before I could do anything about it he gently grasped my hand in his.

"I won't forget this, Alex," he said softly, his piercing dark-brown eyes finding mine.

I squeezed his hand briefly trying not to flinch at the pressure on my palm, then quickly released it, laughing as naturally as I could. "You *are* a soft lad," I teased, trying to keep things light. I didn't want things to go in the direction he seemed to be taking them. "How's the leg now? Come on, were you lying about needing a hospital?"

Max stretched out his leg, wincing as he did so, and we both looked at his knee. I couldn't help thinking that since we had arrived in Spain he had developed a really nice tan. "It's not feeling at all good now. Not sure I'll be out on the kite again today."

"You probably need to get an icepack on that, or you'll be stuck on the beach for the rest of the holiday."

"I can think of worse places to be," he murmured, giving me a half-smile. I gave him a brief smile back then returned to watching the waves. My attention was caught by the sun glinting off my bracelet, and I suddenly imagined Callum watching me – watching us – sitting together on the beach. I shivered briefly. This is ridiculous – Max is just a friend, I told myself sternly, and that's how it's going to stay. I was so convincing, I almost believed it.

Temptation

Max had twisted his knee, but a lengthy visit to the local hospital pronounced him otherwise OK after the accident. I was given some enormous dressings for my hands and advised not to swim for a few days. News that I had actually rescued him had quickly got out: it seemed that there had been more people around than either of us had realised. His parents, after they had got over the shock, were furious that he had been so irresponsible. They were also embarrassingly grateful that I had been there to haul him out of the water.

"Really, Max, you need to stop them," I complained to him on one of our twice daily walks. "If your mum buys me another bangle to thank me I won't be able to lift my arm." I glanced down at my wrist where the amulet was almost hidden with silver bracelets, bright plaited silk bands and glittery beads. She might have been overdoing it but at least she had good taste.

"Oh, let her get on with it. She's enjoying giving me a hard time, as if all the exercises weren't enough."

The doctor had prescribed physiotherapy and walking every day to help his knee, and I had quickly fallen into the habit of keeping him company. We walked along the beautiful beach talking about anything and everything: Max was very easy company. He told me all about Kate, the girlfriend he had just split up with, and I told him a little about Callum. I had to be careful, but I wanted

Callum to seem real to other people too. Talking about him was exquisitely painful: I missed him so much, but every day I found myself looking forward to Max's company, and hours and hours would pass where I didn't give Callum a single thought. Talking about him made me feel slightly less guilty about that. I consoled myself by believing that he would understand, he would want me to be having a great time, and anyway, there was nothing between Max and me for me to be feeling guilty about.

So we walked, went to the bars in the evening, and generally hung out, but my favourite time was when we were alone in the morning on the beach. Every day we managed to get a little further as his knee got stronger.

"How are you feeling?" I asked as we approached the small headland that had been our turning point the day before. The tide was coming in so it was dangerous to walk around; to go on we were going to have to climb over the rocks.

"Yeah, not bad."

"Are you up for it?" I asked dubiously, eyeing the tumble of massive stones.

Max flexed his knee a couple of times. "I'm sure it'll be fine. Just pick an easy path for me and stay close."

The least treacherous route was up reasonably high and then down again. As we scrambled to the top Max caught my hand. "Can we wait a moment? I'm embarrassingly short of breath."

"Sure. Why don't we just sit and admire the view?"

"Exactly what I had in mind," he murmured, picking a flat rock and sitting down, his hand lingering in mine. "I can't think of anywhere I'd rather be." He pulled me down to sit close beside him. I could feel the warmth of his arm pressed up against me, his strong fingers still laced through mine. With his other hand he started to count my bangles, and with every touch I felt a jolt of excitement. A small smile played around his lips as he counted out loud. "Hmm, seven. She has gone overboard rather, hasn't she?" I knew that I should edge away, but I found I couldn't move. I was so close I could almost hear his heart beating, and I could tell that it was going as fast as mine. For a moment I was hit with a wave of desire: Max was so gorgeous, so obviously interested in me and so uncomplicated. I knew that if he turned to kiss me, I wouldn't stop him.

I was almost breathless, waiting for the moment to happen, anticipating how his lips would feel, how I was going to react, that it took me a couple of seconds to realise that he was examining the amulet. "I like this one best; it's unusual. This wasn't from my mum, was it?"

"No, I've had that one a while." With a sudden shiver I realised how wrong it was to have Max touching the delicate silverwork over the strange blue stone, and when he put his finger under the band to turn it around for a better look I had to stop him. Gently extracting my hand from his I gave him a small smile and fractionally edged away. I was horrified with myself at just how close I had come to letting go, of betraying Callum.

Max sensed the change. "Everything OK?" He reached over and tucked a stray tendril of hair back behind my ear.

"Everything's fine. Have I not told you the story of this bracelet? I found it in the mud on the bank of the Thames. It was tied to a big rock with a piece of wire." I couldn't help reaching over to touch the stone enclosed in its cage of beautifully plaited silver ropes.

"Really? That was lucky. It must be worth a fair bit of money."

"Yes, I guess." I paused, knowing I had to say something more. "It's Callum's favourite too."

Max straightened up, shaking his head slightly. "I see. Well, I guess round one to Callum then." He smiled as he said it, but I could read a different message in his eyes.

We started to make our way back down the rocks to the soft sand, and the silence between us was becoming embarrassing. I knew that I needed to say something, but everything I thought of seemed really trivial. Eventually I reckoned it was as good a time as any to ask the question I had been putting off. "I know this is a bit random," I asked brightly, "but did you say the other day that you studied Latin?"

"Uh-huh. Just finished the A level, and won't be touching it again anytime soon. Why?" The surprise was evident in his voice.

"I came across an inscription on something recently, and I think it might be Latin, but can't be positive."

"Do you remember what it was?"

"Well, I've no idea how to pronounce it but it was roughly *mor memoriae*." I stumbled over the unfamiliar words.

"Really? Are you sure?"

"I think so. The script was a bit difficult to read, but that's what it seemed to be."

"Can you show me?"

"No, sorry, I don't have the thing with me. It was on a. . ." I hesitated, not wanting to say it was on the amulet because I was pretty sure that he wouldn't be able to see it. "It was on a silver photo frame that someone gave to a friend of mine."

"Can you write it down?" He bent down and picked up a long stick from the driftwood on the water's edge, then pointed towards a patch of smooth sand.

"Oh, OK, I guess I can." I took the stick and started to write, trying to put in as many of the flourishes from the inscription as I could remember. Max stood next to me, a thoughtful look on his face.

"With Latin, a few words can have a number of different translations because they didn't have the same grammatical structure that we do. But this doesn't really mean anything as a phrase. *Memoriae* is memory, *mor* isn't a word I've ever heard of."

"Really? Maybe it isn't Latin."

"Or maybe whoever wrote it didn't know their Latin very well. They might mean *mors*, which would be death."

I stopped in my tracks, remembering the faintly scratched "s" between the words. "Death?"

"Yeah, I guess it could mean 'death of memories'. Perhaps it was a frame which held pictures of dead relatives."

Death of memories. I realised that I had been hoping it would be something more profound, something that might unravel the puzzle. But as it was it fitted the amulet perfectly; describing what they did every day, dead people finding an endless stream of other people's memories. It would be just the sort of inscription that I should expect on something so malevolent. All those poor Dirges, trapped by their amulets, destined never to be freed from the endless grind. I looked at the writing in the sand as a slightly larger wave hit the beach. The gentle sweep of water ran quickly across the flat patch of sand, obliterating the words. I was suddenly overwhelmed with emotion, lost in pity for the souls caught in the hideous existence imposed upon them by the amulet and its strange inscription, my inability to work out how I could save them, and piercing guilt that I hadn't spent more time trying to figure it out.

"Hey." The gentle touch on my arm almost startled me. "What's up, Alex? Why does that make you so sad?"

I couldn't speak, just continued looking at the beach where the sand had been wiped clean. Every trace of the words was gone.

Back at the hotel I locked myself in my room and sank on the bed with my head in my hands. How could I have been so quick to forget my plans to help the Dirges, and how on earth had I so nearly let Max kiss me? I couldn't believe how I was feeling: the guilt and the longing were fighting in my heart. I needed to talk, and there was only one person in the world who would really understand. Mum would go ballistic when she realised I'd used my phone to chat to someone in France, but I'd deal with that problem later. Crossing my fingers that Grace would have her mobile with her I selected her number and listened to the strange beeps and hisses of the foreign phone system. Finally I could hear an echoing ringtone. It went on and on, and I was just about to give up when there was a click followed by a breathless voice.

"Alex? Babe, is that you?"

"Hi, Grace, yeah. How's the holiday?"

"Oh, it's OK. There's not much to do. How's yours?"

"Complicated. I need a speed chat before Mum finds me. She's banned the use of mobiles this year."

"What's up? Who is he?" As usual Grace had got to the heart of the problem in an instant.

"You remember me talking about Max, the guy we always see out here? He was a right geek, but he's got sort of gorgeous since I last saw him. I've been playing it very cool, not flirting or anything, but there's definitely a connection." I paused, feeling my cheeks starting to burn just thinking about it.

"Yes, and?"

"Earlier, we were sitting on the beach, and I realised that I wanted him to kiss me! How can that be possible? I still love Callum, but Max is unbelievably hot."

"*Did* you kiss him?" she asked.

"No, I stopped myself just in time. I still feel awful about it though."

"Why? I mean, you are on holiday."

"What! How can you say that?"

"Oh, come on, relax; enjoy yourself for a change."

I couldn't believe what she was saying. "Right, so is that what you're doing now, eyeing up all the French boys?"

"Of course not, Jack's too important to me for that."

"And Callum's important to me too, obviously," I shot back at her.

"But I've known Jack forever, we were friends before, and this, well this is the real thing."

"And for me this is no different!"

Grace paused for a fraction of a second. "Hon, think about it – it has to be. Apart from the fact that you've only known him for five minutes, he's not even properly alive!" Grace was the only person who knew about Callum, and she believed me because she had seen Catherine when she had been trying to kill us both in Kew Gardens weeks before. It was such a relief to be able to have honest conversations with someone about him, even if I didn't agree with what she was saying.

"That's low, Grace. I love Callum, I know I do, despite the problems. I'm just having a minor lust moment, I think, that's all."

I could hear Grace thinking. "Have you ever considered that you might just be having a minor lust moment with Callum? I mean, it was seriously quick."

"No," I said angrily. "It's absolutely not the same."

"Calm down and listen to me. It could easily be: Callum appears out of nowhere, he's gorgeous, he wants you but you can't have him. It's the perfect recipe for unattainable lust. You have to be realistic, hon."

"I am being realistic. I'm going to make it work."

There was a brief silence, and I could tell that Grace thought I was mad. "Alex, how are you going to do that? It's impossible."

"It's not. I think there may be a way to bring him over. I just can't explain it all to you now."

There was a pause and I could hear the distance between us crackling. "Well," she said, clearly dying to ask me for more details, "in that case, if you're sure, you need to be careful how you treat Max; you can't play with people's feelings."

"I know, and I feel really bad about that."

"You need to stay away from him. Show him you're really not interested."

"I suppose. That's going to be pretty hard though."

Grace paused, and I knew that hundreds of miles away she was giving me one of her shrugs. "That's how it is, babe. It's your only choice now."

"I know. I just don't want it to be and was hoping you had a magic answer."

"Sorry. No magic here."

I knew that she was right, but the thought of deliberately ignoring Max, refusing to walk with him, not going with the others to the beach bars in the evening, wasn't an easy one to contemplate.

"Thanks, Grace. I'm sorry to dump all that on you."

"No worries," she said. "But you *are* going to ignore my

excellent advice though, I can tell. I want to hear all about him when we both get back."

I smiled and rang off, thinking how lucky I was to have a friend like Grace. I sat for a bit, staring out of the window at the bright bougainvillea casting a pink-tinted dappled shadow, watching without seeing as a fat bee buzzed from bloom to bloom.

The conversation had only confused me more, thanks to Grace pointing out some uncomfortable home truths. I *had* fallen for Callum laughably quickly. So was it love? Or was it only lust? How was I supposed to know the difference?

As Grace predicted, I couldn't bring myself to ignore Max completely, but I did try not to be alone with him any more. Luckily only a few days of the holiday remained. I was really firm with him, and myself, and didn't allow anything to happen that might give him the idea I was interested in him. Every night I stood in front of the bathroom mirror trying to imagine Callum's familiar features behind my shoulder or his featherlight touch on my hair or cheek or shoulder. And every night it got increasingly difficult. I was missing him more and more, and couldn't wait until we were home and I could go to the top of St Paul's again. I spent a great deal of time fantasising about what we would say and do when we finally saw each other again, and tried not to remember the times when my thoughts wandered off in an entirely different direction. Thinking of Max was out of bounds.

On the last day my carefully constructed evasion plan failed completely. At the beach I had been volunteered to go to the bar to get cold drinks for everyone, and Max had offered to help. Refusing would have been rude, so we walked away from the group together.

"You've been very quiet these last few days, Alex," he said as soon as we were out of earshot. "Did I do something wrong?"

"No, honestly, it's nothing like that."

"So what is it then?" he pressed. "There has to be something. You've barely said a word to me."

What should I say? Make something up or let him know the truth? I glanced over at him and he was watching me carefully. "I didn't want to hurt you," I admitted slowly, then pushed on quickly. "I didn't want to give you the wrong impression and then have to let you down." I could feel the blood rushing to my cheeks as I continued to stare at the sand.

"What impression was that then?" he asked with a smile in his voice.

"I didn't want you to think that you, well, you know. . ."

"That I would be in with a chance, you mean?"

"Exactly," I replied quickly, grateful that I hadn't had to say the words myself.

"I'm not sure that's the whole story." Max's tone was casual as we carried on walking. "I think that you fancy me too, but don't trust yourself."

"Well, maybe there's a tiny bit of that," I admitted, wondering a fraction of a second too late if the better response would have been to be offended.

"I *knew* it!" Max caught my hand and pulled me round to face him.

"Everyone fancies you, Max, and you know it."

"I don't want everyone, Alex. I only want you."

I finally met his gaze, expecting to see his usual grin, but he was looking steadily down at me with such an open, honest expression that I could hardly bear to look at him. He was so nice, and all I had done was mislead him. I was suddenly filled with shame. "I'm so sorry," I whispered, my voice catching.

Max pulled me into his arms and held me close. "Don't be upset, please," he whispered into my hair.

His kindness was too much and for a second I let go of the pent-up emotion. A sob escaped and I felt his arms tighten protectively around me.

"I'm . . . I'm sorry," I mumbled again into his T-shirt, overwhelmed by the sudden feeling of security I felt.

"Hey, shush. No worries. It's your decision." He gently stroked my hair, reminding me of another touch. I quickly pulled away, keeping my face averted.

"I didn't mean to do that. I'm sorry."

"You already said that several times," said Max gently, lifting my face to look at him. Passion burned in his velvety-brown eyes and I gasped. As I did, he leaned down and pressed his lips on mine. He was gentle and warm, and his lips tasted slightly salty. I couldn't help kissing him back for the briefest of seconds before I came to my senses. I pushed him away, as firmly as I could. He lifted his head and looked at me with a rueful smile.

"I'm sorry, Max, but this isn't what I want."

"Are you sure? I could have sworn—"

"I'm absolutely sure. You're a great guy, Max, and under other circumstances, well, things might be different, but I'm not free."

"Callum's a long way away right now. Can't I lead you astray a tiny bit before we have to get back on that plane tomorrow?" His words were serious but there was a friendly twinkle in his eye.

I smiled up at him. "It is hugely tempting, of course, but I'm a one-guy girl. That's just how it is."

He pulled me into another hug, but this one was more like a bear hug. "Dammit! You girls! What are you like?"

"Loyal, that's what we're like, you cheeky beggar." I squeezed him back and dropped my arms. He quickly did the same and we didn't look at each other as we stepped back. "So shall we get those drinks then? The others will be wondering where we've got to."

"I guess," he agreed, and we continued down the beach. I tried to make light conversation, but all the while I was fighting the wave of guilt and shame that was threatening to overwhelm me. I couldn't believe that I had kissed him back, not when I loved Callum so completely. And I did love Callum, didn't I?

Homecoming

We were all leaving the following morning, flying into Heathrow but from different airports. Max and Sabrina's dad had been very smug that the flights they had got from Seville were half the price of those we had from Malaga. But they had to leave long before us and I heaved an inward sigh of relief as I finally said goodbye to Sabrina and Max in the hotel lobby. He gave me a quick peck on both cheeks but said nothing, and I smiled as brightly as possible and rambled on about how great it had been and that it would be lovely to see them all again before next year.

I watched as they walked to their car, still not quite understanding why the sight of him leaving made me feel so dreadful when Callum would be waiting for me in just a few hours' time. However hard I tried my mind kept wandering to and fro between the dark-haired, solid, available Max and the blond, ethereal, trapped Callum.

The flight seemed interminable but we actually landed at Heathrow slightly ahead of time. As the plane finally rolled to a stop at the gate and all the passengers started to stand up, I called Callum's name quietly. Within minutes the familiar tingle was back and I realised I was choked with emotion, just knowing he was there.

"Hi, gorgeous, you're back early." His familiar tones filled me with longing and I felt more than a little twinge of guilt for the time I hadn't spent thinking about him.

"Hi, I'm sorry, it's difficult to talk now, but I wanted you to know I was back. I'll call you as soon as I can, OK?" I whispered as clearly but as quietly as I could, but it wasn't quietly enough to avoid Mum.

"What did you say, Alex? What's in the back?"

"Nothing, Mum, really. I was just muttering to myself, that's all."

She huffed a little, but didn't quiz me further, which was as well. I so wanted to see Callum, to reassure myself that he was as kind, thoughtful, perfect and, well, beautiful as I remembered. But every time I thought about him, the memory of kissing Max leapt into my mind. I kept shoving it away but it was persistent, and the more it happened, the guiltier I felt. I was really glad that wearing the amulet meant I didn't have an aura: mine would be sure to give away the turmoil of emotions in my head.

We waited for ages at immigration and everyone was getting quite tetchy by the time we finally made it through to the baggage reclaim area. There was the usual scramble for trolleys, then the jostling for position around the luggage carousels. There was no sign of any of the bags despite the fact we'd been stuck in the passport queue for ages. I took a quick look around; there were plenty of places where I could pretend to make a call and speak to Callum. I edged away from the others on the pretence of going to the ladies', fixing in my earpiece as I went. "Callum, I've got a few minutes before the bags arrive. Are you here?"

I had just reached a pillar to hide behind and was anticipating the tingle in my wrist at any second, so the gentle touch on my other arm made me jump. I spun around.

"Alex! Oh, I'm sorry, are you on the phone?"

In my surprise I forgot to lie. "Max? No, not right now. What are you doing here?"

"Our flight got delayed," he said. "So much for Dad's bargain-bucket tickets, eh? Anyway, I'm glad it did. It's given me the chance to say something I meant to say earlier, but chickened out."

I looked up into his smiling, nervous face. As I did, I felt the tingle in my wrist. I couldn't believe it – this couldn't be happening, not here! Callum was right there, listening to every word of this conversation, and whatever Max was about to tell me, I was sure Callum wasn't going to like it.

"Nothing to be said, really," I tried to say in an offhand but friendly manner, not wanting to hurt Max either, and desperately trying to think of a way out of the situation. But my mind had gone blank. The tingle remained in my wrist.

"No, it does need to be said." Max reached up and briefly stroked my face. "I had a wonderful holiday, and that was down to you, and especially our fabulous days on the beach. I'm not going to forget kissing you in a hurry. You're a great girl, Alex, and your Venezuelan boyfriend ought to get over here before someone else decides to try their luck." He bent down and kissed me on the cheek. "Who knows? Maybe it'll be me," he whispered.

I could feel the blood rushing to my face as he ran his hand down my arm before turning to leave. It was only then that I realised the tingle had disappeared too.

"Callum?" I whispered frantically. "Where have you gone?"

There was only silence.

I spent the rest of the journey home in a daze, refusing to get drawn into conversation. Pretty quickly my family gave up trying, instead talking and laughing among themselves about the holiday. I stared out of the window of the minicab, replaying the conversation in my mind. Had Callum heard everything? As there was no sign of him I had to assume the worst.

I tried hard not to think of Max, not to dwell on the way he had stroked my cheek or what he had whispered in my ear.

Once we were back at home it was difficult to get away to call Callum again. There was a small mountain of post on the front doormat, and even after a fortnight the place had a musty, unused air. I took my bag upstairs and looked hopefully in my mirror, but there was no sign of him behind me. I *had* to find somewhere quiet to call him, to get this sorted out. I just had to. I suddenly had a flash of inspiration, jumped off my bed and ran downstairs.

"Mum, do we need some milk?"

Mum looked up at me in surprise. "Well, yes, I guess we do. Are you OK, Alex? You've been very quiet."

"I . . . umm . . . I was feeling a bit carsick, that's all. I fancy a cuppa now, with proper British milk. I'll nip up to the shop and get some." Before she could say anything else I scooped up my bag and was through the door. I hastily shoved the earpiece back in my ear and pulled the little mirror out of my pocket.

"Callum? Are you there? Please, I need to talk to you!"

I was walking quickly, but not so quickly that he wouldn't be able to keep up, and still there was nothing. As soon as I reached the children's playground I grabbed the nearest bench. Sitting down I could use the mirror to scan around. There was no sign of him.

"Callum! Please come and talk to me. You've got the wrong end of the stick, honestly! Won't you let me explain?"

I waited for a moment but there was no tingle in my arm.

I knew that he could hear me, wherever he was, and I was getting desperate.

"Look, at least hear me out, then if you want to go, I'll understand." I couldn't believe that I was actually saying those words. "But listen to me first, please?"

Looking around in the mirror I suddenly jumped. Callum was standing right behind me, but his hood was obscuring his face. He made no move to connect our amulets.

"I don't know how much you heard but you have to believe me when I say nothing happened. That's the honest truth!" There was still no tingle so I tried again. "OK, let me go through the whole thing. Max is a family friend, more a friend of Josh's really, and our families met up out in Spain. So we spent a bit of time together, *as friends*. I know that he would've liked more than that, but I didn't encourage him, I promise. He knows that I have a boyfriend, but he thinks you live in Venezuela, so that's what he meant about how you ought to get here soon." I put the mirror down and held out my wrist. "I love you, Callum. I've missed you desperately. Please come here?"

I sat in silence for a moment, holding my breath. What would I do if he just left, if I never saw him again? I'd already felt the pain of losing him, and I absolutely couldn't stand to go through that again.

After a couple of agonising seconds there was a familiar tingle in my wrist and I exhaled in relief. "Thank you," I whispered. "It was all a horrible mistake, I promise."

"Are you sure, Alex?" Callum's voice was gruff. "I saw the look in that guy's eyes. He didn't think it was a mistake."

"I can't help what he thinks. All I can promise is that I didn't encourage him, and that he knows I'm yours." There was a

54

grunt and then a brief silence. I still didn't dare lift the mirror to look at him. I didn't want to see the anger on his face, anger that I had caused. "Twice I've thought I've lost you, Callum. Don't you remember? Don't do this to me again. I couldn't bear it."

I was suddenly aware of a gentle pressure on my cheek; the lightest of touches, as if I was being stroked by a feather. "I couldn't bear it either," he said in a voice so full of pain it made me flinch. He wasn't angry, but I'd hurt him badly. I slowly lifted the mirror and he came into view behind me. His handsome face was etched in misery, reminding me of the time I had seen him in the crypt of St Paul's, directly under the dome.

"Please believe me: Max means nothing. Nothing! I've been desperate to see you and talk to you again." I lifted my hand to find his cheek, feeling only the subtle resistance in the air, but watching my fingers in the mirror trace a line down to his jaw. His head lifted slightly and his hooded eyes met mine.

"I couldn't blame you, you know. I mean, I'm not much use to you like this, am I?" There was a sudden and bitter twist to his words.

"We've been over this before," I said as patiently as I could. "I don't care. The entire line-up from my favourite band could stand there begging to go out with me, but I wouldn't be interested. I love *you*, Callum. You, and only you."

"I know that, but it can't last, can it? I mean, be honest. We can't go on having a relationship like this, not being able to see each other properly, or hold each other!"

"Why not? I know that being like this," I waved my hand around to demonstrate my point, "isn't ideal, but we have the Golden Gallery! You're as real to me there as anyone else on the planet!" I paused to catch my breath, getting angrier as I thought about his words. "And anyway, what do you know about what I want?"

"I know what you *think* you want, but in a year's time? Two? Three? When you want to have kids? What then?"

"I'm only seventeen, for goodness' sake! I'm not worrying about all that stuff!"

"Exactly." His voice was suddenly low. "You're only seventeen. You should be out with Grace and Jack and all your other friends, introducing them to your new boyfriend, Max."

"Oh pleeease," I muttered, more to myself than to him. "I can't win, can I? You've decided that you're no good for me. Are you leaving now? Is this it?"

"Stop it, Alex. Don't be so dramatic."

"Me?" I screeched at him. "Me? It's you who's got the wrong end of the stick. We can make this work!"

"Really? How exactly? Are we going to live happily ever after? Have you found someone willing to die so that I can stop being a Dirge, is that it?"

"Of course not!"

"So how can we make it work then? You don't even know what you're talking about!"

"Oh yes, I do! I can bring you over now – any time I want."

There was a sudden silence as we both realised what I had said, and I felt my mouth drop open in surprise.

"What?" asked Callum softly. "Explain to me, Alex. What do you mean?"

I looked up at him meekly. "I'm sorry, I wanted to be sure before I told you. I didn't want to get your hopes up."

"Sure about *what*?"

I took a deep breath and looked at his beautiful, tortured

face. I was suddenly aware of the birds twittering in the late afternoon sunshine in the deserted park. Everything was so normal, so ordinary, but what I had to say was anything but. I looked into his deep blue eyes, willing him to believe me.

"When Lucas disappeared, it wasn't because he had managed to steal enough of Rob's memories, it was because I stopped him. I got really angry and the power in my amulet just sort of streamed out when I pushed it against his. I didn't know what I was doing, I just wanted him to stop killing Rob."

It was Callum's turn to sit there with his mouth open in surprise. He opened and shut it a couple of times before finally being able to speak. "You stopped Lucas? With the amulet?"

I nodded quickly. "It was definitely me. But what I don't know, what I have to find out, is what happened to him after he disappeared. If he reappeared like Catherine did, unharmed in the river, then I can do the same to you. But I can't risk it until I know for sure."

"Why didn't you tell me all this before now?" Callum's voice was unexpectedly sharp.

"I wanted to be sure, that's all. It seemed too cruel to suggest it if I didn't know it would work." I looked at him for a moment, tears suddenly threatening to well up. "Is it too late? Have you decided that enough is enough? I still don't mind bringing you over, even if. . ."

"Now you're *definitely* being dramatic," he sighed. "No, you're not too late; I just wish you'd told me before. I could've spent the last two weeks searching the hospitals, seeing if I could find him."

"I'm sorry, I didn't think of that. I just wanted—" I was interrupted by the shrill ringtone on my phone, making both of us jump. "Hang on a sec," I said as I wrestled it out of my back pocket. "Hi, Mum. Oh yes, sorry about that. I . . . umm, met up with someone from school and we've been having a chat. I'll be back in five minutes."

I looked up at Callum. "I've got to go," I said apologetically. "They're waiting for their cups of tea. I'm supposed to be getting the milk."

He gave a short laugh. "Well, you'd better go; don't want them to wait for their tea any longer. But we need to talk some more, Alex. We need to talk *a lot*." His mesmerising eyes were still guarded.

I swallowed nervously. "Sure, we need to go through all the details. I can tell you exactly what happened and then we can both start searching for him." Callum nodded briefly but didn't say any more. I tried again. "Look, it's good news, I know it is. Our only problem is finding Lucas."

"I wish that were true," he muttered under his breath, before suddenly becoming brisk. "I need to go and do some gathering. Will you be in later?" I nodded mutely. "Good, I'll come to the house then." In the mirror I saw him kiss the top of my head very briefly as he stood up to go. But the glimpse I had of his face as he turned away chilled me to the bone. His eyes were bright with tears.

Number

I was no happier when I got home with the milk than I had been when I went out. My beautifully constructed fantasy of how Callum and I would fall into each other's arms, as far as we could, had crumbled away. I sat with my family while they looked through the holiday photos, happy and content, trying hard not to look at the photos of Max that were included in the selection. All the time I felt empty inside.

It wasn't like the feeling I had had before when I thought Callum didn't love me, or when Catherine had stolen the amulet and I thought she had severed the link between us forever. This was all my own fault. The pain in Callum's eyes was down to me, and I couldn't blame him if he decided we were over. He was miserable enough without this. I excused myself from my chattering family and went up to my room. It was still a complete tip; I'd packed in a hurry and left discarded clothes, shoes and make-up strewn across the floor. Without really thinking about it I started to pick everything up, finding a small comfort in restoring some sort of order. I paused at my desk to move the mirror back to its usual position, and as I did I caught a glimpse of a shadowy cloaked figure behind my shoulder, just as the tingle appeared in my wrist.

"Callum?" I whispered as loudly as I dared, relief almost overwhelming me. "Is that you? I didn't expect you back so early."

The hooded figure didn't move but I knew straightaway

from the feeling in my wrist that it wasn't Callum. "Olivia? It's you, isn't it? Come on, come and sit down and tell me what you're doing skulking around like that." I tried to sound as upbeat as possible. Olivia was only a child; no more than twelve or thirteen when she had fallen into the River Fleet and drowned. She was easily upset and had been struggling with the aftershocks of a recent encounter with Catherine.

I sat at my desk and watched as the figure slowly slid into position beside me, her identity given away by the repetitive movements she always made with her hands when she was nervous, linking her fingers and thumbs together in a chain, again and again. I had to keep watching and moving my wrist to keep in contact with her. Finally she threw back her hood. I was ready with a welcoming smile and didn't expect to see the devastated look on her small face.

"Olivia? What on earth's the matter? Are you OK?"

"It's Callum. He's in a really bad way, Alex. What's happened? Please tell me!"

"What do you mean, a really bad way?"

"I've never seen him like it before. He's really down. I thought that he'd be happy that you were back because he's been going on and on about it, but he's in a terrible mood."

The guilt washed back over me again. "It's difficult, Olivia. He's got the wrong end of the stick about something, that's all."

She got straight to the nub of the problem in a heartbeat. "Did you find someone else on holiday? Have you dumped him?"

"No, I absolutely haven't," I shot back quickly, wondering when she'd got quite so perceptive. She was only a kid after all.

"Well, maybe he thinks you have?"

I couldn't explain it to her, I realised; it wasn't fair to Callum.

"I'm sure he doesn't think that, Olivia. He's probably just not done enough gathering today, hanging around the airport waiting for me. You know how it is."

Olivia shrugged in a grudging acceptance that I could be right, her lip quivering.

"Please don't get so upset," I urged, looking at the misery etched on her face. "It's really not that bad. And anyway, when did *you* last go gathering?"

"Umm, I did some this morning," she hiccuped, still trying not to cry.

"None since then? None this afternoon?" She shook her head, keeping her eyes on the floor.

"It's not enough," I reminded her gently. "You have to do more. Remember what Callum is always telling you? You must keep your amulet topped up, especially when you're not feeling good in the first place."

"I suppose you're right. I've still got all that stuff from Catherine to deal with too."

"Oh, Olivia! I'd hoped that might have worked its way out of your system by now."

She gave a little shake of the head. "No chance. I'm stuck with that forever."

When Catherine had first appeared and started tormenting me, Olivia had stolen away some of her most important memories. As a result Catherine had been furious and had promised to make my life a misery. She had succeeded. Olivia knew that it was her fault, and that the memories she had stolen from Catherine were vital; they could have helped me to rescue the Dirges. But once Olivia had taken them they were gone, irretrievably lost. And worse, she'd been left contaminated by their sheer malevolence, and was struggling to keep on top of the spiralling depression that threatened to overwhelm her. I felt terribly responsible for her pain, and really wanted to be able to help her.

"You have to go and gather, Olivia, and I think you should go and do it now."

"I s'pose I could," she agreed, almost petulantly.

"I expect Callum is at the cinema. You'll be able to find him there and come back with him later." I gave her a quick smile, not wanting to overdo it.

"All right, I'll go. I know I should."

"You will come back, won't you? You need to believe that Callum and I are OK. We just had a bit of a row, that's all. It happens." I shrugged as I said it, trying to make light of the whole thing.

She turned her big, sad brown eyes on me, unblinking in the mirror. "I don't want it to happen. I want you and Callum to find a Happy Ever After and take me with you."

My heart twisted. "I know, and we want that too. We just need to find the right way. Now," I announced, becoming much more brisk, "off you go, find some little yellow lights to gather, and I'll see you later."

I sighed with relief as the strange tingle disappeared from my wrist. It was hard work dealing with Olivia, but what she had said worried me. I didn't want Callum suffering so badly, and the guilt reared up again. If only I had been firmer with Max during the holiday he wouldn't have been so sure of himself. For the umpteenth time I relived that hideous moment in the airport, knowing that the two of them were side by side next to me. Poor Callum! I hung my head with shame as I thought of Max's words. It wouldn't have been so bad if he hadn't mentioned kissing me. If

I shut my eyes I could remember every detail of the beach, every look he gave me, every touch, and then of course the fact that I had kissed him back, just a little, before I pushed him away. That was the worst bit, because I knew I wasn't being entirely honest when I told Callum I had done nothing to encourage Max.

It had only been the day before, but seemed like much, much longer ago.

The evening dragged as I waited for Callum and Olivia to reappear. I unpacked my bag and sorted out my washing just to keep busy, glancing in every shiny surface that I passed, but there was no sign of them. As it got later I was less and less convinced that they would be able to come. After a certain point in the evening something in the amulets compelled the Dirges to return to St Paul's Cathedral, where they spent the night in the Whispering Gallery. As a result they couldn't travel that far from London, and there was no chance of my favourite fantasy of walking on the beach with Callum ever happening unless I could make my plan to bring him over work.

I looked at my watch with a sinking heart. The possibility of seeing Callum again was getting less and less likely, and I really didn't want him spending the night worrying about my feelings for him. I decided to give him five more minutes to appear, and then call him. Picking up a load of dirty clothes I took them downstairs to the washing machine. Mum was in the kitchen sifting through a huge pile of post.

"Hi, Alex, that's efficient of you! You're the first one. Do you want to bung it all straight into the machine and I'll set it running before I go to bed?"

"OK. It's pretty much all light-coloured stuff." I picked out one T-shirt as I squeezed it all in. "What about this one, Mum?

Can it go in too?"

She looked up from the letters, her glasses perched on the end of her nose. "Hmm, not sure. Let me have a look at the label." She peered for a moment at the tiny writing on the label. "No, I wouldn't risk it. I'm not sure how often that's been washed before and it might run. We don't want that happening again, do we?" She smiled wryly at me. Not long ago one of my turquoise T-shirts had got mixed up in a pile of white towels and the entire load had turned a fetching shade of pale green.

"I think I might get an early night then, Mum, given that we were up at the crack of dawn. G'night."

"Goodnight, sweetie. I'll pop in before I go to bed." She went back to sorting post and I'd turned to go when she said, "Oh Alex, just a sec, there's a letter here for you." She fished a small, plain white envelope out of the smaller pile and handed it to me. "Looks intriguing!" she said with a smile, clearly being nosy.

"Probably from one of my hordes of admirers," I said, taking the envelope nonchalantly.

"Which one?"

"None of your business!"

She laughed and gathered up a load of pizza delivery leaflets. "It was worth a go! You never tell me anything these days." She was smiling but I knew she was desperate to know what was going on. I used to tell her everything when I was younger and I knew she missed that. And I had been particularly opaque since meeting Callum. No wonder the whole thing was driving her mad.

I ran back upstairs with the letter unopened in my hand. It was thick paper: a proper envelope, not one of the self-sticking ones, with my name and address handwritten carefully on the front. I shoved the mess off the futon and threw myself down, sliding my finger under the flap as I did. Inside was a matching sheet of paper, folded in half. I smoothed it out over my knee, a frown instantly forming on my brow.

Alex, please call as soon as you can. We have something important to discuss.

Underneath was a mobile phone number, written in the same careful hand. I turned the paper over. There was nothing on the back. The envelope gave no clues either, the postmark smudged and unreadable. It was just the message and the number, with no clue who it was from.

Frowning even harder I reached for my mobile and punched in the number to see if it belonged to someone I knew, but there was nothing. That wasn't so surprising though, as I had managed to destroy my phone about a month ago and hadn't been able to transfer all my old numbers. Now I only had those I'd actually called since.

My thumb hesitated over the green button as I caught a glimpse of the time. It was too late to be calling someone I probably didn't know. I deleted the number and lobbed the phone back on to the desk, sitting back and looking at the ceiling. I would worry about that tomorrow, as I had more immediate things to think about: how to bring Callum over and save him from an eternity as a Dirge.

I smoothed the stone in the amulet, catching a glimpse of the tiny layers of gold, which made flecks of light deep inside. It was almost impossible to explain the feeling that it gave me, the feeling of power and strength. I stretched my arm out experimentally and concentrated on the beautiful bracelet, thinking back to what I had done to Lucas. Then I had pushed – shoved – with my mind while our amulets had been connected. I tried pushing again, thinking about getting the energy needed to help Callum escape. A strange coiling sensation slowly grew along my arm, and as I watched the amulet began to glow.

Startled, I let my arm drop, shaking it as if to get rid of a persistent fly. The strange glow disappeared immediately.

"Wow," I couldn't help breathing out loud. As I sat there looking at the amulet an extraordinary feeling of calm settled over me. And with that sense of calm came a clear and absolute knowledge: I could save Callum and all the other Dirges. I just knew it.

I was worrying too much about what happened to Lucas. We might never find out and spend the rest of our lives fretting about it, getting more and more frustrated and never risking bringing Callum over. But now I was positive: I knew that if I tried, he would end up exactly like Catherine. The only difference was that instead of using the power in my memories to make his escape, I was going to channel that power through the amulet.

I felt as if an enormous weight had been lifted from my shoulders. My decision was made and I couldn't help smiling to myself. The only question left was when to do it.

I was still sitting on my futon looking at the amulet when the tingle in my wrist announced Callum's arrival.

"Hi," he said hesitantly.

"You came! I was about to call you before it got too late." I started to lever myself up to move to my desk.

"No, don't move. We can talk here. You look comfortable."

I settled back in my seat. "If you want. I do prefer looking at you though."

Callum coughed in a strangely self-conscious manner. "Did you do something with your amulet this evening?"

66

"Why? Did you feel something?"

"About five minutes ago my amulet glowed briefly. I think some of the others did too, so I came right over to check everything was OK. Have you been up to something?"

I couldn't tell where he was so I had to assume he could see my face, which I knew was going red. There was no point denying it. "I might have given the amulet a little test, I admit. But it was only for a second."

I could hear Callum's sharp intake of breath. "So it *was* you? Really?"

"Of course. Why would I lie about it?"

There was a sheepish edge to his voice. "I wasn't sure if I believed you before, about what happened with Lucas. I thought it was just a coincidence that he disappeared when you pushed your amulet on to his."

"Callum, I know I can channel the amulet's power, and I know that it's going to work, and I think we could do it anytime we like. We just need to decide what we want to know before we try. Would you rather wait for proof or just go for it? After all, Lucas could have been swept away in the river and never found again. We could spend the rest of our lives searching for an answer that never comes."

"I know," he sighed. "I've been thinking that too."

"But it's up to you," I whispered. "I'm not going to force that one on you." I reached up to try and find his face but couldn't. "Where are you, Callum? Let me see you."

"I'm right here," he replied in a strangely gruff voice, and I felt a soft touch on the side of my face. "Are you sure about this?"

"I know it will work, I just know it."

"No, that wasn't what I meant. Alex, are you absolutely sure that you want me to come over? I'll have no memories, no money, nowhere to go, so I'll be entirely dependent on you. You need to really want this to happen, I couldn't bear to be a burden. . ."

"Will you stop it! You'll never be a burden, and we'll work out the rest when you're here." I paused for a second but he didn't say anything. "Honestly, Callum, I don't know what else I can do to convince you that it's you I love, no one else. What else can I say?" I needed to see his face so I grabbed the mirror off the desk and found him beside me, staring pensively out of the window.

"I love you so much, Callum. Let's not waste any more time like this."

Finally he turned towards me, the beginnings of a wry smile on his face. "You can be very persuasive when you want to be, can't you?"

I laughed, relieved.

"So how do we do this?"

"Umm, as far as I can tell, we need only each other and the amulets, and to make sure that the river isn't too high. I guess that we should check out the tides and the recent weather reports. I don't think there is anything else much we can find out."

"Did you ever find out what the inscription meant?"

"Oh yes, it means *death of memories*, or something like that. I think it just describes the function of the amulet."

"How did you find that out?"

My heart sank. "I, umm, I asked someone who had been studying Latin."

"Who was that then?" He smiled at me at last. "Who do we need to thank for that?"

I couldn't tell another lie, as tempting as it was. "Max," I whispered.

There was a long silence. "Max?" he said eventually.

"Yes, he's just done Latin A level," I blustered.

"You shared our secret with Max?"

"Of course not! I just asked him to translate the words!"

I could see Callum become very tight-lipped, and for a moment I thought he might disappear again. He continued to look at me with disappointed eyes. Finally he spoke. "It's getting late, and I have to get back to St Paul's. You must be tired too." He paused and raised his free hand as if he were about to stroke my hair, but dropped it before he touched me. "We'll talk more tomorrow, if you want to."

I really, absolutely had had enough, and the words exploded out of me before I thought about their effect. "Don't you *dare* speak to me like that! I've just told you – proved to you, actually – that I've got the power to help you, and all you can do is whinge about a conversation with someone unimportant when I was on holiday!" I glared at him, but before he could speak I carried on. "I mean, how much do you want this? I thought that you wanted nothing more than to escape. Why are you making it so difficult?"

Callum was staring at me, open-mouthed in shock, and I realised I didn't want to hear his excuses. I whipped my arm away from his, folding them both tightly across my chest with the amulet tucked out of sight. "I don't want to talk about it any more now. *You* come and talk to me tomorrow when you're ready." I turned away from the mirror so that I didn't have to look at him, my heart racing and the blood pounding in my temples. When I glanced back a few seconds later he had gone.

Stalker

I spent the night pacing the room, worrying about the effect of what I had said on Callum. It was harsh to speak to him like that when he lived in constant misery, and I knew that I shouldn't have snapped, but sometimes he made it really quite hard. I tried not to think about how much of my mood was down to my feelings of guilt.

It must have been well after three in the morning before I finally stumbled into bed and into a restless sleep. When I woke I automatically reached for my pocket mirror, waiting for the now-familiar tingling sensation in my wrist. I wasn't going to be the one who called first, but I didn't have to wait for long.

"Morning," I said carefully.

Callum sighed heavily and finally looked up, dark circles under his eyes. "I'm sorry, I'm behaving like a complete idiot. It's all just been a bit of a shock, that's all."

I reached over, using the mirror to check exactly where he was, and gently touched his mouth, immensely relieved that he was back. "These are the only lips I want to kiss, and I want to kiss them properly as soon as possible. Can I come to the dome later? We can make plans there as well as anywhere, and then we can get on with it."

He gave me a brief, lopsided smile that didn't quite reach his darkened eyes. "I suppose I could see what I can do."

"If you can get the Golden Gallery shut I'll leave you in no doubt about who it is I love, I promise you." I stroked his face, feeling the whisper of something insubstantial.

Without another word Callum moved closer and in the mirror I could see he had wrapped me tightly in his arms. As usual I could only just feel it. "Don't let's argue," I said softly, leaning in towards him. "Life is difficult enough without making it worse."

"That's true." I felt his mouth move against my hair. "I'm sorry, really I am."

"Me, too." I smiled at him as I sank into his arms, my heart filled with longing and hope.

The dome of St Paul's Cathedral was the only place where Callum appeared to be real, and then only to me. Previously he had been able to ensure that the gallery was closed for maintenance on each of my visits by influencing the dreams of the guy in charge. I wasn't hopeful that he would be able to do it at this time of the morning. After Callum left I was getting ready to leave when I spotted the folded sheet of paper on the desk. Who was sending me such strange notes? There was only one way to find out. I reached for my phone and tapped in the number, shutting my bedroom door carefully before I pressed the call button. The phone rang once before clicking to voicemail.

"You have reached the phone of the Reverend Waters. I'm sorry I can't take your call right now, but please leave a message after the tone and I'll get back to you."

I snapped it off instantly, dropping the phone on to the futon as if it would contaminate me. Her again! What on earth could she want?

Reverend Waters worked in St Paul's, and she had spoken to me after my terrible visit to the top of the dome when Catherine had the amulet. I had been in a bad way and she had tried to help, but at the time I wasn't about to start explaining about Callum to a complete stranger – I'd have been locked up. I had seen her on other visits to the cathedral too, but had always managed to avoid talking to her.

How did she know where I lived? And what on earth could she want with me? As I made my way into central London my mind kept circling back to that question until I came up with the only possible answer: she had seen me ignoring the "Closed" signs up to the Golden Gallery and I was about to get into trouble for trespassing. I couldn't afford for her to stop me, not when I was so close to patching things up with Callum. And after we had talked and sorted out what we needed to do, I was going to bring him over. If she wanted to confiscate my annual pass after that, then I couldn't care less.

I jumped off the bus at St Paul's and looked around. There was no sign of Reverend Waters but I didn't want to risk walking into the building without checking out things properly. I sat on the steps in the sunshine and pulled out my little pocket mirror, ready to call Callum and find out about the dome.

As usual the Dirges were drifting around the crowds, picking up a fresh happy memory here and there. I saw a man with a bright-yellow aura suddenly become the focus of activity. Two Dirges started to converge on him from different directions and there was a brief tussle between them before one of the dark, hooded figures shoved the other out of the way and passed their amulet through the little light. The light immediately blinked out and, as I watched, the man's expression grew puzzled. Whatever it was he had been enjoying remembering, it was gone forever.

Sighing, I looked away. However unfair it was, there was no way that I could condemn the Dirges for what they did. This wasn't their choice. It was the only way they could make their existence bearable.

"Hey, that's a big sigh. Are you OK?" Callum's arrival was, as usual, preceded by the strange tingling in my wrist.

"I'm fine. Just watching a couple of your colleagues scrapping over a particularly juicy memory. I can't believe that you have to live like this. It's all so wrong!"

"Tell me about it," he said with feeling.

"No luck with the dome?" I guessed.

"None whatsoever. The usual guy is off, and his deputy is much less susceptible to my suggestions. I'm sorry."

"It's not your fault," I said, trying to hide my disappointment. It was going to be much easier to convince Callum that I meant what I said if I could actually hold him close. We were back to square one. I reached for his hand and squeezed. "I can still climb up there. Granted, it won't be as good as when we're alone, but we could be together for a little while. Worth a go?" I gave him my best winning smile.

"It's always worth a go to me," he said, finally returning my smile. "You ready?"

I hesitated for a second. "I need you to do me a favour first. There's a vicar in there," I gestured over my shoulder towards the cathedral, "and she wants to talk to me. I really don't want to talk to her. Can you see if the coast is clear?"

"Really?" he asked, puzzled. "Why does she want to talk to you?"

"I have no idea but she sent this to the house." I dug into my

73

bag for the piece of heavy-duty notepaper. "That number went to her voicemail. It's all she sent." I could see Callum peering over my shoulder as I looked at the paper with distaste. "It's a weird thing to do though. The only thing I can think is that she might have spotted me climbing over the barriers and she wants to tell me off, but I'm not sure why she's being quite so mysterious about it."

"OK, so we need to avoid her then. What does she look like?"

"Quite old, grey hair, wearing one of those long black cassocks. I've seen her on the cathedral floor and at the Whispering Gallery."

"Why don't we go in by the crypt entrance and then sneak up the stairs? I can go ahead and check out the gallery before you have to walk around."

"OK, sounds like a plan. You go and make sure the way is clear and I'll be right behind you."

It was a Sunday so the place was heaving with people. I picked my way through the crowds loitering on the steps in the sunshine, listening to all the various languages and accents, and finally made it to the side entrance to the crypt steps. It was cool and dark inside and the long, quiet corridor felt a world away from the noise and bustle just above.

Starting to walk between the café tables I kept my head down and my hair loose to conceal my face. "Is the coast clear?" I hissed as I approached the main part of the crypt.

"No sign of anyone, just keep on going."

"OK, let's get through here as quickly as possible." I had my season ticket ready in my hand as I approached the gate. The guy behind the desk seemed very bored and was about to nod me through when he suddenly sat up.

"Excuse me, miss, can I take another look at your ticket, please?" His hand was stretched out towards me.

"Umm, yes, of course. Is there a problem?"

"Just had a few forgeries through lately, that's all," he replied, not looking at me but consulting something out of sight on his desk. "All clear. Enjoy your visit." He passed the ticket back to me and looked towards the next person in the queue. I grabbed the ticket and hurried through the entrance, not looking back. I walked directly to the bottom of the stairs. Climbing up from here meant that I missed walking under the dome, but it was much more discreet. I didn't look around for Callum as I knew that he would be keeping away from me. Down in the crypt the influence of the dome on the Dirges wasn't good: it seemed to magnify the horror and suffering visible on their faces and they tried to avoid going there. So I was surprised when the tingle reappeared in my arm as I started walking up the steps. Callum's translucent figure was visible walking next to me.

There was an urgent edge to his voice. "That ticket guy made a phone call as soon as you were out of earshot."

"What! What did he say?" I stopped dead on the stairs.

"Keep walking," urged Callum. "I didn't hear all of it, but I'm pretty sure it was about you. He said something like 'If you want to talk to her you'd better get over here now.'"

"Crap! He must've called the vicar. I don't want to see her, not today."

"We don't have to go up the dome if you're worried."

I turned to look at him as I continued trudging up the endless steps. Seeing him next to me always made my heart sing, regardless of what else was going on. "No way. I want to get to the top. I'm not giving up the chance of hugging you properly, even if it is a bit public, just because some weird vicar wants to give me a piece of her mind." The last few words were somewhat indistinct. "Can't talk and climb, Callum. Getting puffed. See you at the gallery." He turned and smiled at me, a smile of such longing that for a second I forgot the pain in my calves. Then he was gone. I carried on climbing.

I hurried on up the stairs as quickly as I could manage, pausing only as I got to the landing at the Whispering Gallery level. "Callum?" I called quietly. "Is it OK to go through?" Once I started walking through the narrow little passage to the gallery it was difficult to turn back, and then once I stepped on to the gallery itself it was easy to see everyone and there was nowhere to hide.

"No sign of her," he announced as he appeared suddenly next to me, his wrist by mine. He stayed with me as I negotiated my way around the gallery, past the Dirges who were sitting in their seats, invisible to all the other visitors. A few of them looked up at me with curiosity, but most of the others shrank away, hiding behind their hoods as Callum loomed behind me. Once safely through the little door that led to the next set of stairs I stopped for a moment, realising that I had been holding my breath.

"Was Olivia there, Callum? I didn't see her."

"I didn't see her either. I'm not sure exactly where she's got to. Maybe she'll be up at the Stone Gallery." He paused for a second. "Are you OK? Ready to go on up?"

I stood up straight and took a deep breath. The next spiral staircase always seemed to be the worst: round and round in tight circles with no features to tell you how close you were to the end. "Ready," I agreed, and set off.

As I reached the next level up Callum appeared again. "I've checked down from the top. The vicar's not up here, and I can't see her on the stairs so we'll have a bit of time. If she's old, she's not going to be racing up here at any great speed."

"OK, that's good, so we can relax a bit."

"Yes, panic over. But no time to waste, eh?" He smiled at me, his hand becoming more solid in mine. I gave it a quick squeeze.

"No, none. Let's go."

There was no need to jump over maintenance barriers, as the Golden Gallery was still open. It was a bit of a blow, but seeing Callum in public was still better than not seeing him at all, and the closer I got to the top of the dome, the more excited I was about putting my plan into action. He stayed with me as I walked up through the latticework of wooden beams and iron staircases, and each time I looked at him he became more and more solid.

"Come on, give me a break," I puffed as we reached a little landing and he strode on to the next stairs. "I normally have a bit of a rest here. Why are you walking with me today?" Normally he met me at the top, which gave me a few minutes to compose myself after the lengthy climb. He was not seeing me at my best, red-faced and gasping.

"Now the others know you are here, I'm not letting you in here alone, not after what happened before."

"Oh, good point. Do you think that someone else might try to hurt me?"

"I'm pretty sure none of them would dare, not with Matthew keeping watch."

"Was he? I didn't see him."

"He's had to lay down the law, making sure that they all behave themselves around you. It's easier now Lucas has gone though; he was always the worst."

"Was that why everyone was so wary of me back down in

the Whispering Gallery?"

"Probably. They've been given some very clear instructions about leaving you alone." His voice was tight, and I knew that he was remembering the fight on this same staircase not long ago, when Lucas nearly managed to get me to take off the amulet. I shuddered briefly.

"There's no need to worry, Callum. I'm not going to take it off ever again. None of them can hurt me, not now I know what they could do."

He made a non-committal grunting noise. "Look really, I'll be fine," I continued, still wanting to catch my breath. "I can't talk any more now. I'll call you again at the top." I smiled briefly at a passing tourist, who was obviously curious about who I was talking to. I made a bit of a show of getting out my mobile and pressing the cancel button, but left the earphones in place. Callum disappeared up the steps and I concentrated on getting up to the next landing.

It was hot and stuffy in the dome, and stepping through the open door on to the Golden Gallery was a huge relief. Callum was instantly by my side, and it took all my self-control not to hurl myself into his arms. As no one else could see him, that would have looked too odd. I pretended to make a call. "Hi, Callum, I made it – top of the dome!"

"So I can see," he said drily. "If you come round to the east side there's not so many people there and we can sit together for a while if you want."

"It's what I've been waiting for." I smiled back. The gallery wasn't as busy as it had been on previous visits, with no snaking queue of people shuffling around. Small groups were gathered at the railings, pointing out some of the various landmarks that were so clearly visible from this vantage point. There were no actual seats, but the carving on the stone wall made small ledges where it was possible to rest. I could finally feel Callum's strong fingers laced through mine and I squeezed them tightly.

I sat down on the small stone ledge next to Callum, leaning against him, his arms holding me close. I could feel his heart beating through the thin white shirt he always wore. I adjusted my earpiece with a deliberately exaggerated movement, although no one seemed to be paying me any attention.

"Oh, Callum, I've missed you so much!"

"I know, and I'm really sorry about everything," he said in a voice heavy with emotion. I could feel him kiss my hair, properly this time, not just the faintest hint. It took all my self-control not to swivel around and kiss him properly. "It's just that I've missed you so badly; I guess I got jealous."

"Really, there's no need to apologise. We're here now, and that's what matters, nothing else." His hand was stroking the length of my hair and back in a tantalising fashion. "What's really annoying is that your maintenance man is away. I'm not sure how much of this I'm going to be able to stand."

"Do you know," he murmured, kissing down my neck from my ear to my shoulder, "you are utterly in my power for once. I think I like this!" He continued stroking my arm as I tried hard not to wriggle.

"You're impossible!" I laughed, relieved at how easily his black mood had been lifted by just being up here.

We sat for a while, then I got up to stand by the railings, Callum right behind me. It wasn't the same as hugging him properly, but he could hold me tightly, and I could hold his arms, kissing his hand when no one was close by. The Thames glittered in the sunshine below us. I stared unseeing out across the panorama of London, thinking about my plan. I knew I could save him, and I could do it any time. Within minutes he could be a mass of sparks and we could be together properly by this evening. So what were we waiting for?

"You're very quiet," observed Callum. "What's bothering you?"

"You could be here tonight, Callum, by my side. You only have to say the word."

He sighed heavily. "I know. I've thought about little else since yesterday." I saw his long fingers trace the shape of the twisted silver on my wrist. "And I've come to a decision. You seem really convinced that it will work, and if it does, I'm with you properly. If it doesn't, I die. But I can't live like this. I love you too much to be so far away from you all the time. Given those choices, I want to try."

I turned to look at him, ignoring the strange looks from a passing tourist. His eyes were dark with emotion, the gold flecks flashing as he moved. "Are you sure? If we do it now there's no going back." I tailed off as it became obvious I was being overheard. I picked up my phone and gave an angry look towards the middle-aged couple who were lurking just a little bit too close to us.

"I'm sure. You'll be able to do the same for Olivia and the others afterwards, won't you?"

"I don't see why not. It doesn't seem to wear me out at all."

"Then it's time to take the risk," he said firmly. "I'm no use to you like this, am I?"

"It's a much harder question to answer up here, where I can see you properly." I lifted his hand and pressed it to my cheek, feeling its warmth and strength. "Back home, where you're insubstantial – well, that's easy. Here, you're already as real as me."

He held me tighter for a moment. "I think we should do it," he whispered, running his hand down the length of my arm. "And I think we should do it now."

It was time. I had expected to feel some panic, some worry about whether I was wrong, but I was strangely calm. I felt so sure that I wasn't going to kill him, and that we had the rest of our lives to be together. I looked round; he was watching me closely, a small frown wrinkling his forehead. I was almost bubbling with the thought of it all, of being able to sit quietly reading, resting my head on his chest, of eating meals together, of finally getting the opportunity to walk along a beach, hand in hand. I knew what I had to do.

"It's a big decision," I whispered back, and for a second I thought I saw a shadow cross his eyes. "A big decision, but one that I'm happy to make with you." The frown disappeared as his face creased into a huge smile.

"Great! So where shall we do this? Here or somewhere else?"

The butterflies were already setting off in my stomach, but I didn't let myself think about the consequences of it going wrong. Lucas had disappeared, and there was no reason to suppose that he wasn't safe and well somewhere, just like Catherine. It was time to do to Callum what I had done to Lucas.

"No time like the present." I smiled at him. The gallery was fairly quiet for a moment. It was as good a time as any. "OK," I said, my mouth suddenly dry. "Here's the plan. You put your amulet with mine, and I start to push with my mind. As soon as you disappear I'll run down to the riverbank. The tide is out so it'll be easy to fish you out and I'll take you home. Sorted!"

I could see the fear momentarily on his face. "I love you, Alex. Whatever happens, I want you to remember that." He leaned forwards and kissed me gently on the lips, and I knew that he thought he could be kissing me goodbye.

"I love you too," I replied, looking deep into those mesmerising eyes, trying to sound as confident as possible. "See you on the other side!"

He held out his wrist and I positioned mine next to it. "Ready?"

"Ready."

Callum's amulet was pressed up hard against mine and I held his wrist tightly as I felt the power in me grow. It was a wave, rising as it travelled up my arm from the twisted silver. The stone started to glow. I turned all my attention to the amulet, ignoring everything else going on around me.

"OK? Can you feel it yet?"

"It feels weird, as if it's warming up somehow."

The strange coiling sensation was back, wrapping around my wrist. I took another deep breath, feeling the strange and unnatural power growing within me, ready to be unleashed.

I pushed.

Torture

There was a sudden explosion of sparks and I felt myself being thrown backwards across the balcony. I hit the stone floor with a thump. Callum had been thrust in the other direction, so I scrambled up quickly to check that he was being consumed by the light. But he was sitting on the floor, looking absolutely normal with no sparks or glittering lights tracing their way across him. He was peering curiously at his amulet and a quick glance at mine showed that the glow was beginning to fade.

"Callum? Are you OK? What's happening?"

"Nothing as far as I can see." He sat up and stretched out his arm, examining the amulet from every angle.

"Is it OK? We've not broken it, have we?"

"No, it seems fine. That was freaky."

I realised that I was being watched by a small crowd of tourists, so quickly bent down and pretended to pick something off the floor. "Ah, found it!" I moved the mouthpiece for the phone and spoke clearly into it, shrugging and smiling at one of the tourists as I did so. "Sorry about that, Callum. Where were we?" I went back to leaning on the rusted golden railing and looked out at the far horizon. Within a second Callum's arms were tight around me.

"What happened there then?" He was struggling to keep the disappointment out of his voice.

"It was weird. It started out feeling exactly like it did last time, when I stopped Lucas, but then, well, it was almost as if someone had put in a barrier and the power rebounded back to me." I rubbed my backside carefully. "It packed a bit of a punch."

"Tell me again what you did to Lucas – *exactly* what you did."

I cast my mind back to that terrible day only a few weeks previously when I had chased after Catherine, then Rob, and finally ended up fighting with Lucas. "Rob was kneeling on the floor. Lucas was standing in front of him. I had just put the amulet back on after Rob had torn it off his wrist. Lucas put his hand out and Rob suddenly went rigid." I shivered despite the warm summer's day.

"Carry on," Callum encouraged gently.

"I stepped between them – as far as I could see in the reflection in the mirrored building anyway. I thrust my amulet into Lucas's and pushed, just like I did just now."

"So your amulets were in the same space?"

"Yes. Ooh, do you think that's it?"

"It could easily be. Up here I'm solid to you and your amulet, so we can only get them alongside each other. When you attacked Lucas your amulets were lined up in the same way ours are when we talk. I bet they have to be in the same space."

"Yes! That's bound to be right! So our plan would have worked anywhere but up here."

"I guess. Unlucky, eh?" He squeezed me tightly for a moment and bent down to kiss my cheek. "Can we try again downstairs?"

I flexed my fingers. "I feel fine. It doesn't seem to affect me at all." I looked down at the Thames far below. "We should probably be by the riverbank anyway, so I can raise the alarm the minute you appear in the water. It was a bit stupid of me not to think about that earlier."

"OK, shall we go now?"

"Might as well." I quickly glanced around me at the balcony. For a moment we were alone. "Kiss me, Callum, quickly."

He didn't need to be asked twice, twisting around so that I was pressed close to his chest. His soft lips found mine, and for a moment I drowned in his touch, taste and smell. His mouth became more urgent and I couldn't help responding. Suddenly he broke off, breathing heavily.

"I need to be over there with you," he said in a husky voice. "Come on, let's go and get it done." With a final squeeze he released me, then grabbed my hand and started pulling me towards the "down" exit.

I laughed, holding tight to his hand as we slipped through the narrow doorway. Almost immediately his fingers became less firm, and as we descended there was quickly nothing for me to hold on to. But there was a new and exciting urgency to our plans, so I continued following down the treacherous stairs as quickly as I dared, the memory of his kiss still lingering on my lips.

We were nearly at the bottom when there was a flurry of activity among a small crowd of translucent figures. I could see a swirl of cloaks and Callum suddenly pulled up.

"What's up? Who's there?" I called as I saw him deep in conversation with someone.

"It's Matthew. Give me a minute, will you?"

The tingle went from my wrist as he and Matthew continued. Matthew was pointing, and whatever he was saying it obviously wasn't good news. I sighed. I was getting used to things going badly around me in the cathedral. I left them to it and stepped through the door into the bright sunlight of the Stone

Gallery. Quickly checking around that the strange vicar wasn't lurking nearby, I moved to the edge where I could admire the view and talk comfortably into the phone when he returned.

After a few minutes Callum was back at my side. I glanced up at his face, and even in the daylight I could see that he was ashen.

"What? What's happened now?"

His voice was urgent. "Matthew says there's something you need to see before it gets moved. Please come now, we have to hurry."

"OK, I'm coming, but why don't you tell me on the way?"

"It's right here." We had reached the strange fibreglass shelter that covered the entrance to the top of the stairs. Inside was a seat where the security guard or guide usually sat. It was a hard plastic seat, and absolutely unremarkable.

"What am I looking at?" I asked, puzzled.

Matthew suddenly came into view on my other side, and he walked quickly to the chair and pointed. Next to it in a small stack were a number of magazines and papers. On the top of the pile was a copy of the *Evening Standard*, rather dog-eared and folded open. "Quickly, take it!" urged Callum.

"Really?" I scanned around but the guide was nowhere in sight. Some tourists were approaching though, so I snatched the paper and ran down the tight spiral staircase. Callum kept pace with me easily, but by the time I emerged at the Whispering Gallery I was monumentally dizzy.

"I'm going to have sit down for a moment or I'll fall over," I hissed, sinking on to the closest part of the bench. None of the Dirges were nearby. I used the paper to fan myself briefly. "That was not a good idea. Right, what am I looking for?" As I spoke

I smoothed the paper out over my knee. It had the usual range of stories on the page, from celebrity watching through to minor disasters.

"There," exclaimed Callum, pointing towards the bottom of the page.

I read the headline and my blood ran cold.

Mystery River Man Tortured

Police confirmed today that they are setting up a murder inquiry after post-mortem results showed that a man pulled out of the Thames last week had been tortured to death. Identifying the man as 76-year-old Lucas Pointer, Chief Inspector Megan Sharman admitted they had few clues. "From the injuries observed at the post-mortem it was clear that the unfortunate Mr Pointer was systematically tortured, then dumped barely alive into the Thames. Although he was rescued in a matter of minutes it was impossible to save him. Our investigations are ongoing, but have been hampered by the fact that Mr Pointer was reported missing by his wife, Emily, fifty-three years ago. Mrs Pointer passed away last year, believing her husband to be dead. This was a horrific crime perpetrated by someone cruel and callous on a helpless old man, who suffered terribly. If anyone has any knowledge regarding this incident, or the whereabouts of Mr Pointer in the intervening period, please contact the incident room."

I couldn't breathe. I tried to reread some of the details but it was impossible; my hands were shaking too much. "I killed him," I whispered. "Me. I killed him." The paper dropped to the floor as I pressed my hands to my face, a huge tidal wave of fear threatening to engulf me. Callum was looking at the report again, trying to read it where it had landed by my feet. The panic was getting worse. I cupped my hands over my nose and mouth, trying to take shallow breaths, but it didn't help. "I've got to get out of here, right now!" I tried to speak calmly but I failed miserably. Several heads turned to look in my direction as I got to my feet. I stumbled blindly for the stairs down and it took a moment to realise that someone was trying to talk to me.

"Alex! Calm down. You need to get a grip." I stopped in surprise at the unfamiliar voice.

"Ma . . . Matthew?"

"Yes. Get back there and pick up the paper. It's an old one; you won't be able to get another easily and you'll need the details. Come on, *now*, before someone else takes it!"

I stopped and hung on to the cast-iron balcony rail, trying to make sense of what he was saying. "What?" I shook my head. "I don't understand." There was a sharp edge to my voice. All I wanted to do was get away; to get away and to run as far as I could.

"Pick up the paper! You need to know more, like the date it all happened. Do it *now*!"

"OK, OK, I'm going." It was easier to do as he asked than to stand there and work out his reasoning. As fast as I could I made my way back to the seat, past several groups of tourists trying out the famous acoustics. One group had just sat down where I had been, and a middle-aged man was reaching for the paper.

"Sorry, that's mine. I dropped it," I said, rudely snatching it out of his hand. Before he had time to react I was gone, walking as quickly as possible back around the balcony to the main staircase. The Dirges melted away as I approached, but I would have walked straight through them anyway. I didn't have time to mess about. The tourists were worse: they had no sense of urgency and were ambling gently through the little narrow corridors to the top of the stairs. I was ready to scream by the time we got the landing and I could overtake them. Trying hard to fight the panic I started down the stairs as quickly as possible. I blanked my mind, thinking only of my next action. Get down the stairs. Get past all the tourists. Don't run. Don't let the weird vicar see you. Get to the door. Get to the door. *Get to the door!*

My hands were clammy, the newspaper sticking to my palms as I pushed my way through the exit turnstile. Leaving the cool quiet of the cathedral I burst through the revolving door and on to the steps, blinking in the bright sunshine. I still had to be further away. It wasn't safe. I needed somewhere to hide, to think. I started to walk as quickly as I could, desperately trying not to draw attention to myself by running.

I didn't stop until I was at the river. The tide was low, exposing beaches of mud and shingle on the South Bank at the far side. Under Blackfriars Bridge the water lapped gently and benignly at the edge. It was quiet, with only the occasional pedestrian passing by. I found a seat and sank down, pulling in my knees to make myself as small as possible. Not only was I a murderer, I'd come within a whisker of murdering Callum as well. My head knew that they were all already dead, but my heart told me something quite different. My mouth felt like sandpaper and I had to hold on tight to stop shaking. My mind circled around that terrible moment when I had fought for Rob. I had wanted to stop Lucas, but did I want to torture him? If that had been the choice, if I had known, would I have still done it?

I wrapped my arms around my head, trying to block out the images that were swirling around in there, but one more awful fact surfaced: not only had I tortured and killed Lucas, I'd made him old. *Old!* Would I do the same to Callum?

Finally there was a familiar tingle in my arm, and Callum's shocked voice in my head. "Alex? Keep still, will you?" The voice faded in and out and I realised that I was rocking violently backwards and forwards. I tried to stop but it was almost impossible. In the end I sat on my hands, but still couldn't stop my head and shoulders.

I tried to speak but nothing came out, my mouth was so dry. I tried to swallow a couple of times and tried again. "I made him old, Callum, then I killed him. We can't do it; I can't do that to you. What if our experiment this afternoon had worked? We'd be fishing your tortured body out of the river there. We can't do it!"

"Shhh." I could feel his hand on my hair, stroking it rhythmically. "But we didn't do it. We stopped and I'm still here."

Another wave of despair washed over me. "But this means that I can't – we can't – try again. I'll never be able to rescue you." My voice rose to a wail as the tears started to stream down my face. All the consequences of what it meant were piling up: I couldn't save him after all and every plan I had was crumbling. "I can't bear it!"

"I know." His voice was hollow, beaten. "I almost wish it had worked earlier. At least that way I would have gone into it thinking it was going to work and by now it would all be over."

"You can't want that, not really. You can't honestly want to die."

The silence answered my question.

"We don't need to do anything, not yet," he said eventually. "But you have to remember that none of us is here out of choice. All of us would take the chance of oblivion even if it meant another painful death." There was another pause. "We have all died already, remember," he added softly, "and if I can't have you..."

I couldn't believe that we had gone from the excitement of planning being together to him effectively asking me to kill him.

"This can't be happening, it just can't! It's so unfair!" Without thinking about it I was rocking again, holding myself tight, trying to will the whole thing to go away, when Callum's voice cut across my thoughts.

"Alex!" he hissed. "It's the vicar. Look, she's running this way!"

Spinning round I saw Reverend Waters staggering towards us. She saw me leap up and tried to increase her pace, but was obviously exhausted. "Alex, please, don't go," she gasped. "We need to talk about. . ."

But the last thing I needed now was a telling-off. Clutching my tattered newspaper, and with panic threatening to tear my insides apart, I turned and ran.

Realisation☺

This time I didn't stop until I got to Waterloo, and there I only paused briefly to talk to Callum. The running had helped clear my mind; I was exhausted but able to think straight.

"Callum?" I called as I stood on the concourse waiting for my train's platform to be announced. "Callum, do you think you can find out what that vicar wants? I can't believe she'd go to so much trouble just to tell me to stop jumping barriers in St Paul's."

He obviously started talking before the tingle reached my wrist, so I missed half of what he was saying. ". . .how she came to be under the bridge, can you? I mean, she can't be that fast, she's ancient. What do—"

"Wait!" I interrupted him. "Back up – I didn't get half of that. Didn't you see where she came from?"

"Nope, no idea. It's almost as if she knew that's where you were going."

"She can't possibly have known that. I didn't know myself until I was almost at Ludgate Circus. I don't like her. She's freaky." I had a quick scan around of the crowd. "Are we safe here? Did she follow us again?"

"No, I watched her. She followed you along to the Embankment and I thought that she might get a cab but then she turned around and went back. Once I was sure she wasn't following I came to find you."

"OK, well, my train is going in a few minutes, so why don't you have a look round at the cathedral and see if she's gone back there. We need to know more about her, and what she wants."

"OK. I'll come to your place later. Call me if you need me before then."

"All right." I felt the featherlight touch of his lips on my cheek and the tingle was gone. The noise and bustle of the station reinvaded my consciousness and I couldn't help dropping my head and letting my long blonde hair obscure my face, just in case. There was no point in making it any easier for her or whoever else she might have told. I walked towards the barriers, shoved my ticket into the little slot and made my way as calmly as I could on to the platform.

On the train I wedged myself into the furthest seat in the carriage where no one could see me, and looked again at the crumpled paper in my hand. Half the newsprint was smudged where my sweaty palms had been clasping it, but I could still read the item. It was so awful I didn't know which bit was worse: not only had I killed Lucas, but it had been a hideous, painful death. And somehow in the process I had made him old. Was that because he had become the age he should have been?

The wave of panic I had been controlling threatened to break through yet again as I thought of how close I had come to doing that to Callum. He could easily have been dead by now, or writhing in pain and ageing before my eyes. We were so lucky that it hadn't worked.

London started to slide past my unseeing eyes as the train began its long, slow journey to Shepperton. I smoothed the paper out across my knee again, looking for the date. The story had come out two days after my fight with Lucas, so it was nearly a month old. For a moment I wondered at the coincidence that had led me to it. Before I had gone on holiday I had been scouring the Web for anything like that, but had missed it completely. Why had the killing got such little press coverage?

I guessed that they were not having much luck with their murder investigation, as there was absolutely no evidence that would point them towards me, and nothing else that they could suggest was a cause of death. But the fact that they wouldn't be able to prove it was me didn't alter the fact that I had done it; I had tortured Lucas to death.

I shut my eyes and pressed my knuckles into the sockets, trying to get the image of his face out of my head. But it just made it worse. I remembered in graphic detail watching the rush of glittering sparks envelop his body, sweeping across his face and into his bellowing mouth, covering him completely until there was just a momentary outline showing where he had been. The mass of sparks had then cascaded on the floor into a puddle that had disappeared very quickly down a nearby drain.

At the time I had just been relieved that he had gone, and only later started to piece together the possibilities; that I had been responsible for stopping him, and therefore that I could do it again and save Callum. And I had been particularly happy over the last month or so knowing that I could do it without the help of Catherine. I hadn't cared that she had run away; in fact, I had been delighted to see the back of her. She had taunted me as she had left and I bet she knew that any attempt I made to save him would result in his death.

I was back to square one again, with a boyfriend trapped in another dimension who was suffering horribly every day, no useful plan to rescue him myself, and with a guilty conscience to boot.

It was all so unfair! I wrapped my arms across my head, trying to make myself as small as possible in my seat, and unsuccessfully trying not to think. But the dramas of the day wouldn't go away, circling my head until I was ready to scream.

I was relieved when the train finally stopped at the station and I could start to walk home; sitting still wasn't doing me any good at all. As soon as I was away from other people I called for Callum and he was at my side within minutes.

"Hi," I asked as brightly as I could manage. "Did you have any luck in finding her?"

"No, no sign of her at all. But now I know what she looks like, and that she's in the cathedral a lot, it shouldn't take me long to track her down." He was keeping pace with me easily as we walked up the narrow residential road. I flicked open my little mirror so that I could see him.

"This is all so weird. It's like she's stalking me."

"I know." Callum sounded rattled. "Your trespassing theory does seem a bit lame, and if she's trying to convert you she's got a strange way of going about it. What the hell can she want?"

"The first time I met her she thought I was going to jump off the dome. Perhaps she still thinks I'm suicidal?"

"Well, maybe, but it still seems pretty unlikely."

"I've had enough of this. I've got to find out what is going on, with her, and with this." I waved the newspaper at him. "I need to get on the Internet and start getting answers to some questions."

I could see him frowning in the little mirror, obviously deep in thought, his soft lips pressed together in a hard line. "Yes, you're right," he said eventually. "How about you go and check out what happened to Lucas, and I'll go and see if I can find out about the mysterious Reverend Waters?" He peered across at my watch. "I'll be back later to find out how you're getting on, if I can do enough gathering in time."

I was instantly contrite. "Leave her until tomorrow; you need to make sure that you have what you need. It's been a pretty traumatic day, and doesn't that mean that you have to do more gathering?"

He shrugged. "Some, I guess. I'll do what I need to do. I promise I'll be back later though, and with as many answers as I can find."

I marched up the road as quickly as I could, desperate to get back home where I might be able to find some solutions to my problems. The smell of someone's barbecue drifted across the path, and I glanced through the open gate as I passed. A group of teenagers were standing there, cans in their hands, laughing over some shared joke, and for a second I had a momentary pang of longing; longing to be normal. The thought of being able to go to a party with Callum tore at my heart. Earlier I had been so sure that I could help, that it was just a matter of time before I brought him over, but now . . . now I knew I was deluding myself. It made me realise that Catherine had been telling the truth: the only way I could do it was with her involvement, and she would never, ever agree to help us.

I wished that Grace was home so that I could talk to her about it, but she was still on her family holiday and would be for another few days. For now Callum and I were going to have to sort out this problem on our own.

When I finally got back to the house I could see that Dad's car was missing. Hopefully that meant that both Mum and Dad would be out and I could slope off up to my room and my laptop without being sidetracked. I slipped the key in the lock and crept inside. It was immediately obvious that I wasn't in luck. I could hear the washing machine churning and Mum giving Josh a hard time about something. I glanced longingly at the stairs and wondered if I could get away with just sneaking up there, not telling anyone I was home. I had just decided to go for it when the kitchen door burst open and Mum appeared with a basket of washing under one arm.

"Oh, hello, Alex, you're back. You've been gone for hours; I was beginning to wonder when you might turn up. Right, you take these, fold them up and put them all away where they belong, then bring me back the basket." She barely drew breath as she thrust the overflowing laundry basket at me. She was obviously having one of her rare "being efficient with the household chores" sort of day, so I was relieved that I'd missed most of it.

"Hi, Mum, good to see you too," I mumbled under my breath as I staggered up the stairs, trying not to drop too many of the socks balanced on the top. I worked as quickly as I could and dumped a pile of clean holiday clothes in everyone else's bedrooms. Sneaking into my room I quickly opened up my laptop and switched it on, intending only to get some basic information from Google before I had to go back downstairs. But as ever I was sucked in and within minutes I was lost. Most of the reports had come out in the last two weeks while I had been away, but even so I couldn't believe that I hadn't seen one of the early ones.

Lucas Pointer had been identified by his dental records, and one account I read suggested that his body had been burned beyond recognition. Finally I came across a picture. Taken about fifty years earlier, it was black and white and very grainy, but the familiar cruel eyes stared out at me. I couldn't help shivering. From that picture it looked as if he had always had a nasty side, and hadn't just been turned by being a Dirge. *And you killed him*, I reminded myself. Even though I knew that death was what he'd wanted, I still felt a huge pit opening in my stomach every time I thought about the pain I had inflicted with it.

I was just searching for other articles on his death when I heard Mum calling from downstairs. I quickly shut down the computer and picked up the laundry basket. She wasn't in the mood to be kept waiting.

Downstairs I could see through the kitchen and out into the garden. Josh was mowing the lawn, his face a picture of gloom.

"Right," she announced in her best no-nonsense voice. "You have a choice. You can finish doing the washing or you can come with me to the supermarket. Which is it going to be?"

That wasn't a hard decision. The washing would take minutes. "Washing, I guess."

"Fine. There's a load to take out of the machine and hang on the dryer, there's another load of beach towels in the bathroom, and there's a small pile of hand washing on top of the machine." I groaned inwardly. Maybe not such a smart choice after all, and she hadn't even finished. "And when you've done that, can you please sort through all the rubbish which I've taken out of all your pockets and is currently on the window sill in there. I'm sure most of it can go in the bin."

"Yes, Mum." I quickly picked up the basket and got out of earshot before she could add anything else to the list. I busied myself noisily for a few minutes until I heard her call goodbye, and the door slammed behind her. Once the car was safely out of the drive I nipped out into the garden.

"Hey, having fun?" I tapped Josh on the shoulder as he walked the mower down the grass, leaving a slightly wobbly stripe.

He jumped.

"Oh, hi, Alex." He pulled his earphones out and I could hear the heavy thump of the bass even over the noise of the mower. "I didn't know you were back. Did you see Mum?"

"Uh-huh, and I've got a list of chores as long as my arm. Has she been like this all day?"

"Yup. It was a good call being out when she got back. Unfortunately I was still in bed, and she took that as a bit of a personal affront."

"Well, I'm going to do a bit of mine then have a coffee. Want one?"

"Nah, you're OK, thanks. I'm roasting. I'll get this done and grab a beer." He plugged the earphones back in and restarted the mower. I walked slowly back into the house. I didn't want to do any of it, but Mum was going to expect it done by the time she got back, so I reckoned it was as well to get on with it. I rolled up my sleeves and got to work.

An hour later I was roasting too, and looking forward to a long cold drink when everything was done. I grabbed a plastic bag and started gathering all the junk that had come from the pockets. I debated checking every piece, but if it hadn't been missed so far, what was the point? Finally I dropped the lot in the bin outside.

I had only just got myself a drink when Mum reappeared, and I hoped that by offering to bring in the shopping I might be able to slip away afterwards and get back to my laptop. We quickly got everything put away and I made her a cup of coffee. I could see Josh mouthing the word "creep" at me with a grin as he finally came in, covered in grass clippings. I raised an eyebrow at him.

"I've got some e-mails I need to answer, so I'll be upstairs if you need me," I said as casually as I could manage.

"OK, sweetie," said Mum absently, looking at her BlackBerry. "Oh, did you go through all that stuff from everyone's pockets?"

"Yup. Well, I put it all in the bin."

"What was the stuff from St Paul's?"

"I'm sorry?"

"There was a card, from St Paul's. Some vicar called Veronica Waters. Why on earth did you have that?"

I stared at her, my mind racing. *Veronica* Waters? The creepy vicar was called Veronica?

"Alex? Are you OK?"

"Oh, yes, sorry. I was thinking about something else. Umm, I don't know. Someone fundraising the last time I went there I expect. I guess I should probably have kept that one." I smiled and made for the door. "I'll just fish it out," I said over my shoulder as I made for the door. My heart was pounding as I threw open the bin. She was called Veronica. She had given me the little card after I had been helped down from the top of the dome when Catherine had the amulet. I hadn't read it but had stuffed it in the back pocket of my jeans where it had stayed until Mum had taken it out when they were washed.

If she was the same Veronica a whole new list of questions needed to be answered.

I had first heard of her from Callum, when he had been telling me a bit about his life. Veronica was a Dirge who had apparently been a bit wild, always taking memories from late-night party-goers. Then she had managed to get away: someone had found the amulet and it had given her the chance to escape. She, like Catherine, had obviously become real again, and somehow Catherine had known all about her. If Veronica was the same person as Reverend Waters there were things which I had to ask her.

I quickly retrieved the bag from the bin and silently ran upstairs, carefully shutting my bedroom door before upending the contents of the bag on the floor. It didn't take long to find the card. Small and white, it had a little logo with St Paul's in the corner.

Reverend Veronica Waters

I looked at the phone numbers, then scrambled to my feet to get the letter from my desk. The mobile number was the same. I sat back down with a thump. It *was* her, but what did it mean? And why was she so keen to talk to me? There was only one way to find out. I picked up my mobile and punched in her number.

"Hello, Reverend Waters here." The voice was warm and friendly.

I swallowed hard. "It's Alex." My mouth was so dry it was barely more than a whisper. There was a sharp intake of breath then a momentary silence.

"Alex, thank heavens! We really, really need to talk. You know who I am, don't you?" Her voice became more guarded.

"I've just worked it out."

"I'm sure it's a shock, but we have no time to waste."

"What do you mean?"

"I'm not able to talk right now. I'm on the train to Shepperton."

"What! What do you think you're doing?"

"You kept running away; what else was I supposed to do?"

I couldn't have her coming to the house, not with my mum still bustling around downstairs. "Not here," I muttered, thinking fast. "I'll meet you at the garden centre down the road." I didn't really want to be anywhere alone with her, and the garden centre would have plenty of people wandering about.

"I'll be there in about an hour," she said.

"I'll tell Callum to meet us there. He's off gathering at the moment."

She was suddenly sharp: "Just us, Alex, that's really important. There are things we need to discuss that we shouldn't share with anyone just yet."

"Well, I'm going to tell him that I'm meeting you. He'll get worried."

"Please don't tell him, or any of the other Dirges, anything about this. At least listen to what I have to say first. What harm can it do?" She had a very firm, no-nonsense tone.

"That attitude's got me in trouble before," I muttered, mainly to myself, remembering the time Catherine fed me a load of lies about Callum and drove a wedge between us. "OK, I'll see you in a bit. Go to the café in the garden centre."

The phone went dead. I slumped back into the futon, massaging my temples to get rid of the headache that was threatening to make an appearance. Why did everything have to be so complicated? I hated not being straight with Callum: there had been too much of that over the last few days. I wondered what could possibly be so desperate that she couldn't tell me on the phone, and why she was so determined that I didn't tell the Dirges about her. She hadn't exactly been hard to spot before, hanging about at St Paul's all the time. But there was no way to work it out; I was just going to have to wait.

There was plenty to occupy me. I started to search the Internet for information about Lucas, but it was difficult to get hold of anything in addition to the basics of the original story. The facts about his life were very sketchy as they were from so long ago, and some of it seemed to be made up. I was almost ready to give up when my phone beeped with a text.

I reached over to see who it was, hoping for a light-hearted distraction from one of my friends.

Hi, hope you got home OK. Will be in Richmond tomorrow, was wondering if you fancied a drink? Max x

The memory of Max's easy smile caught me off guard and for a moment I was overwhelmed by the possibility of doing something normal with someone uncomplicated. I sighed as I reread the message.

"That's a big sigh. What have you found out?" Callum's silky voice was back in my head and I smiled. Whatever other rubbish was going on, he was there for me. And he didn't need any more pain.

"Oh, nothing, that's the problem," I said, smoothly flicking the phone off and reaching for the mirror. There was a tiny hint of suspicion on his face and for a moment I wondered if he had seen the message, but there was no way I was mentioning Max again, not after the last time. "I've got to go and do some dull chores too, so I've only got about twenty minutes."

"Ah well, this will have to do for now." His long fingers traced a path down my arm. "Much as I'd like to sit and do this all evening, I don't have that long before I have to do more gathering too. Is there no more news about Lucas? Didn't you manage to find out anything else?"

"No," I said, angling back the lid of my laptop so that he could read the screen. "Look, nothing useful at all. They don't seem to have published any information about how he went missing, or any of the details of how he died. It's all very odd."

"At least we can be sure it's him. That photo is pretty creepish." He nodded towards the screen as I scrolled through a couple of items. "So according to that, he had been a Dirge for fifty-three years."

"So it seems. How long did he think he had been there?"

"It's really hard for us to tell, and I didn't spend a lot of time talking to Lucas, but Matthew guessed about twenty-five or thirty years. I asked him earlier," he added in response to my sharp look.

So he'd been there twice as long as they thought, then. I made a mental note, but didn't think it was fair to bring it up. Callum was ahead of me though. "So although I think I've been here about ten years, in reality it could be longer. Much longer. I could easily be twice your age."

"There's really no point in worrying about that, is there? I can't bring you over anyway, not now." My voice caught on the last bit and I dropped my gaze.

"Hey, none of this is your fault, you know. In fact, you've given every one of us hope."

"What do you mean? If you're talking about Catherine I have no idea where she is, and she won't help anyway. That's if she was telling the truth about being able to in the first place."

He paused for a moment and then spoke so softly I had to strain to hear. "You can set us free, Alex. You can release us all."

I stared at him in horror. He meant every word. I finally found my voice. "You can't mean that. I'm not going to kill you!"

"But you have to. Matthew will be coming to ask you, to arrange the details." He smiled at me gently. "Don't forget that we are already dead. All you'll be doing is moving us on." He stroked my hair with his featherlight touch, an unreadable look in his eyes. "You're our only hope. Matthew wants you to do it as soon as possible."

I sat back, aghast. How had this happened? They wanted

me to murder their entire community.

Callum continued to sit there, the strange look on his face. I couldn't sit still, so leapt up and started pacing my small room. I could see in the mirror that he was watching me, waiting.

I finally slumped back down again. "Is that what you want, really?" I asked in a small voice.

"No, you daft girl, what I really want is to be over there with you, real and alive like Catherine, but I have to face facts." His kind tone turned bitter.

"I can't do it to you, Callum. I just can't. I can't hurt you so badly that you end up looking like you've been tortured to death!"

"Not even if I ask you to?" He looked at me unblinkingly. "You love me, Alex, I know, but at this point it's our only sensible choice."

"I'm not going to discuss this. There's no way it's going to happen. I'm not going to line you all up and inflict that on you one by one."

Callum shut his eyes for a moment, pinching the bridge of his nose. "Fine, let's leave it for now. But we will need to talk about it again, and soon." He paused for a second as we heard Josh walk past my bedroom door, then carried on in a quieter tone even though there was no way Josh could hear him. "In the meantime, have you been able to find out anything about the dodgy vicar woman?"

"I've been concentrating on looking for reports on Lucas," I whispered back, avoiding answering his question. "Did you have any luck at the cathedral?"

"None," he said gloomily. "All I can do is follow her if I happen to see her. I can't go rummaging through the files and find out where she lives, I have to wait for someone to leave it out and that could take forever."

I hesitated for a second, but decided to give Veronica the benefit of the doubt. Another few hours weren't going to hurt. "I'll keep looking until I have to go out. There has to be some information about her somewhere." I made a move for the laptop, as if I was about to start searching.

"Leave that for now – let's just sit for a bit. I think we deserve it after the day we've had." In the mirror I could see him holding me tightly, his left arm with its amulet across in front of me and superimposed on my right arm, his head behind my right shoulder. Even the day of worry and pain hadn't affected his staggering good looks. My heart leapt into my mouth as I watched him. I still couldn't believe that someone so beautiful and so kind wanted me. And what was even harder to believe was that he truly wanted me to murder him.

I wasn't going to let that happen. If Veronica couldn't tell me something useful then I was just going to have to find Catherine, wherever she had disappeared to.

Veronica

I persuaded Callum that I needed to go and do my chores, and he went off gathering. Part of me hoped that he would follow me and see Veronica as it seemed so unreasonable to keep it from him, but I resisted the temptation to give him a hint. As I walked up the road to the garden centre I kept trying to imagine what it was that she wanted to hide from the Dirges, but could come up with nothing. Not wanting to be late, I arrived in the café in plenty of time and crept along behind the racks of pot plants to find somewhere to watch unobserved, wanting to check her out when she arrived.

But she was early too, and was at a table facing the entrance, hands folded in her lap. She wasn't reading or checking her phone, but was just sitting watching the entrance intently. There was something strange about the way she sat, as if she was used to waiting. I wondered again what she could possibly want to tell me and why she was being so weird about it. I watched her for a couple of minutes, but it really wasn't going to get me anywhere; the only way to find out what she wanted was to go and ask. I stood up straight, tossed my long hair over my shoulder and walked purposefully into the café.

As Veronica saw me a huge smile lit up her face, doubling the lines etched in her skin. "Alex! You came. I'm so pleased to see you." She stood up and took a step forward.

"Hello, Veronica." My smile was more guarded and she immediately pulled back from what might have been an attempt to hug me. Until I knew what she wanted I was determined to be cautious.

"Please, Alex, do sit down," she said. "I'll get us some drinks. Coffee or tea?"

"Coffee, please." I sat at the small table while she went to the counter. She wasn't wearing her cassock or even a dog collar, just ordinary old-lady clothes. She looked particularly unthreatening, and a bright-yellow light flickered above her head. She returned with the drinks and a couple of large chocolate-chip cookies.

"So, Alex, here we are at last. It's good to have the opportunity to talk."

I nodded briefly, wanting to hear her story first.

"So you know who I am then?"

I stirred my drink for a few moments, wondering how to put it. "I don't know for sure, I'm just trying to join the dots, but I know that a Dirge called Veronica was able to escape years ago, and I'm guessing that was you." I looked at her. "Am I right?"

"Yes, that was me. It's a long time ago now."

I nodded and sat back, considering her for a moment. She had a weathered face, one that looked like it had seen a lot of life, the wrinkles forming well-worn creases on her forehead and around her mouth.

"You managed to come over safely then?"

She nodded, rubbing her wrist absently. There was an old scar still puckering the skin there. "Safely for me, anyway," she said, looking at the floor.

"You killed someone." I kept my voice as low as possible so as not to attract attention. "You knew what you were doing."

"I know, and I live with that every single day." She looked back up again. "You've got no idea, no idea at all about how bad our lives are as Dirges. We would all have done anything to escape, anything, and all I expected was oblivion. Now I live with the perpetual guilt."

"It's a shame that Catherine didn't have quite the same take on things," I muttered.

"You know Catherine?" she asked sharply.

"Of course! She nearly killed me trying to escape."

Veronica looked at me in surprise. "It was your memories that brought her over? So how are . . . I mean, you're alive. How did that happen?"

"It's a long story. Before we talk about me, I'd like to know what's going on. What have you been following me for, and why didn't you sign the note you sent?"

She took a sip of her tea before answering. "I didn't know what you knew and how you would react. I thought it best not to do anything that might alarm or panic you, and thought my name might do that. I thought you'd just call the number out of curiosity and I'd get the chance to explain before you told anyone." She looked up from her cup. "I assume you've not said anything to your parents?"

"Huh, too right! They would have had the amulet off me instantly." I considered her warily. "So tell me what you know about Catherine then, as we have her in common at least."

"I've been waiting a long time for Catherine, or someone like her. Every day I scour the papers, looking for reports of people plucked from the river, people with no memories. I also have access to some of the reports from the river police, given my position, and I routinely visit all the nearly-drowned when they are in hospital, just in case. But I never had any luck. I'd almost given up hope when I visited a woman who had been rescued from near Blackfriars Bridge and was recuperating in Guy's Hospital. She had no visitors and the staff were concerned because she had such violent mood swings. It was clear as soon as I saw her scarred wrist and started to talk to her that she had been one of us, that she was a Dirge."

I realised that I was fidgeting with the spoon on my saucer and, not wanting my nerves to show, carefully put it back down before sitting on my hands. "What did she say?"

"The talk didn't go as well as I'd hoped. She's a troubled soul, and was obviously struggling with the memories she had inherited."

"Good; she didn't deserve them anyway," I huffed, unable to keep the dislike out of my tone. "So come on, what happened next?"

"She got pretty upset, and the staff suggested that I leave it until the next day. But when I went back she had discharged herself and gone. I've had no sign of her since then."

"She came to find me instead, to start making my life unbearable. Was that because of something you said? Did you tell her something that made her give me all that grief?" I could feel my voice rising so made a determined effort to keep it down. I leaned over the table towards her. "What was it you said to her that didn't go well?"

"It's a long story, and I think I'm going to have to tell you a bit about my history for it to make sense to you. Is that OK?"

I looked into her eyes and saw only compassion there. "I'm sorry, I didn't mean to, well, you know." I stumbled over the words, knowing that it was time to start sharing. "It's just that Catherine made my life a complete misery for a while, and I've no idea why."

"Thank you, I'll explain it as well as I can." Reverend Waters took a deep breath. "When I was a Dirge, when I was . . . like them, I wasn't very nice. I can remember all of that so clearly, but like all the others, nothing from before."

"Nothing at all?" I couldn't help interrupting. "When you came over didn't you get back the memory of how you ended up as a Dirge? That's what Catherine said she'd got."

Veronica gave me a rueful smile, her weathered face folding into soft lines. "You know, perhaps I would have done if I had been sober enough to remember anything. But it seems that I fell into the Fleet in some sort of alcoholic haze. There's nothing to remember."

I stared at her, stunned. "What? What do you mean?"

"I was a mess, that's what I mean. I was obviously a needy, addictive type before, and that didn't change when I found myself stuck with the others in St Paul's. I had been young and beautiful and I became very, very angry. I spent my life stalking the bars and clubs of London, feasting on the memories of those who were busy drinking there. I found I enjoyed the drunken memories rather more than the sober ones."

Looking at the well-groomed elderly woman next to me I found it hard to picture her stalking drinkers and preying on their alcohol-sodden thoughts. I struggled to find something to say as she paused, waiting for my reaction. "I know, I don't look the type, do I?"

"How long is it since you came back over?" I said at last.

"It's been many, many years. When I was a Dirge I was in my twenties, I guess, but a lot of water has passed under the bridge since then. So now, I don't actually know how old I am, but I've been here for over forty years." She paused, looking out across the room but not seeing the other people in there. "Over forty years of waiting to try to do what's right." The last was just a whisper and I struggled to hear her. "And now you've arrived, and we can fix it all!" Her sudden change of tone startled me.

"I'm sorry, I'm not sure I understand."

"Not to worry, Alex, not to worry. I'm getting ahead of myself. It's just so exciting to be back close to the amulet again after all this time." She looked at my wrist. "May I?" she asked, lifting my hand.

"Umm, sure. I'd just rather not take it off, if that's OK with you."

"Quite understand, quite understand," she muttered as she started examining it closely. I was struck by the familiarity of her actions, moving the amulet back and forth as if to catch the light, and was horrified when I remembered why. I had looked at the amulet like that when I had been trying to get it off Rob outside the office in Soho. As subtly as I could I drew my arm back in, forcing her to let go.

"So, umm, you were partway through telling me about your life as a Dirge?" I prompted, keen to move her back to her original subject.

"Yes, true. I was." Veronica sighed and sat back, taking a long sip of her cooling tea. "It's not a happy tale, but then, I guess, none of them are. I don't remember anything about drowning, I think I must have been unconscious when I took that last fatal breath of Fleet water, so I don't know anything about exactly where I was, unlike the others. And as I wasn't aware of drowning, I didn't have the same level of despair that most of them do. What I had was a huge, vast amount of rage. I couldn't believe that I had ended up in that situation, that I, Veronica, was stuck in that hideous place. I mean, it wasn't possible; someone was going to have to save me."

She described herself in a self-assured tone, and I wondered again who she had been before. She sounded like she felt that she was someone special back then, important even. Perhaps she had been a celebrity in her day. Everyone was equal as a Dirge though, even though some *were* different. She was different because she had anger, not despair, and Callum was different, too. He had hope: when he had died, when he had taken that last breath, he really, really expected to be saved. I wondered if the amulet automatically chose to connect to those who felt less creeping horror and depression than the others did.

"So what is the first thing you do remember?"

"Oh, that's easy. Finding myself on the riverbank, soaking wet, with the mother of all hangovers." She looked at me briefly. "You know, that bit never went away. My personal purgatory was to spend eternity with the worst hangover in the world. Anyway, I found myself lying on the little beach at the side of the river, near to where the new Waterloo Bridge now stands."

"*Now* stands? That bridge has been there forever! When on earth did you die?"

"You must know that none of us know that. All I can tell you is what has changed in that time. When I arrived on that beach, London was very different to the city you see today. I think it must have been around the early nineteen hundreds. There was a different bridge across the river there then, with lots of arches, and on the southern bank were some small beaches at low tide. Just rough bits of scrubland really, full of rubble and discarded rubbish. It smelled terrible. I tried summoning help as soon as I could stand up, but the only people nearby, poor people picking through the rubbish that had been washed up, just ignored me completely. I remember getting pretty cross with them." Veronica paused and gave me a weak smile. I half-heartedly smiled back, trying to encourage her.

"Callum told me that Catherine had done much the same thing, ranting and shouting at the people when she realised that they couldn't see, hear or feel her."

"I probably would have had a lot in common with Catherine. It's a shame I never got to know her properly."

"Actually, she's really not very likeable, so you've not missed much," I muttered. "So when did you realise that you were . . . different?"

"I dragged myself up to the street, and noticed that I was wearing a full-length cloak. For some reason that surprised me, but I didn't know why. It was at that point that I realised that I had no other memories at all. It was most peculiar. I knew the names *of* things, like the Thames and Somerset House – and St Paul's, of course, but I realised that I had no idea of who I was, or where I lived or who were my family. You have no idea of how frightening that can be."

I made a non-committal grunting noise, not trusting myself to speak. That was exactly how Catherine left me when she took my memories to come over. And it was exactly how Veronica would have left the poor person she attacked too, I thought, but I kept silent. I didn't want to bring up something that might upset her, not when there was so much to find out.

"I decided to keep the cloak because, well, I had nothing else. So I started to walk towards the bridge, hoping that I might see someone who I knew, or might know me, and then I stumbled across a crowd of people. There was some sort of disturbance going on and the police were there. I worked my way around the edge of the crowd to get closer to the policemen, trying hard not to draw too much attention to myself. I didn't know who I was, but I was pretty sure that I didn't belong there, among the thieves and villains living around Waterloo. No one took any notice of me at all, which I was initially grateful for. I thought that maybe the cloak made me blend in. Little did I know!" Her laugh was harsh. "Of course," she continued, "once I found a policeman it was only a matter of minutes before I realised I was in a completely different type of trouble.

"I had approached one of the police officers, one who seemed to be issuing orders. I stood by him for a minute but he didn't acknowledge me, so I tapped him on the arm. Or rather, I *tried* to tap him on the arm. My hand went straight through him. I couldn't stop myself from screaming, and then realised that the noise had no effect on him either. I had no idea of what I had become. . ." Her voice faded out and I could see the tears working their way down her creased cheeks.

I reached out to take her hand, giving it a quick squeeze. "You don't have to tell me, you know; I do understand."

"No, it's OK, I know; I'll be fine. It's just never being able to speak about any of this before makes it harder to do so now. But it will do me good, and there's no point in being self-pitying." She took a deep breath and wiped the tears from her face before carrying on. "I tried all day to get someone to register that I was there, to move things, to shout into people's ears, but nothing; no response from anyone. I continued for hours and hours, working my way across London, chasing people. At some point I crossed the river, but I'm not sure when I did that. I was in the West End when all the theatres started to empty out, and I was worn out trying to capture anyone's attention. It was dark, and I was sitting at the side of the road, hungover, angry and very sorry for myself when I noticed the lights."

"What lights?"

"The little dancing lights above the theatre crowd's heads. Almost all of them had these faint little bouncing glows, like fireflies or something."

I nodded in agreement. "That's what I thought they were too, when I first saw them."

"You can see auras? How have you managed that?"

"It's part of the long story. Essentially, Callum copied all my memories into his amulet as Catherine was stealing them, then later, when the amulet was put back on my wrist, he was able to download them all back into me. Ever since then I've been able to see the happy auras."

"I didn't realise that you could see them too. Is it just the happy ones, or can you see the others as well?"

"Mostly the yellow ones, but I can sometimes see the red and purple if someone is feeling it really strongly. They all seem to be much clearer in St Paul's than anywhere else."

"Hmm, interesting. So you know that I'm happy to have found you at last." She smiled warmly at me, the little yellow light confirming her words.

"I've got quite good at filtering them out, really. Unless I'm thinking about it, I don't take much notice of them. It can be useful when I'm talking to my mum though; I know when it's a good or bad time to ask for a favour."

"I can see how that would work." She smiled again briefly, then her gaze wandered off to the distance and the yellow glow faded as she started to talk again. "So, I realised that I could see these strange lights over everyone's head, and I was puzzling over that when I felt the strangest sensation." She paused so I raised my eyebrows at her. "There's absolutely nothing I can compare it with in real life. It was like I had been summoned by something I didn't understand. I was being pulled through the streets of Soho, across the darkened spaces of Lincoln's Inn Fields, towards the east. Stopping wasn't an option; I couldn't even think about not following the urge, which was getting stronger all the time. And all the while I was getting angrier about the fact that any of this was happening at all. I didn't want to believe it. I was pushing through the oblivious crowds when I stepped through a child. I must have picked up her aura by mistake, because at that point I still hadn't realised that I had an amulet, but as I picked up that little yellow flicker I felt a wave of relief. No, relief isn't the right word, because I was still desperate afterwards. I imagine it is closest to someone who is dying of thirst being given a thimbleful of water. It was welcome, but I needed more, and it wasn't until that point that I knew I was missing something. But I hadn't realised what I had done, so I carried on following the urge to move eastwards.

"Eventually I ended up at the front of St Paul's. It was dark, and most of the people had gone from the streets. The urge to move towards the building was positively painful, so I started walking up the steps. I was looking at the front, at the huge doors, when I realised that a dark shape had just appeared *through* those closed doors. Someone dressed in a long dark cloak. Someone like me."

"Matthew?" I guessed.

"Yes. He had been nominated by the leader to gather the newcomer into the fold."

"The leader? That wasn't Matthew then?"

"No, when I became a Dirge the leader was a man called Arthur."

"Really? The only Arthur I heard Callum mention was a guy who stalked weddings, but that's all. Would that be him? What happened to him?"

"I've no idea. He was leader until I left."

"Callum did tell me that they sometimes vote for a new leader. They must have voted him out, I guess. Had he been the leader for a long time?"

"A fair while, I think. Time is difficult to gauge over there, so I'm not sure. Maybe they voted him out because of his behaviour. He and another Dirge had a – well, it wasn't a fight exactly, but they were battling to take control of something."

"What was that?"

"My human."

"What? Your human?"

"Yes, the man who had found the amulet and had made a connection with me. Traditionally that made him mine. It was my chance to get away, to escape the life, to die, or so I expected. But Arthur and Lucas both decided that they ought to be allowed to go; Arthur because he reckoned he had been there the longest, and Lucas because he was the nastiest."

"I know Lucas or, rather, I did. He found a way of escaping."

She raised her eyebrows in surprise. "Well, if anyone could, he would." She paused for a second before continuing. "Well, they explained what had happened. Of course, I didn't believe them; it all seemed so preposterous. But there I was, with the amulet fused to my wrist, waiting to make me its slave. The next few decades have begun to blur a bit really. My life became an endless round of seeking and capturing memories, trying to keep the amulet full enough to stay sane. As I said, I found that I had a preference for memories gathered from people who had been out drinking, who really didn't seem to notice or care that their thoughts had gone missing. I would wait on the streets outside the pubs and bars, and catch them as they were leaving. I guess in the mornings they just couldn't remember the night before. I got very good at it, and because I was the only one who really liked the drunken thoughts, I didn't have much competition.

"And then, one day, everything changed. I was walking down the Strand late one afternoon to go to the King's College University bar, as the students always started drinking early, when I suddenly had this peculiar vision. A middle-aged man's face, looking intently at something I couldn't see." She hesitated and then sighed. "Poor Daniel, he didn't deserve it."

"So he was the guy you ... you ... killed."

"Killed. Yes, ultimately I did. And I regret it every day of this life." She looked away, unable to hold my gaze.

"So where in the Thames did he find the amulet?"

"He was walking on the riverbank near Kew when he saw it washed up on a little beach. He climbed down to get it. His first thought was to take it to the police to see if it had been reported missing, but then he looked closer and realised that it had been in the water for many years. He knew that it was valuable, and he realised that he could sell it for his fund.

"Daniel was a vicar, and his parish church was falling down. Congregations had drifted away and some people had stolen the lead from the church roof. He urgently needed to raise cash to help repair the building. He had started the fund but it hadn't been going well. Poor Daniel, he wasn't much of a salesman and he had terrible trouble convincing any of his flock to contribute. He thought that finding the amulet was the answer to his prayers.

"He walked home with the amulet, cleaning it as he went, and that was when I got my first glimpse of him. I was in St Paul's at the time and couldn't help exclaiming at the vision. Everyone became really excited; it had been a long time since the amulet had been seen. But there was an immediate fight. Some of the others thought it was wrong that I should be the one chosen, as I hadn't been a Dirge for as long as some of the rest. But no one was going to get anywhere unless Daniel actually put the amulet on. When he was holding it I got the visions, but to use him to escape I needed him to be wearing the amulet, to give it some power. And I knew from what some of the others were saying that I needed *him* to be wearing it, not someone else, not his wife, or someone who would buy it from the jeweller's. My connection was always going to be the best with him.

"Luckily from the visions I could see roughly where he was, and the fact that he was wearing a dog collar made it easier to track him down. I finally found him in the vestry of his church, considering the bracelet. That night it was fairly simple to invade his dreams and plant the idea that the bracelet would only be safe if he was wearing it, that no one would be able to steal it from him. Once he put it on the process was simple. . ."

"Did you manage to work out how to talk to him?"

"No, I never learned that particular trick. You must ask Callum sometime how he worked it out. No, I just appeared behind him in the mirror and the windows. Scared the poor man nearly half to death too."

"I can imagine," I murmured, remembering just how frightened I had been when Callum started lurking behind my shoulder.

"So I just stalked him, waiting until he had started wearing the amulet for a while and then ramped up the sudden appearances. He really thought he was going mad. I was trying to be with him all the time, to make sure that I was there when he took it off, that I would be the one with the chance to go, but it was hard. I had to keep gathering, obviously, and he didn't spend a lot of time with happy people. Every time I left his side either Arthur or Lucas were at his heels, hoping to snatch the opportunity. It got to the point that I knew something had to be done, or I was going to miss my chance to go. I couldn't face the rest of eternity in that miserable existence, but I couldn't be sure what to do. Then the decision was taken out of my hands. . ." She paused again, looking at the floor.

"What happened?" I prompted gently after the silence continued for a few minutes. She looked at me with eyes that were full of pain and remorse.

"Daniel had worked out that the amulet was the cause of all his problems, and he wanted to be rid of it. He was no longer concerned about making money out of it; in fact, he considered it downright evil and as something sent by the Devil to tempt him. So he wound a wire around a large rock and attached the amulet to it. As soon as he did that I was able to strike. He was so relieved to be dropping it over the side of the bridge that he didn't notice that I was taking away every memory of it. By the time he realised something was wrong it was too late: he couldn't stop me."

I couldn't watch her as she described the process; it was all too familiar, too hideous. I didn't want her to see the accusing look that I was sure would be in my eyes.

"And as I sucked away the last memories, I was conscious

of Arthur and Lucas fighting to get close to me, to get a share in the spoils. That was the last memory I had as a Dirge. The next thing I remember was being hauled into a boat in the middle of the Thames, miles downstream. It all goes a bit fuzzy for me then."

"Why? Did you start drinking again?"

"Certainly not! I've not touched a drop since I came back over. It was having all Daniel's memories, that was what made things difficult. For a long time I couldn't really get to grips with the fact that I, Veronica, had the memories of a middle-aged vicar, at the same time as remembering my time as a Dirge. As soon as the doctors realised that I had no past, and that they didn't believe what I was saying, they immediately locked me up in a psychiatric hospital. I was there until I could work out what I was supposed to be telling to whom. That took a while, I can tell you."

"So how long were you locked up for?" I asked, appalled.

"About fifteen years. I was nearly institutionalised when finally they decided I wasn't a danger to myself or others and let me out. I had a diagnosis as a schizophrenic as I had two clear sets of memories, but no one believed that both were real. For a time I doubted it myself."

Veronica paused, stopping to pick up her coffee spoon and stir the dregs of her cup. I realised that I was holding my breath, waiting to hear the next details of how she actually managed to integrate with society after life as a Dirge. That's what Catherine was dealing with.

"So there I was, on the streets with nothing, nothing but hazy memories of life as a parasite and very clear memories of Daniel's calling to be a vicar. So I went to the church. They looked after me and gave me a home, gainful employment and, eventually, education." She smiled at me briefly. "That bit wasn't too hard as I already had all of Daniel's memories of being in the seminary, so I sailed through."

"But did you believe it? I mean, did his memories bring faith into your life, or did they change you?"

"The memories – any memories – can't change your personality, but they can modify your reaction. I had been an addictive person, I'm sure of that, and that didn't change; I still am. But with Daniel's memories I was able to change the focus of that addiction, to channel that into a wish to repent and pay back my sins. Daniel didn't deserve to die, and I have spent the rest of my new life trying to make up for that."

"So what did you do?"

"After training in the Church I was assigned to a parish in the north, an inner-city area with a great many problems. I think that I was able to help some of the troubled people there, and I believe Daniel would have approved. Of course, back then there were no women vicars, so I was more of an assistant than anything else, but that changed in time. And then, when I retired, I decided to devote whatever time I had left to trying to help the Dirges. I couldn't join the staff at the cathedral. It's far too competitive to get into one of those roles, but it's possible to become a Friend of St Paul's, a volunteer who helps with all the visitors.

"I had first gone back to St Paul's when I was discharged from the hospital. It was strange, returning to the place. I wasn't sure what I would feel, if there was going to be any evidence of what I had been through, but it was just like any other church. I tried to make myself known to the Dirges, but I have no idea if I was successful. After the time spent in the hospital I no longer looked much like I did when I was one of them, so I guess they didn't recognise me. And of course I look even less like my twenty-something self now."

"I've not heard anyone mention you, except as a master at stealing drunken thoughts," I admitted. Veronica nodded sadly, the cloud of purple above her head thickening.

"That's what I thought," she agreed. "I knew that I had a futile task, but I had to try, to be there, just in case. And then you turned up." For the first time in about ten minutes she looked straight at me. "You turned up and I knew that my waiting had been worthwhile. I just had to be a little bit more patient."

"What do you mean?"

"When I came back over, when I got my life back, I learned something. I learned how to save the Dirges, to set them all free." A huge smile lit up her face as she reached over and grabbed my hands. "Together with you, and the amulet, we can release every last one of them from their suffering."

My heart almost stopped. She knew what had to be done, how to rescue Callum and bring him to my side! He could be with me after all. It was all I could do to stay in my chair. I couldn't believe that I hadn't realised that she would be able to help.

"You can do it too? Catherine said that she could, but then she lost the memory. She says she wrote it down, but if you know how then I don't have to try and find her!"

"I've been waiting to do it; that's why I wanted to talk with you. It's time the Dirges went home."

"But, Veronica, that's fantastic!" I couldn't help exclaiming, then lowered my voice as I saw other heads in the café turn to watch us. "How would it work? What do I have to do? When can we start? Catherine wouldn't tell me anything."

"Well, it's pretty straightforward really. We just need you, the amulet and me, and all the Dirges gathered together."

"And then what?"

"Well," she started, leaning over the table in a conspiratorial fashion, "we all form a huge circle: the Dirges, and you and me. We'll have to be next to each other, then when you and I touch you can channel the energy from the amulet around the line. With both of us there it will be like making an electric circuit."

We both looked at the amulet for a moment, its rich colours glinting in the halogen spotlights of the café. I could almost feel its potential. "Is that all I have to do? Push the energy? We don't need anything else?"

Veronica nodded enthusiastically. "No; between us we can do it. My waiting is done; I can finally set them all free."

Her enthusiasm was catching. "That would be brilliant! I mean, it will take a bit of explaining, all these people suddenly appearing in the river, and we'll have to make sure that there are enough lifeboats around so that no one drowns, but I'm sure I can work out a way to do that!" My mind was racing with the sudden and exciting possibilities; Callum could be here with me in days. I was almost breathless with my excitement as I quickly thought through all the various logistical problems we would have to overcome. I was smiling to myself as I thought of being there on the riverbank when Callum came ashore in one of the lifeboats; the kiss we would share. . .

Veronica's voice interrupted my thoughts. "Alex, I don't think I've explained this very well."

"What do you mean?" I asked, still smiling.

"When I said that we could release them, I mean, well. . ."

"Yes?"

"It will allow them to finally die," she sighed gently. "What we have to do is kill them all."

125

Persuasion

My heart sank as I realised what she meant. For a moment she had given me hope that there was a better way out for the Dirges, but the crushing disappointment was back.

"Look, Veronica, I've worked out for myself how the amulet can kill them, but surely there's a way to save them all instead?" I sat back, folded my arms and glowered at her, my excitement ebbing away. Why was everyone so convinced that the only way out was death?

"Well, there *is* another way," said Veronica, "but we don't have a chance of making it work."

I looked at her through narrowed eyes. "Why not?"

Veronica looked down at the table, shaking her head. "We need Catherine. She's the only person who can bring them over alive. And she won't do it. She made that very clear."

I knew it! "I really hoped that you weren't going to say that," I said. "Are you sure there's no way that I can do it?"

"You have the power, Alex, with the amulet, but you *will* kill them. You've already tried, haven't you?"

I felt a shiver run down my back. "You knew? Why didn't you tell me?"

"I *have* been trying to talk to you, if you remember." Veronica couldn't quite keep the exasperated tone from her voice.

I felt myself slump. "I saw the paper: I know I did it. You'd better tell me what else you know."

She quickly explained: she had been reading the police reports and had seen the news of the body in the Thames, but as the person had been tortured she had dismissed it as unrelated to the Dirges. It hadn't been until a few days later when she was reading another report that she had come across the photo of Lucas.

"That shocked me, I can tell you, seeing my old enemy scowling out of the paper like that. It was the last thing I expected. So I started to do a little digging. And then I found the report in the *Evening Standard*, and I knew that you and the Dirges needed to see it. I waited until I heard that you were back in the cathedral, and left it somewhere where it wouldn't go missing, but where it would be spotted by the Dirges. They obviously found it."

I nodded once. "Matthew spotted it while I was up at the top with Callum. I had no idea that I had done that to him, none. I was just trying to stop him from hurting Rob, that's all."

"You don't need to explain to me, and neither do you need to worry," she said, leaning forward and dropping her voice. "No one can possibly connect you to that."

"But there's a murder inquiry, it said so. The police will be checking out everything."

"I can assure you that they won't. The investigation has already been wound up."

"How do you know that? And why would they stop?"

"I know because I have friends in the police, especially the river police. I've made it my business to get to know them all. They've stopped because no one really understands what happened to him." She paused for a moment as a young couple struggled to get their double pushchair past us, smiling automatically at the two chubby little babies sleeping peacefully inside.

"Do you know the details?" I prompted, as she seemed lost in her thoughts again.

It took her a second or two to refocus on me. She sat up a little straighter in her chair. "Well, it seems that he was found alive in the river, but suffered some sort of cardiac arrest – or heart attack – when they were trying to help him. He was covered in a network of black lines – scorch marks – which they think mean that he must have been tortured. But it was after he died that the strangest things happened. He was on the ambulance trolley, covered in a blanket, when he spontaneously combusted. The fire was brutal, and although there were plenty of people to hand, within minutes there was almost nothing of him left. He was identified by his dental records."

The cold sweat of fear that had started to creep up my back threatened to overwhelm me. Burned! I had tried to do that to Callum. He too could easily be lying on a mortuary slab as a blackened pile of bones and teeth. I bit back a sob, hiding my face in my hands.

"There was even worse, though. It was clear from the old dental records who it was, but it didn't tally at all with the report from the guys at the lifeboat station who dragged him out of the water. They described him as a man in his twenties, otherwise fit and healthy-looking, with an identifying tattoo. The teeth and the tattoo matched the missing person's description perfectly, but the man who was missing would have been well into his seventies. They can't work it out."

"So he didn't get old?" I peered out from between my fingers.

"No, he just went up in smoke."

"Oh, don't, please!" I begged. "I can't listen to any more!" I pushed back my chair and made for the nearest exit, hoping that the fresh air outside would help to clear my head. It didn't help much, but at least I wasn't looking into those pale-blue eyes, eyes that knew far too much. I circled around for a few minutes before finding a shady pillar to lean against. Why had she told me all that hideous detail about how Lucas had died? What was the point? If she wanted me to help her to kill them all, she was going about it the wrong way. I was pretty sure some of the Dirges would hesitate too, once they knew what was involved. I knew that I couldn't keep it from them; it wasn't fair.

If Catherine was the only one who might be able to bring them over alive it was clear that I had to find her, and persuade her to help. I shut my eyes and took a deep breath. I never wanted to see her again in my life, and now I had to go begging to her. But before I could do that I needed some proper answers.

When I returned Veronica was still sitting in the nearly empty café, waiting patiently as if she knew I'd come back. I sat down opposite and put my hands on the table. "OK, Veronica, we clearly need to work together on this. But I don't think you've been entirely straight with me. I want to know three things." I started to count them off on my fingers. "One, how did you know about me and Callum? Two, what do you know about Catherine? And three, if we could persuade her to help us, what does she need to do?"

For the first time Veronica looked uncomfortable, but I pressed on. "Come on then. How did you know? How did you find me, and how could you possibly tell what I was going through?"

"I didn't," she admitted with a little shake of the head. "It was all a huge stroke of luck. I didn't even realise that it was possible for the Dirges to speak to the humans. One day, when you went to St Paul's to meet with Callum, I happened to see that." She gestured at the amulet. "It's not the sort of thing you forget, not when you have one welded to your wrist for decades. You were behaving very purposefully, going straight up the stairs, so I followed you. I took the lift so I was up at the Whispering Gallery by the time you got there, and I saw the way you walked carefully around, as if you were trying to avoid a long line of invisible people. I knew you could see them, I just knew it, so I followed you up to the Stone Gallery. You were gone when I got up there, though, as I was a bit slow up the stairs. I searched all round and asked the staff at the exit if they had seen you, but they didn't remember seeing you go down. So I searched again, and realised that the only place you could have gone was up, past the closed sign for the Golden Gallery.

"So I followed. It's a long way for someone who's not as young as they were, you know, so I took my time, praying that you weren't already coming down the other side. When I finally got to the top I stayed behind the door and listened. I could hear your conversation – just the one side of it, as if you were on the phone – but I knew that you were talking to one of them. The things you were talking about, the problems, the need to discuss everything with Matthew, it all fell into place. I knew that you were going to be my link. So I made my way downstairs and waited. And waited. What were you doing up there all that time?"

My cheeks flamed as I remembered. Kissing had been pretty high on the agenda for most visits. "Oh, well, you know," I started to mumble until I realised she wasn't waiting for an answer.

"Eventually you came back down and I stopped you to look at your ticket. Do you remember?"

I shook my head. "If I had just spent the afternoon talking to Callum I wasn't likely to remember anything else."

"Well, your season ticket has your name on it, and a reference number, so I could find out where you lived. There was no phone number though, and you're not in the directory so I couldn't just call. At that point I just needed to be sure that you would be back to the cathedral as often as possible. I needed to force you to come, so I thought I would try and make you a bit afraid, so that you would be back to talk to the Dirges about it."

"What did you do?" I asked suspiciously.

"I broke your window."

"That was you?" I exclaimed, almost jumping out of my chair, remembering the cold early morning air rushing into my bedroom and the mysterious note that I had found wrapped round a golf ball.

She looked at her shoes and nodded mutely. "It was the only thing I could think of, to get you back up to London as quickly as possible. I wanted to confront you somewhere where I knew we could find a large gathering of the Dirges, to talk to them at last."

I was speechless. Why would she do that? I had spent weeks worrying about who had thrown that ball, and my list of potential suspects had been quite large enough to not have to wonder if there was someone else involved. I realised I was sitting there with my mouth open and snapped it shut. I sat back and folded my arms. "That was a mean thing to do," I said eventually, "and your timing was terrible. There were three people falling over themselves to make my life miserable already; I didn't need anyone else."

"I'm so sorry; I had no idea at the time. I just wanted to finally implement my plan, make everything all right again. I was so excited; I had thought that with Catherine turning me down I had lost my chance, but there you were, and the whole thing was possible again."

"So if you were so keen to confront me in front of the

Dirges then why the secrecy now?" I asked. "Why can't Callum be listening to this?"

Veronica leaned forward. "Whatever you did when you took on Lucas, it made the amulet much more powerful. I wanted to talk to you first before the Dirges knew that, knew what had happened to Lucas, otherwise they'd never have left you alone. It would've given them such hope, you see. You and I need to decide what to do for the best, especially if you want to involve Catherine."

"OK – Catherine. Tell me about her. You said earlier that it was the conversation with you that turned her against me. I deserve to know what all that was about."

Veronica tucked a stray strand of her steel-grey hair behind her ear before she spoke, her eyes fixed on the table between us. "When I came round after stealing Daniel's memories, I couldn't remember how I died because I think I was probably too drunk to notice. But I did have one shiny new memory, one startling new fact; I knew the way to put all the Dirges out of their misery. It gets given to all of us who are resurrected."

"How can you be sure of that then? That it comes to all of you?"

"Because I asked Catherine, and she has it too, but she refused to help me," Veronica answered eventually, looking out of the window. "I was so excited when, a month or so ago, I saw that police report about a girl who had been pulled out of the river but who had no memories, and I knew that the time had finally come. As I said, I went to the hospital and confronted Catherine. She absolutely refused to help. In fact, I've rarely seen someone angrier with life. She clearly thought that draining someone of their memories would kill her, and she was horrified to find that it actually propelled her back into life. I tried to get her to see sense, that none of the Dirges deserved the existence that they have, but she wasn't to be swayed. She refused to tell me where I could find the amulet so I was back to square one again until I caught the glimpse of the amulet on your arm in the cathedral."

"So let me get this straight," I said as it all slowly sank in. "You and Catherine both knew – just knew, as if by magic – that if you could find the amulet you could release all the Dirges?" She nodded. "And knowing this, Catherine still stole the amulet from me to try to sell it?"

Veronica nodded. "She's really not nice, that girl."

"And you knew all this time." I sat back and folded my arms, exasperated. "Why did you leave it so long?"

"I know, that was . . . stupid of me, I admit. I just didn't want to frighten you with my plan until I was sure that you would see my point of view. You seem pretty balanced, and I can't imagine that you will sit idly by and let them continue suffering."

"You knew all this when you first stopped me in the cathedral, but you didn't say a word."

"I know, and that really horrifies me now; we could have prevented so much anguish." She was pressing her hands together as if in prayer. "And then the next time – well, by then it had already gone."

I was still taking in that I hadn't been alone, that there had been someone who would have understood. I stared down at my cup, shaking my head as she continued.

"What can I say? I was wrong, and I knew it as soon as I saw you again. That next time you went up to the top of the dome, when you couldn't find Callum, were you going to jump? That's what the wardens thought, and that was why I wanted to talk to you. But of course by then you had lost the amulet so there was no point in discussing my plan. You looked so lost, so forlorn. I longed to tell you what I knew; that you weren't the only one who missed them, but I had to wait, and hope that you would do all you could to get it back. You looked like a capable girl, and certainly one with a lot of passion. I was sure that you would be able to get it back from whoever had taken it from you."

"Why not just tell me? Why give me the cloak-and-dagger clues?" I finally asked, dumbfounded.

"It worked though, didn't it? It wasn't long before you were calling me."

"But in the meantime the amulet had nearly been lost."

"Look," she said, grabbing my hands and holding them tight. "I'm sorry, I made mistakes, and it was only because of your resourcefulness that you saved the day. And now I'm begging for your help. We can free the Dirges from their constant misery, using your amulet, and we can do it right now. But if you won't even consider that, you'll have to find Catherine. She's the only one who can bring them back to life."

"Why? What is it that Catherine can do that you can't?"

"I'm old, Alex. I've been here a long time, and I don't have the energy and the power that I had when I first returned. I'm worn out. I can still help you to release them, but only someone newly resurrected can make them live again. If you get Catherine to help, and help soon, they'll all have a second chance at life, whether they want it or not. All I can offer them is eternal peace."

I pulled my hands away and sat back in my seat, then took a few sips of cold coffee while I considered this new information.

"What would I have to do, whichever way we do it? How will it work?"

Veronica looked suddenly animated, sitting up straight,

her aura flashing bright yellow. She reached over and stroked the amulet reverently. "The key to everything is this, as you know, and we need to harness its power; we need to sort out our plans and—" Glancing up at my face she suddenly stopped. "Oh, Alex, I'm so sorry, you look distraught. This isn't easy for you, is it?"

I shook my head slowly, appalled at the thought that I was going to have to ask Catherine for help, but at the same time relieved that there was someone else involved, even if it was a slightly flaky ex-vicar.

"Shall I get some more drinks? Give you a few minutes?"

"Thanks," I said. "There's a lot to think about."

"Of course. I won't be long."

I watched her walk away in a daze. I still couldn't believe that she had been the one lurking outside my house throwing golf balls. She absolutely didn't look the type. She must have been well into her sixties, with greying hair cut into a severe bob. She wore no make-up, and her clothes were functional rather than fashionable. She looked like someone's grandma.

There was so much information to take in, so much that I didn't really understand. What were the implications of some of the things she had told me? She'd kept her personality when she had stolen Daniel's mind, but had been affected by his thoughts. Would that mean that the same would happen to Catherine? Over time, would she turn into a nicer person because of my memories? And would it be straightforward to get her to return to London or would I have no choice but to put Veronica's other plan into action? There was only one way to find out.

I rubbed my thumbs under my eyebrows, trying to relieve the headache that was starting to throb just above my eyes. Even though it was going to be a nightmare, I had to find Catherine.

Search

I sat with Veronica for another half an hour, listening to her talk about releasing Dirges, but my mind was elsewhere. There was no way that I was going to do it if it meant that I had to kill them all horribly; I wasn't going to have that on my conscience. I needed to work out how on earth I was going to find Catherine.

As we parted she extracted a promise from me that I wouldn't say a word to the Dirges just yet. I could see her point: it was their very existence we were talking about and I didn't want to mislead them about what I was going to be able to do. It was best to say nothing until I knew if there was a chance that Catherine might help.

It was difficult not to discuss it with Callum when he came over briefly later in the evening, but I managed it. There were a few occasions when he looked at me oddly but I carried on and he asked no questions. I didn't feel good about it though.

The next morning I wasn't up until late morning. Mum and Dad had gone to work and Josh was still sound asleep when I let myself out for a walk to try and clear my head.

I was on my way back when I was almost knocked off my feet by a large chocolate-brown Labrador puppy jumping up at me.

"Hello, Beesley!" I said, rubbing his ears as he enthusiastically tried to nibble my belt. "You've grown while I've been on holiday.

You're quite the big dog now." His tail whipped back and forth, tongue lolling out of the side of his mouth. "What have you done with Lynda?"

I looked around. The puppy seemed to be on his own so I took a firm hold of his collar and walked with him back to his house. It looked deserted. Lynda's car was missing and there was no answer at the door. I walked around towards the side gate. It was firmly locked but the bottom of it was a chewed mess of splinters. Beesley had obviously been working on his escape plan all morning.

"What am I going to do with you, you daft dog? You can't go back in there, can you? Home with me, I guess then." His soft brown eyes twinkled. This was clearly what he had in mind. Shaking my head I took a firmer grip on his collar and went home.

Josh was awake, eating a sandwich and reading the paper. He raised his eyebrows as Beesley burst into the kitchen.

"Hello. You've been out dog hunting, have you?"

"Ha! Collecting waifs and strays actually. I found him on the road. He's escaped from his back garden."

As Josh and I discussed how to get hold of Lynda, Beesley was wreaking havoc in the kitchen, pulling over the bin, then jumping up to put his front paws on the table to steal a piece of bread which he then chewed up messily, leaving wet crumbs all over the floor.

"It's no good, I'm going to have to take him for a walk, just to wear him out. If I hang on to him, could you find me a bit of rope to use as a lead?"

Josh grunted in agreement, reviewing the remains of his lunch, and quickly returned with some old rope. It seemed tough enough so I tied one end to his collar and made a loop at the other end, which I could put over my wrist. Making sure I had my earphones with me I let Beesley drag me out of the house.

I struggled to keep Beesley to heel as I put the earphones in. He had got much stronger and much, much harder to control. Tugging hard, I finally got him close to me and looped the rope around my hand.

"Callum?" I panted, already out of breath. "Hi, I'm back. I seem to have got the dog for the day, so why don't you bring Olivia over?"

By the time I made it to the little field with the swings the tingle was in my wrist. "Hi, gorgeous," he greeted me, his honeyed tones making me melt as usual. "You look like you're struggling there!"

"Oh don't. He's been a nightmare. He escaped from home so I don't know quite how long I'm going to have him for. Is Olivia with you?"

"Yup, she heard the word dog and was almost here ahead of me. Look." He couldn't point so I quickly scanned around to see if I could spot what he was talking about. I didn't have to look far. Beesley had suddenly sat down, a soppy look on his face, his nose moving from side to side as if he was following an invisible fly.

"Well, she can come again!" I laughed. "Instant obedience! I can't believe that she's got him so well controlled."

"She's been here every day while you've been away, playing with Beesley in his back garden. He adores her."

I had introduced Olivia to Beesley a few weeks earlier, and the two of them had immediately hit it off. Before I had gone away on holiday she had come with me on several walks with the puppy and I had got to know her quite well. Callum loved her like a sister and was terribly protective of her. I knew he was delighted that the two of us got on so well, but he was always warning her to be careful. Too much fun with the dog during the day meant that she had to do a lot more gathering of happy thoughts and memories to keep her amulet full, and that wasn't always easy.

"How's that worked out?" I asked Callum softly. "Is she getting better at doing her own gathering?"

"Yeah, it's been good for her. A bit of responsibility and focus seem to have helped. Much like they've helped me, I guess!" I felt the whisper of his lips brush my cheek. "Now, you and I need to talk. Matthew was keen to join us today but I've put him off until, well, we get it all sorted."

I sighed. Why was it all so complicated? "Sure. Let me just tie up Beesley and then I can get out the mirror."

I walked to the bench in the furthest corner of the field, one near the small ford across the stream, dragging Beesley in my wake. I tied my end of the makeshift lead to the iron leg and let him go. The rope only just allowed him to reach the water, but I could see that he and Olivia were enjoying themselves, splashing around in the shallows.

Getting the mirror out of my pocket I angled it so that I could see Callum's face. He was watching Olivia, seeing her run and skip and laugh with the dog, and I could see the love and tenderness that he felt for her reflected there.

"I can't do it," I said softly. "I can't torture her to death, Callum, any more than I can torture you. Please don't ask me again."

He dragged his gaze away and his eyes met mine in the mirror. The pain on his face was evident. "I know it's cruel to ask but it's worse for her to have to stay. You can see that, can't you?"

I shrugged, not wanting to answer. I really wanted to tell

him that there was a possibility, a chance that we could save them all, but Veronica was right. Knowing that they could be saved but that it depended on the malicious whim of his sister wasn't worth discussing. She was bound to disappoint them. As I watched him and stole the odd glance at Olivia too, I knew what I had to do. I had to use all my powers of persuasion to bring Catherine back and get her to help. And if that failed, if that last hope was taken away, only then would I do as Matthew asked. In the meantime, though, there was a way to tell him half the story. I carefully worked out what I was going to say as we watched the dog in silence for a while, Callum's arms folded around me, his free hand gently stroking my arm. Every so often Beesley would come running back with a stick, which he dropped at my feet expectantly, waiting for me to throw it towards Olivia. He was easily pleased.

"You know," I ventured after about the tenth throw, "I think I should see if I could track down Catherine."

"Really? Why would you want to do that?"

"She knows *something*. I know that Olivia took the memory from her by mistake, but Catherine told me that she had written it down. I didn't care at the time because I thought I knew how to save you, but of course it turns out that I don't. Maybe she knows something different."

"I don't know," said Callum dubiously. "You're hardly best mates, are you? What makes you think that she would help?"

"Well, nothing really. I'm sure she'll be as obstructive as ever. But don't you think it's worth going to ask? She's had a bit of time on her own now. Maybe her outlook has changed."

"I think you're mad," he said, ruffling my hair, "and clutching at straws."

"Maybe, but if it's a straw that might bring you over to me I have to grab it, don't I?"

"I suppose. But do you even have any idea where she is?"

"No, not really," I admitted. "But she can't have disappeared off the face of the earth. She doesn't have a passport so my guess would be that she's still down in Cornwall where Rob said she was going."

"If he was telling the truth, of course."

"I know. But didn't you see her on the train to Exeter or Truro or somewhere?"

"I guess. It was the West Country line. That was weeks ago."

"Why would she move on? She's as likely to be there as anywhere else."

He paused for a second, considering my response. "OK, what if you're right? What are you going to do then? Cornwall's a big place."

"I'll start stalking her again on Facebook. Maybe there's a clue that she has given away. Maybe she's talked to one of my friends – I can ask them all and see."

Callum shrugged. "If you think it'll do any good. Then what'll you do?"

"Go down there and talk to her; get the information I need."

This time he actually snorted with derision. "Alex! Get real! She hates you *and* me. There's no way she's going to be helpful. The only thing she'd like more than leaving us to wallow in misery is to watch us all die horribly."

"It doesn't mean I can't at least try," I retorted.

"I know, I know." He was instantly contrite. "It's just that, well, having lived with her for so long, I know what she's like. But you do have some winning ways, so you never know. It's worth a shot." I felt the gentle stroking of his hand down the length of my hair and relaxed back towards his touch. In the mirror I could see his mesmerising blue eyes, the gold flecks flashing briefly in the sunlight as his glance flicked towards Olivia for a moment. Olivia was oblivious to us, deeply engrossed in her game with Beesley. "I don't want to leave you either," he whispered, his soft lips finding my neck in the tiny reflection. I could feel the faintest of touches as he worked his way up to my jaw line, and slowly, slowly along to my mouth. Kissing Callum was always bittersweet: his gentle touch filled me with longing for more; more that we couldn't possibly have. But I didn't stop. I didn't know how many kisses I had left.

After a couple of hours Olivia and Callum had to go and find some memories. Luckily the local cinema was showing summer-holiday films: lots of romantic comedies, which meant both of them could scoop up dozens of happy thoughts in double-quick time.

Once they were gone and the dog was securely tied up in the garden I fetched my laptop and started my search. Facebook was the obvious place to start. Catherine had set up a profile some weeks earlier when she had first started tormenting me, and had used it to become friends with a lot of my friends. I started with the so-called friends who didn't actually like me much, and Ashley was the top of that list. I scoured her page for any interaction with Catherine. There was an awful lot to trawl through. Ashley was clearly taking the summer holidays as an opportunity to really spread a load of gossip. She talked a lot of drivel, I realised, as I worked through page after page. Eventually I gave up and found Catherine's own page. I needed to see the detail and I wasn't down as one of her friends, but I knew who was. She had attempted to get friendly with Grace a few weeks before, and I knew Grace's password. I logged on quickly and was momentarily distracted by the familiar photos. An unexpected wave of loneliness suddenly swept through me; I really missed Grace and was glad that her holiday was nearly over too. It was always so much easier to deal with problems if I could discuss them with her first. She'd know the best thing to do.

I realised I was staring into space and mentally shook myself: I had to rummage through all the information on Catherine's page. Angling the screen to get the best view I started reading.

After an initial flurry of activity, Catherine had gone pretty quiet. There was no location given either.

"Come on!" I muttered to myself. "There has to be some way of finding her!" I couldn't believe I was drawing a blank quite so quickly. Some detective I was.

"What's up, titch?" Josh's voice made me jump.

"Oh, Josh! I didn't hear you coming."

"Just creeping around so that mutt doesn't see me." He nodded out towards the garden where Beesley was, for the moment, lying in the shade of a tree, pink tongue lolling out of the side of his mouth.

I decided that Josh might be able to help me. "Actually, it's good you're here, techno-geek that you are. I'm trying to find someone and I'm not having a lot of luck."

Josh pretended to be offended for five seconds, but his curiosity was piqued. "Anyone I know?" he said.

"Well, now, don't jump down my throat, but it's Catherine River."

Josh looked at me sharply. "Are you having a laugh? Why on earth do you want to find that nasty piece of work? Have you forgotten she attacked you and left you for dead!"

I pulled a face. "No, I hadn't forgotten. I just really, really need to find her. Are you still connected to her on Facebook, on that other account where she pretended to be Cliona?"

"Who knows? I don't think I unfriended her, but she might have done it to me."

"Would you have a look? I really need to find where she is. I think it's somewhere in the West Country but I don't have very much more information than that."

He looked hard at me, and I did my best to look like I knew what I was doing. "I don't think this is a good idea, you know," he muttered as he reached for my computer.

Within a few minutes he had found what he was looking for. "Here we are, still a friend. That woman's a psycho, remember. Don't do anything stupid." He turned the laptop round to face me.

"Thanks, Josh, you're my favourite big brother in the whole wide world."

"Ha ha," he said. "See you later."

I turned my attention back to the screen, anticipation making my heart beat faster. Catherine had pretended to be an old penfriend of mine, Cliona, when she befriended my brother. It was an ideal alias for her to hide behind. I started to flick through the pages and read all the conversations. This account was even less active than the other one. She had obviously done what she wanted to do in manipulating Josh but wasn't into making conversation. I continued to scan the entries, but the further I went, the less likely it would be that I would find something that she had given away, some inadvertent clue revealing her location.

After an hour I pushed the laptop away in frustration. I was absolutely no further forward. Glancing out into the garden I could see the late afternoon sun casting purple shadows into the corners. Beesley continued to sleep contentedly, which was surprising given that it must have been his teatime. I really ought to take him back home, I thought, watching his tail swish as he dreamed some doggy dream. I was just about to get up when the tingle appeared in my wrist. I knew immediately that it wasn't Callum.

"Hello?" I said carefully.

"It's me, Olivia. I'm sorry, Alex, but I wanted to talk to you without Callum around." Olivia's soft voice was even quieter than usual.

"Oh, hello, Olivia, I wasn't expecting either of you back so soon."

"I gave Callum the slip. He thinks I'm gathering in screen four, where they're showing that new film about the honeymoon. He says he can't stand watching it again this week."

"You won't have long before he notices then, I guess." I waited, but she said nothing. "Come on, Olivia. If you want to talk to me you're going to have to tell me what's on your mind."

"There's a rumour going around. Matthew was trying to keep it quiet, but people are talking. Is it true? Are you going to kill everyone? Can you even do that? No one will tell me what's going on!"

I sighed. "Who's been telling you all this?"

"Apparently there was a newspaper report about Lucas being dead. We know that he's gone, and the rumour is that it was something to do with you. Is it true?"

It was going to be pointless denying it. "Well, yes," I admitted. "When I was trying to stop Lucas from hurting Rob I did something that killed him. I didn't mean to, I didn't know exactly what was going to happen, but I did. He's dead."

There was a sharp intake of breath and then a silence, which continued until she could stand it no longer. "It's not fair! They never tell me anything. They think I'm too young to understand but I've been here for years and years and years. I just don't get any bigger. Why won't they treat me like a grown-up? I've as much right to know what's going on as anyone else, haven't I?"

"Shh, Olivia, don't shout in my head. I've not discussed this with anyone but Callum so far, not even Matthew. No one is keeping anything from you. What do you want to know?"

"Are you going to do it?"

"I need to do what's best for everyone, and I don't know what that is yet."

"So you might? You might kill us all?"

I bit back a sigh. It was always difficult getting into arguments with Olivia. To her, everything was absolutely black or white, with no shades of grey at all. "I need to talk to Callum, and to Matthew, and I've not had the chance to do that yet, but—"

I stopped dead as I heard the front door open. I didn't have my mobile phone anywhere in sight. "Crap. I've got to go. Someone might hear me talking to you! I'll speak to Callum, OK?"

"If you say so," she said grumpily, "but I want to know what you decide to do. I'm not too young, whatever Callum thinks, and he needs to understand that."

"OK, I'll talk to him," I hissed through gritted teeth as I turned around. It was Josh, and he wasn't alone. Max was walking into my kitchen.

Investigation

It took a couple of moments to regain my composure. "Max! I didn't know you were coming round."

He gave me one of his most devastating smiles. "I was in Richmond so Josh and I decided to make an evening of it. We've come back to dump the car and grab a sandwich, then we'll be heading out." He paused for a second. "Fancy joining us?" he added, a bit too casually.

"Umm, thanks, but I can't go out tonight. I've got to wait and look after the dog until our neighbour comes back." I gestured out into the garden, where Beesley was still sound asleep.

"He doesn't look like he's too much trouble," laughed Max.

"You have no idea. Earlier today he escaped by chewing through a solid wooden gate."

"Impressive." Max smiled and turned away from the window back towards me. I was suddenly conscious that Josh was nowhere to be seen. "It's good to see you, Alex. Really good."

I didn't know what to say so I just smiled and quickly looked away. Where had Josh got to? "Do you want a coffee to go with your sandwich?" I winced at how inane I sounded but at least it gave me something to do. Moving across to the far side of the kitchen, I picked up the kettle and filled it with water. Deliberately not turning to look at Max I stood the kettle back on its stand but as I reached for the switch long, tanned fingers encircled mine. He was right behind me.

I stood completely still, my skin prickling where he was touching me. Then I felt his lips brush the top of my head. "Give me another chance, Alex, please?" he murmured. "I really enjoyed the time we had together in Spain, and I think you did too."

I started to object, but as I drew breath to speak he continued. "Look, I know about the other guy, the one who's abroad, and I understand. But he's not here, is he? Why not at least come out with me a couple of times? It can't hurt and you've nothing to lose."

I could feel the strength in his fingers as they continued to hold mine. He was standing close enough behind me that I was conscious of the heat from his body. He took my silence as a good sign and carried on.

"I thought that maybe we could just go and get a drink – nothing more, just a drink. We are friends after all, and then take it from there. The thing is. . ." He paused and turned me round so I was facing him, his hands resting on my shoulders. "The thing is, I can't stop thinking about you, Alex, and I just needed you to know that. I reckoned it was time for me to come and fight for something I really, really want."

I tried to keep my eyes firmly fixed on a button on his shirt, but there was no doubting the sincerity in his tone. I couldn't stop myself from looking up at him.

"You're really sweet, Max, but I just can't. I'm sorry." I dragged my eyes away from his face; looking at those soft lips made me remember that kiss on the beach, remember how he tasted.

He grimaced. "'Sweet' wasn't really the word I was looking for. I was hoping for irresistible."

"I'm sorry," I repeated lamely, mentally shaking myself. "But I love someone else, and that's all there is to it."

His warm fingers traced a line down my cheek. "OK, I believe you." He bent down and briefly kissed my cheek before stepping back, hands raised in surrender. "But I think it's only fair to warn you that the fight isn't over yet. I'm not giving up that easily." His dark eyes twinkled. "You need to watch out, Alex Walker. I'm a man on a mission!"

I quickly turned my attention back to the kettle so he couldn't see the tears welling in my eyes. Tears that appeared from nowhere and which I didn't understand.

Thankfully Josh reappeared soon afterwards, so I could make my escape. He gave me a pointed look as I left the kitchen and I realised the two of them had clearly hatched the plot together. I'd thought it was only girls who did things like that. Ignoring my big brother, I made for the garden, walking down to the chair that was hanging from a sturdy branch in the shadows at the end. I really hoped that Olivia had disappeared after she left me, and hadn't hung around to witness the scene with Max. I didn't want her getting the wrong idea and telling Callum before I had the chance to do so.

I called him as soon as I sat down. It was gloomy under the tree in the fading light, so I didn't worry too much about anyone in the house seeing me talking to myself. There was no instant response and yet again I began to panic. What had she heard, and what had she passed on?

"Come on!" I muttered to myself, willing him to appear. At that moment the tingle was back.

"You're very impatient this evening," observed Callum, his voice even.

The only thing for it was to tell him everything. "I'm just really glad you're here. Max just turned up out of the blue with

Josh and it all got really awkward."

"Yeah, I saw him just now," he said. "He's sitting in your kitchen drinking a beer."

"Oh no, is he still here? I thought the two of them would have gone down the pub by now."

"You're in trouble, Alex, you know that? You need to be careful."

I felt my mouth open wordlessly like a fish. There were too many possible ways in which I could be in trouble, and I had no idea which one he was talking about. Was he about to leave me because of Max? Were some of the Dirges coming to get me? Did he know about my conversation with Veronica? "What . . . what do you mean?" I managed finally.

"Max. He's pretty determined to win you over. I overheard a bit of their conversation as I came through."

"Oh. Really?" I tried not to sound relieved that it was only Max he was referring to, though that was bad enough. "What was he saying?"

"He was telling Josh how frustrating it is that you are so loyal to your boyfriend," he started.

"Well, I am loyal," I interrupted. "It's perfectly true."

"But that as the boyfriend lives in Venezuela he reckoned it was worth another go." I felt him stroke my cheek in exactly the same way that Max had done, only the touch was infinitely lighter. It made me wonder if he had been watching. "And that soon enough he'd wear down your resistance."

"He's wrong, as you know."

"Don't burn all your bridges, Alex," he said in a voice so soft I struggled to hear it.

"What? What are you talking about?"

"He seems to care, and he's persistent. I guess he really likes you."

"So?"

"I'm just trying to be realistic. Going to find Catherine is a wild goose chase, and even if you do track her down, there's no guarantee she'll give you the magic formula for bringing us all back to life. In the end, you're going to help us die because you know that's what we want. And when that happens you'll be pretty upset, and it would be good to know that there was someone around to comfort you."

"Are you telling me to go out with Max?" I hissed. "That's too creepy for words. And I don't want him, I want you!"

I felt the tiniest squeeze as his arms tightened around me, and to my surprise he laughed. "Good answer!"

"Were you testing me?" I tried to turn the relief in my voice to outrage.

"Oh, maybe just a little. Give me a break, will you? The guy looks like a male model."

"He's not a patch on you."

"You poor deluded creature," he answered, and I could hear the smile in his voice. I wished I had the mirror in my pocket to enjoy another look at his mesmerising blue eyes.

"Did you see Olivia just now?" I asked. "I had to get her to go in rather a hurry, and I'm not sure she's all right." I didn't want to spoil his good mood, but I was worried about her.

"No, I haven't seen her. Is she upset about something?"

"She wants to know what's going on. She's heard the rumours going round over there and she's fed up being treated like a child and having everyone exclude her from their plans."

"How did they find out about it so soon? That's all I need.

Anyway, there aren't any plans, not yet."

"I know that, but she obviously thinks there are."

"Well, I wish she hadn't found out. She's too young to have to worry about all this stuff."

"Me, too," I said with feeling.

I felt his arms move around me. "Don't let's talk about this now. There's no point. Let's enjoy the time we have together." I nestled back in his embrace and tried, unsuccessfully, to forget. Callum was gently stroking my arm when he suddenly stopped.

"Oh, and guess what? I came across another of your admirers this afternoon."

I sat up in surprise. "Who?"

"Rob. Yet another man captivated by your beauty and sunny temperament. Ow!"

The swipe I'd aimed at his head had obviously found its target. Rob had very briefly been my boyfriend before I met Callum, and he had ended up working with Catherine to steal the amulet and sell its story to the papers. I had only just stopped him, and that was when I had inadvertently killed Lucas. In the fight Rob had lost all of his most recent memories but otherwise seemed OK. He had forgotten what a terrible boyfriend he'd been, and that I didn't want to have anything to do with him any more.

"So come on, where did you see him?" I asked impatiently, tapping my foot.

"I saw him in the pub when I was on my way to the cinema. He was on the phone, talking about how he had been planning to ask you to go down to the place that his family had rented over the summer."

"Oh no, not that again. It's such pain having to say 'no' to everything twice with him. Did he say anything else?"

"Actually, he must have been talking to someone who knows you, because he said something like 'When I bring her down you're going to have to leave. Even if she's your friend I want the place to ourselves, if you know what I mean'. It was perfectly clear what it was he had in mind. He's a right charmer, isn't he?"

I agreed absent-mindedly. Something was niggling at me, something that was important. I searched back through all our mutual friends to see who the mystery person on the other end of the call might have been, what the link was, but nothing came to me.

"Hey," said Callum after I had been brooding on it for a while. "Come on, it's not that important. Do you want me to start stalking him again? Not that I fancy the idea much."

"Nah, don't worry, he's not worth the effort. He's not worth *any* effort, the little worm," I added with some feeling. I was about to expand on that when Beesley leapt up and raced towards the house, barking wildly.

"It looks like Lynda's home and come to collect. I'd better go inside."

"Time for me to go and find Olivia then, make sure she's done enough gathering for the night." He gave another stroke of my hair. "I guess I'll see you tomorrow."

"I'll be here, I'm not disappearing on my road trip just yet, not when I don't know where to go."

"OK, till tomorrow then." There was a brief silence, then I felt a gentle touch on my lips. "I love you, Alex," he said quietly, and with a sudden flurry he was gone before I could reply.

"I love you too," I whispered into the gloom, before walking slowly towards the house where I could see Mum talking to Lynda. I really wished Rob would take a hint. It was so annoying that he couldn't remember important conversations, or how abominably he had behaved, trying to lure me and then Ashley into his little love nest in Cornwall.

"Cornwall!" I stopped dead in the middle of the lawn. Rob had been talking to someone about being in Cornwall. Could that have been a coincidence? Was it possible that he had been talking to Catherine? I ran upstairs, making my excuses as I went through the kitchen, and fired up the laptop. It was always grindingly slow in the evening, and I wished we had a faster Internet connection. I had checked Rob's page when I had been looking for Catherine and there had been nothing useful there. Nothing had been added since then, and I pushed the laptop away in frustration. I was going to have to wing it.

The easiest way of getting information out of Rob would be to tackle him face-to-face. It wasn't a pleasant prospect but, given he still seemed interested in me, I had the opportunity of manipulating him to get what I needed. I didn't even feel guilty at the idea: Rob definitely deserved it.

Looking at my watch I saw that I might get him before he went out so I pulled my mobile out of my pocket and scrolled through the names.

"Oh crap, crap, crap," I said to myself as I realised it was yet another of the numbers I had lost when I'd drowned my phone. I had re-entered most of them, but I hadn't expected to need Rob's details. I looked down the list to try and decide which of my friends would have his number and wouldn't mind giving it to me. Probably not Ashley, I thought with a half-smile. Jack would be the best one, I realised. I pressed the number quickly.

Jack was one of my oldest friends; our families had been socialising together since Jack's brother and Josh had been in primary school together. He was currently going out with Grace, which I was delighted about. The two of them made a great couple and clearly adored each other.

"Hi, Alex, what's up?"

"Hi, Jack. Oh you know, the usual. Not seen you for a while. I hope you've been behaving yourself while Grace has been away?"

"Are you checking up on me?" he asked with a smile in his voice.

"As if! I'm sure you're looking forward to her coming back tomorrow even more than I am."

That was pushing him too far; he was never going to admit that, even to me. "Is it tomorrow? I'd forgotten."

"You're such a terrible liar! Don't worry, I won't tell her how much you've been pining, I promise. I was just after a favour, actually."

"Really? You stun me. Come on then, what do you need?"

"Rob Underwood's mobile number."

That did stun him. "What on earth for? Have you forgotten all the grief he gave you?"

"No, course not. I just need to talk to him, that's all. Can you text me his number, please?"

"OK, but be careful, Alex. He's acting really strangely. That memory-loss business has messed with his mind."

"I will, don't worry. So when are you and Grace off to the Gower?"

"Later this week, so I'm sorry, you're not going to get much time with her."

"I know, it's all right for some, skipping from one holiday to another. I shall prise her away from you for at least one night out before you whisk her away though."

155

"Good, she'll want to do that. OK, so I'll send you Rob's number now."

"Cheers, Jack," I said. "See you soon."

Seconds after I put the phone down it beeped. Rob's number had arrived. I sat for a moment rehearsing in my mind what I wanted to say, then took a deep breath and picked up the handset again.

"Rob, it's Alex."

"Oh, hi, Alex, how are you?" The surprise was evident in his voice.

"Fine, thanks. Look, I was just wondering if you were around tomorrow?"

The surprise was instantly replaced by smugness. "Well now, let me see . . . yeah, I think I can squeeze you in somewhere."

"Great. Coffee maybe? Hampton Hill High Street?"

"Sure, I can do that."

"OK, so how about ten o'clock outside the theatre, then we can see which café has space?"

"Whoa, ten o'clock? That's a bit early."

"No point wasting the day, is there?"

"I'm glad to see you're keen. OK, for you I'll do ten o'clock. See you tomorrow."

"Yeah. See you, Rob."

He was going to be unbearable but I needed to get the information and he was much more likely to give it to me if he thought he was in with a chance. The thought of spending any time with him made my flesh crawl. He had proved just how shallow and mercenary he was when he tried to sell the amulet, and I had no regrets at all that he had lost his memories of all those few weeks. I also didn't feel at all guilty about manipulating him; I couldn't think of anyone who deserved it more.

I had a quiet evening, planning how I was going to get the information out of Rob without making him suspicious. Josh and Max had gone out, and my mum was curious about why I hadn't chosen to go with them.

"You two seemed to be getting on so well in Spain," she suddenly started as we loaded the dishwasher before she went up to bed. "Why didn't you want to go to the pub with them?"

"I just didn't, that's all."

"I mean, it's pretty clear that Max fancies you."

"Oh, Mum, please stop! I really don't want to discuss this."

"But he seems like such a nice lad."

"He is a 'nice lad', Mum, which is why I don't want to encourage him. It wouldn't be fair."

"Not your cup of tea then?" she pressed.

"No, not my cup of tea." I turned my back and picked up a stack of plates, hoping that it would end the conversation, but she wasn't done.

"In that case, you may want to scarper. Max is going to be staying the night, and they'll be back soon."

I stopped dead, rattling the crockery I was carrying. "Oh, right. I'll just load these and get out of the way then."

Mum lifted the plates out of my hands. "Go now, before you drop something. I can finish off. What are you doing in the morning?"

"I'm meeting some friends in Hampton Hill at ten, so I'll get the train. They'll still be sound asleep that early, I'm sure. Goodnight."

"Goodnight, sweetpea," she murmured, turning back to the

dishwasher. I headed for the stairs.

I was only just in time; less than ten minutes later I heard the two of them downstairs, laughing in the kitchen. Part of me really wanted to go and join in, but I knew that it wasn't fair. I sneaked out to the bathroom when it sounded like they were mid-conversation, and heaved a great sigh of relief when I made it back into my room without being spotted. I crept into bed and turned out all the lights except my little reading light; I didn't think there was any point even trying to sleep. But I must have been tired because when there was a tap at my door it jolted me awake.

I was momentarily confused. Why would someone be knocking at my door? I was just trying to decide whether to ignore it and hope they went away, or answer and find out who it was, when the door slowly swung open. Max wouldn't just come into my bedroom, surely? I held my breath as the silhouette in the doorway finally became clearer.

"Josh!" I hissed. "What on earth are you doing?"

"Oh, sorry, I was trying not to wake you up. I need the futon for Max. The air mattress has sprung a leak."

"What? Oh, OK. Look, just dump all the stuff from it on the floor over there." There was much stumbling and cursing as Josh attempted to wrestle the futon mattress off the chair. In the end I got out of bed to help him.

"Here, like this," I said scathingly as I freed it easily. He gathered it up and tried to manoeuvre his way around my tiny room without knocking too many things over. I opened the door so that he could get out just as Max was coming up the stairs. He smiled as he saw me.

"Hi, Alex. Sorry to disturb your early night. See you in the morning, maybe?"

"Uh, yeah, maybe," I stammered. "Goodnight." I stepped back into the shadows, suddenly conscious of the skimpy summer pyjamas I was wearing. I shut the door behind Josh as quickly as I could and jumped back into bed, flicking out the light. But by then I really couldn't sleep, and I was very aware of the footsteps that stopped outside the door ten minutes later. I held my breath and listened to the old floorboards creaking as eventually the steps continued to the bathroom.

I set my alarm really early and was out of the house long before anyone else was up. The train was full of commuters looking as if they would all rather be on holiday and I was glad when I got off after a few stops. I was ridiculously early so I went into the park. The only people out seemed to be dog walkers and joggers, so I ambled down the long path until I could find a quiet bench. As I approached the first one I realised that a stag was sitting not far away. He lifted his head, antlers catching the sunshine and fixed me with a beady eye. I knew that generally the herds of deer that roamed Bushy Park weren't dangerous, but I never liked getting too close to the stags. Some were huge, and to my mind, all of them had a mean look about them. I quickly moved on to the next bench.

There was still a slightly cool edge to the air but the sun was warming the wooden seat. I checked my watch: I had over an hour before I was due to meet Rob – plenty of time to talk to Callum. The bench had an armrest that was at the perfect height for my mirror, so I set it up and pulled out my earpiece. "Callum? Are you around? I'm in Bushy Park."

There was silence for a few moments before the tingle reached my wrist. It still made me shiver with anticipation to know that it meant he was right there beside me, even when I couldn't actually see him.

"Morning, gorgeous." His deep voice held a hint of surprise. "I didn't expect to find you here." I angled the mirror so that he came into view. The sun was catching the blond streaks in his hair and made his blue eyes sparkle.

"It's a long story. I'm meeting Rob later."

"Really? What for?"

"Because of what you told me yesterday. Do you remember that you said he was having a conversation with someone about getting out of his parents' rented house in Cornwall?"

"Yeah – what of it?"

"I think it's Catherine. We know she went to Cornwall, that the two of them were hatching plots together before. Maybe she's staying at his cottage."

Callum's eyebrows shot up in surprise. "Of course! Why didn't I think of that? It makes perfect sense."

"So what I need to do is find out exactly where the place is. I'm not exactly sure how I'm going to wrangle it out of him. Any bright ideas?"

"I suppose you could just ask," he said dubiously.

"I know, but I don't want him getting the wrong impression, not again. It's really annoying that he only remembers fancying me and not the rest of it."

"Of course," Callum said slowly, looking out over the park. "I could do something about that."

"What do you mean?"

"I could take those memories away. If you want me to." He shrugged. "It wouldn't be difficult; all you have to do is talk to him about it and then I can pounce."

"But what about your principles? You don't like taking real memories, I know."

"I don't like him making you feel bad either. And it's something I *can* do for you."

I smiled at him. "It's tempting but I think I'll get more out of him if he thinks he's in with a chance. Maybe later."

"All right." I saw him ruffle my hair, laughing. "I didn't think I'd get away with that. It was worth a go though! I would so love to wipe you from his memory completely, the lying little—"

"Stop it!" I interrupted, laughing too. "You really are terrible, you must—" I broke off as a piercing scream made me jump. Looking up from my mirror I saw a toddler pointing at me and drawing breath for another wail as she turned and ran for the safety of her mother. "Whatever's the matter?" I muttered to myself, then froze as I looked around.

I had been so engrossed in my conversation with Callum I hadn't noticed what was going on around me. Three large stags were standing behind me, all nearly within touching distance. That close up they were huge, especially since I was sitting down. I could see the soft velvety noses twitching as they stretched even closer. And I could see the hard, sharp points on the ends of the antlers too.

"Umm, Callum, this must be you. They don't normally do this." I spoke as quietly and as evenly as I could, not wanting to startle them. Those antlers could definitely do a lot of damage.

"I knew there was a reason I didn't normally come into the park," he laughed, clearly amused.

"Do you think that you could walk away, please, nice and slowly so that they follow you?"

"They're not going to hurt you."

"That's easy for you to say, Mr No-real-body-to-damage. Please, walk away now!"

"All right. Go back to the gate and I'll catch up with you there." The tingle went and I continued sitting completely still for a moment. Finally I risked moving my head a fraction. I could see the three stags walking together in a line away from the path. Other deer were wandering up from different directions. I turned the mirror to see the whole scene and if I could glimpse him. Generally he arrived and left too quickly to actually see him walking about, but this time he was there, perfectly reflected in the little mirror. I had to suppress a giggle. He was doing a full-on Pied Piper impression, cloak blowing in the breeze, beckoning the deer to follow him. He saw me looking and waved, then blew me a kiss with a flourish and a bow. I pocketed the mirror and headed back to the gate.

Road Trip

As I had anticipated, Rob started sleazing all over me the minute he arrived, and I found it really hard to keep the distaste out of my voice as we queued for drinks.

"So, Alex, good to see you. What's brought about this sudden change of heart then? Have you realised that you actually do find me completely irresistible?"

"No, delightful as you are, Rob, don't forget that you're going out with Ashley, not me."

"Where have you been? I split up with Ashley weeks ago. Right now I'm single and loving it."

My heart sank. He was going to be even harder to control without the threat of Ashley to slow him down. "Oh, I didn't know that. I've been in Spain for the last two weeks."

"And you've come back looking even more gorgeous. Great tan!" He caught hold of my hand and lifted my arm, pretending to examine it from every angle. I gently extracted it.

"I know I shouldn't sunbathe, but I do find it hard to resist. Not that I can do it for long though."

"Shame I wasn't there to help you with your suntan lotion," he said with a definite leer. It was too early to tell him what I really thought; I needed information first. So I smiled tightly and changed the subject.

"Shall we take these through to the garden out the back?" I

gestured to the coffees.

"What don't we get them as take-outs? We can go into the park where it's nice and private." He ran his hand down my spine, making me jump.

"I've ordered them in proper cups so that we can stay here." I made my voice as firm as possible. I wanted Callum to be able to listen in, and that obviously wasn't going to be possible in the park.

"OK, if you want. We can always go for a walk later."

I ignored the last comment and led the way out into the tiny walled garden behind the café. It was disappointingly quiet, the little cast-iron chair and table sets all empty. Rob looked around and nodded. "Not bad, not bad at all." The oily tone in his voice was making me want to scream.

Once we were settled he leaned over, his elbows on the table. "Come on then, Alex, I'm not daft. What's up? Why the sudden need to talk?"

This was the difficult bit. Exactly how was I going to be able to get the information that I needed? I had been arguing with myself about the approach all morning.

"The thing is, Rob, I'm worried about a friend of mine. We, um, had a bit of a row and she's gone away. I could really do with her address so I could write her a note and apologise."

He looked at me with a puzzled frown. "So why do you want to talk to me?"

"I think you might know where she is. Her name's Catherine. Catherine River."

He sat back in surprise. "You know her?"

"I sort of introduced you a couple of months ago. It's probably during that time you can't remember."

"Really? It was you? She didn't mention that."

164

"As I said, there was a bit of a row. Do you know where she is?"

"Sure, she's staying at the house we've rented down in Polzeath. Not for much longer though. In fact, she should be leaving today or tomorrow."

I tried not to let my excitement show. "Oh really?"

"Yeah. It was all a bit tricky. After I had lost that chunk of memory, when you found me in London, she rang me. It was very odd. I mean, she clearly knew all about me, and I had absolutely no memory of her whatsoever. But I had agreed to let her stay in the house, it seems. Mum went a bit mental when she found out, but as I've been sick she let me off." He paused for a second to take a slurp of his coffee. "So how do you know her then?"

"Oh, from way back. We were at primary school together and she came back to the area recently." I felt a bit guilty lying to him but I wasn't going to tell him the truth, and the tale about school was what Catherine had been telling people when she appeared in June. "You said she was going to be leaving?" I asked as casually as I could manage. "Do you know when? I'd really like to write to her."

"No point in doing that. She'll be gone tomorrow and the post will miss her. Why don't you send her a text?"

"I lost all my contacts when my phone got wet."

"You want it?" he asked, pulling his phone out of his jeans pocket.

"Umm, yeah, that'd be great."

He quickly scrolled down through his lists of contacts, pressed a few keys and within seconds there was a bleep from the phone in my pocket. "There you go. So what did the two of you argue about? Was it a proper catfight?" I could see him struggling not to leer again.

"Please! Nothing so exciting. She was trying to manipulate a friend of mine into doing something she wanted, and I didn't think it was right, that's all."

"And now you want to make up?"

"There's stuff we need to talk about. Are you sure that she won't get a letter? I've got one ready to send."

"You can try if you want, but I reckon you'll miss her."

"So what's the address?"

"I don't know! I've never been there. We're going down for the first time next week. The plans all got scuppered by me being in hospital. Dad's been moaning about the wasted cost for ages."

"Any chance you can find out exactly where it is?" I asked as lightly as I could. "I mean, how did you tell Catherine where to go?"

Rob looked puzzled for a moment. "I have no idea. My memory is still a bit patchy sometimes. I suppose I could ask my dad. I know roughly where it is, but that's not much good for a letter, is it?"

I took a deep breath and tried not to scream. He wasn't being deliberately obstructive, not really. "If you could ask today, that would be brilliant. I just think it's easier to explain things in a letter than a text." I tried to relax my fingers, which were gripping the sides of my chair in frustration. "So I know you've not been there, but what's the place like? Does it overlook the sea? Easy walking distance to the front?"

"Yeah, we've rented a place just up the road before. It's on the hill overlooking the town, near to the fancy new hotel. Mum likes it because she can go and use the spa when the rest of us are surfing."

"Sounds cool. When are you off?" Relaxing my fingers wasn't working so I picked up my coffee cup.

"At the weekend, although I could be persuaded to go down a few days early, make sure she's left the place all neat and tidy." He leaned forward and let a finger gently graze down the edge of my arm. The yellow aura above his head pulsed brightly. "Fancy coming with me? You'd love it down there."

"Rob, we've had this conversation several times now, and I'm not going to change my mind. Just because I'm here doesn't alter that."

He was about to answer when there was a spectacular noise from the other side of the wall, making us both leap in our seats. His coffee shot across the table and mostly landed in my lap.

"What the hell was that?" he shouted as the strange baying continued. It sounded a lot like animals trying to kill each other.

"Maybe it's the stags fighting in the park. It's just the other side of the wall," I bellowed over the noise. Then as suddenly as it had started it stopped, and I found myself shouting into the silence. "Wow. They are noisy beasts." I looked down. "Um, Rob, I seem to be rather a mess – I'm going to have to go home and change."

"Sorry about that," he said, gesturing towards my wet clothes. "You can come and dry off at my house if you want." I was about to accept as it would be an excellent excuse to get him to search for the address when he continued. "Everyone's out today. We'd have the place to ourselves."

"Thanks, Rob, but I'd better get home. When you get back will you check that address for me?"

He looked disappointed, and for a fraction of a second I wondered if the drink in the lap had been deliberate. "Sure. Well, let's go then, shall we?"

As we walked towards the door of the café I glanced at the reflection in the glass and the tingle appeared in my wrist. Directly behind me was Callum, grinning broadly. He had obviously enjoyed his game of winding up the stags.

As I sat on the train the coffee began to dry, turning everything I was wearing sticky and uncomfortable. I didn't really want to go home as I wasn't sure what time Max would be leaving but I didn't have a great deal of choice. The train slid past the dull office blocks and suburban houses and I tried to think of any other alternatives as I stared out of the window. At one station a man in a yellow jacket was changing the posters in the advertising boards on the platform, tearing down pictures promoting the latest Hollywood blockbusters. How things had changed, I realised. Just a few months ago I would have been off the train trying to negotiate with the guy to have one of the old posters to add to the collection on my bedroom wall. But not any more; now I had real dramas to occupy me.

I pulled out my phone, wondering if I should send Catherine a text. I just couldn't think of what to say that would compel her to talk to me. I suspected that if I tried I might make things worse. Sighing, I put the phone down in my lap and returned to looking out of the window. When it erupted into life a few seconds later I was able to answer it almost instantly.

"Grace! You have no idea how good it is to hear your voice!"

"Hi, babe, are you still having boy trouble?"

"The worst! As soon as you get back I'm going to bore you rigid about it. I need help." As I said it I realised just how much I wanted to talk to her, to test my theory and also have some uncomplicated girly gossip. "When do you get back? Is it tonight?"

"I'm already here. The drive up through France was quicker than we thought, so instead of staying over another night we got a ferry yesterday evening and got home at about midnight. So what's up? Did you and Max get together, or is everything still OK with Callum?"

"There have been a couple of complications, to be honest."

"Complications? How can it be even more complicated? I'm coming over now!"

"Actually, Grace, I'm just about to get off the train at Shepperton. Can I jump on the bus and come to your house? I think one of the complicating factors may still be at my place."

"Now, that sounds intriguing! Of course you can. See you in a bit."

It wasn't long before I was sitting in Grace's kitchen in a borrowed pair of shorts, giving her all the details of my holiday and the problem that was Max. Finally, though, I had to get to what was really troubling me. "Actually, Max is only a small problem in comparison. There's much worse: it looks like I'm going to have to find Catherine again."

"No! Why? She's a psychopath who tried to kill you. Why would you possibly want to find her?"

Instinctively I rubbed my arm where Catherine had hit it with a golf club earlier in the summer. Although the bruising was now gone it was still a bit tender. The blow had been aimed at my head and could easily have killed me if I hadn't moved at the last minute. Approaching Catherine was going to be a dangerous business, but I had no choice.

"I thought that I knew how to rescue Callum, how to make

him human again, but actually I don't. In fact, when I tried it on someone else, when I was trying to save Rob, it turns out that he died properly."

Grace looked up at me quickly, the implications of what I was saying slowly sinking in. Her mouth opened soundlessly as I carried on.

"I want Callum to live! I can't lose him again, not for a third time. And there's worse." I buried my face in my hands, not really wanting to say the words. "The process seemed to torture the guy really badly too. I can't do that to Callum."

Grace recovered her voice. "Oh, Alex, that's horrible! How did it happen?"

I gave her a quick summary of what I had done. She already knew a fair bit of it, but I had glossed over the details of saving Rob because it had seemed a bit weird. She paced up and down the kitchen as I told her about it, throwing in the odd question, a huge frown on her usually flawless features. Finally she stopped and looked at me with her hands on her hips.

"So let me get this straight," she said, the frown deepening. "You think that Catherine – and only Catherine – has the ability to help you bring the Dirges back to life. Why can't Veronica do it? She's an ex-Dirge too."

"Her power to help has faded because she's been over here for so long and is so much older. She can only help me put them all out of their misery. Catherine, though, as she's so recently come over, can help me to keep them alive." I struggled to keep the tears in check as I thought about it again. "If there's a chance, any chance at all, that I can save Callum I have to try. I can't just kill them all."

"But that's what they want, isn't it?"

"Only because they think there's no other choice."

She looked at my reddened eyes and gave a wan smile. "OK, you have to find Catherine, I agree, and make sure you've tried every alternative first." She hesitated a moment, then grabbed my hand and waited for me to look at her. "But the thing is, Alex, you will have to think about it; you're going to have to be prepared to make that decision. Doing anything else is unfair."

"I know, but not yet. I can't give up Callum just yet." I could barely say the words.

"All right, not yet." She patted my hand as if she were comforting a child, and pulled a scrunchie out of her handbag. Pulling back her long dark hair into a messy bun, she scooped up a notepad and pen and sat opposite me at the table. "Time to go to work."

"Thank you. I knew you'd help," I sniffed. I blew my nose loudly, making her tut. "So I know where Catherine is, roughly anyway, but she's leaving today or tomorrow, and I don't know where she'll be going. I could get the train but it doesn't go anywhere near Polzeath. There is one way of getting there but it's a bit of a last resort."

Grace lifted her head from her scribbling. "What's that then?"

"Rob offered to take me."

"Are you mad? You know what he's after."

"I know," I said miserably. "But it would get me there, wouldn't it? I'd just have to be very firm with him." It would be a complete nightmare, I knew, but it *was* a means to an end.

"That'll never work. Of course," she said chewing on the end of her pencil, "there is one alternative that you haven't thought about."

"What? Anything's better than Rob."

"Ask me. I could drive you down there this afternoon."

"Really? But what about—" I stopped as she put her hand up.

"If I couldn't do it, I wouldn't have offered. Now, are we on? Ready for a road trip?"

It was surprisingly easy to get ourselves organised and to make our excuses. The most difficult bit was saying goodbye to Jack and Callum. It was particularly hard on Grace as she hadn't actually seen Jack since before she had gone on holiday. They snatched an hour together before she drove to my house to pick me up, but that was all. I managed to speak to Callum briefly.

"I don't understand your rush," he complained, trying hard to keep his amulet and mine together as I whirled around my room throwing clothes and bits into a small bag. "I mean, I know she'll be moving from Rob's place, but she won't go far."

"We don't know that. She might jump on a train and end up in Scotland."

"I suppose. But do you really think she might help?"

"If there's any chance, any chance at all, that she can help me to understand how I can bring you over alive, I have to go and ask her. And I have to persuade her to talk to me first."

"That's where you're going to struggle," he murmured, taking the opportunity to hold me briefly as I sat at my desk to gather my make-up bag.

"I know, but I have to try. I've nothing to lose."

"I know, me neither. I only wish I could help."

"Well, there is something you could do," I asked, trying to smile. "Can you see my hairbrush anywhere?"

He ruffled my hair gently, not quite managing to smile back.

"Over there, by the box of tissues. Will you be away long, do you think?"

"No, I'll probably be back tomorrow. Grace is going to the Gower with Jack later in the week, so she's got to be here to pick him up. I'll be back before you know it." I stopped trying to pack and gazed at him in the mirror. His mesmerising blue eyes were full of worry, and his free hand was twisting around a lock of my hair.

"There's something you're not telling me, Alex, I can tell. And I know," he continued as I started to protest, "I know that you'll be keeping something from me for a good reason. Come back to me quickly, that's all I ask. I don't want to waste any more time than we have to."

"I wish you could come with me," I murmured, reaching up to stroke his face. His long fingers covered mine as he gave me a long, searching look.

"I wish I could too. Please be careful."

"I will, and I'll be back soon." I gave as much of a smile as I could manage.

"When you come back, we need to talk some more about what Matthew wants you to do. What I want you to do," he added in a quiet voice, suddenly looking away.

"I've already told you, I won't do it."

"Think about it. Ask Grace. I know that it's a hard thing to decide on your own." He bent down to kiss my shoulder and I couldn't see his face, but I was sure I heard a slight break in his voice. I was about to reply when there was a sharp knock at the front door.

"That'll be Grace. I have to go now. I won't be long, I promise."

"I love you, Alex. Please, please be careful. Catherine's dangerous."

"I know, and I love you too. See you tomorrow, I hope."

I quickly wiped my eyes as I threw my rucksack over my shoulder and made my way down the stairs, catching a glimpse of Callum behind me in the big hall mirror. Josh was just letting Grace in.

"Hi, are you ready? Got everything?" she asked with a smile.

"Pretty much." I lifted my bag so she could see that I'd packed. "I just want to get a few bottles of water from the fridge."

She followed me into the kitchen and stopped dead. Max was sitting there, looking gorgeously dishevelled. Neither he nor Josh had been up for long. It wasn't often that Grace was lost for words but this was one of those times.

"Grace, this is Max, a friend of Josh's. Max – Grace."

He gave her a lazy smile. "Morning, Grace. I've heard lots about you."

"Oh . . . sure." She turned to give me a look that clearly told me what she was thinking.

I scooped the water bottles out of the fridge and made for the door. "Come on, Grace, we need to be going. No time to waste, remember?"

"Um, no. Right, well, nice to meet you, Max. See you, Josh," she said as I pulled her gently out of the kitchen. Josh nodded at me briefly over his bowl of cereal. Max was obviously pleased at the effect he was having.

"See you, Alex. Drive carefully and remember what I said." He looked at me steadily for a moment, then winked.

Grace didn't regain her composure until we were sitting in the car. "How on earth do you do it, Alex? Three of them falling all over you, all drop-dead gorgeous!"

"I know, I can't believe it. All these years of waiting and suddenly I'm overwhelmed with choice. I just wish I knew what I was doing differently."

"So I can absolutely see how Max would be a complication."

"Yeah, and it got even more complicated when Max kissed me at the airport in front of Callum."

"Ouch! That can't have gone down well."

"Tell me about it. I think I've convinced him it was all a misunderstanding but it's been a bit of a struggle."

"Complication is about right," she sighed, before turning her full attention to the M4.

The journey down to Cornwall took hours. We stopped briefly for a sandwich somewhere near Bristol but otherwise kept on going. I called Rob mid-afternoon and managed to get an address out of him. Punching the details in Grace's rather basic satnav we followed the instructions, not realising quite how much further Devon and Cornwall stretched beyond the end of the M5. We seemed to be stuck behind caravans forever and were sitting in a traffic queue when my stomach began to rumble again.

"It's nearly seven o'clock. How did it get to be so late when we still have so far to go?" I wailed, exasperated, drumming my fingers on the dashboard.

"I don't think my driving has helped much, has it?"

"You've been brilliant. There's no other way we would have got to where we need to be in time." That probably wasn't true, I realised, as I said it. The train and a taxi would have got me there about an hour ago.

"But I'm not exactly speedy, am I?"

"You're going to get us there in one piece, and that's what

counts," I said, giving her a smile. She was absolutely right though. I had had to bite my lip several times to stop myself from shouting at her to put her foot down. "Anyway, the gizmo says that we'll be there in half an hour. I just hope I can convince Catherine to come back with us. She'll have to if she's going to be any help with the Dirges."

"If anyone can do it, you can," Grace said supportively if inaccurately.

"I do love your optimism, Grace." I smiled wryly to myself. "I mean, I've got to try, there's no other choice, but she's a monstrous cow."

"I wonder how much of it is because of her big secret and how much is just because she's an evil witch?"

"Not a clue. I've puzzled and puzzled over it, and so has Callum, but I don't have any idea. I know that she knows how to save all the Dirges: she told me that she had written it down so whatever Olivia took from her is irrelevant. But if that's all it is, why does she hate me? What have I got to do with it? What can I possibly have done to her to cause all this loathing?"

We lapsed into silence as there was no answer. Catherine's hatred for me was epic. I thought back to the horrible things she had done to me since she had come over: malicious e-mails, stealing all my money, attacking me with a golf club, and finally stealing the amulet so that she and Rob could sell it and expose all the Dirges. It was a campaign of terror and I had been hugely relieved that she was out of my life.

The closer we got to Polzeath, the less likely I thought it would be that she would help me, even if we could find her. What was I doing dragging Grace all the way to Cornwall for a complete waste of time? The whole thing was mad. I thought about how we could plan our approach to Catherine, but absolutely nothing sensible came to me. I was going to have to cross my fingers and wing it.

I stared unseeing out of the window as the beautiful Cornish countryside swept past, wishing Catherine wasn't my only hope. But if there was a chance I could save all the Dirges, however small, I had to take it.

Dusk was beginning to fall as we made our way along the little country lanes that led to Polzeath, and the birds were flying low across the hedgerows. We hadn't seen much in the way of civilisation for ages.

"Not a lot going on round here," said Grace, keeping an eye out for large vehicles coming towards us on the wrong side of the road, which seemed to be how they drove in Cornwall. "Honestly, with all this space you think they'd make the roads straighter."

"I'm pretty sure it doesn't work like that," I tried to laugh. "I think the farmers might object."

"I don't think I'm ever going to be a country girl," she sighed. "I bet you can't even get a decent cup of coffee out here."

"It's supposed to be the place to go, you know. Lots of surfing shops and fit guys in wetsuits."

"Well, no harm in looking, I suppose. But I still bet I can't get my skinny mochaccino."

"You might be surprised," I murmured. "Rob comes here, remember."

We finally found ourselves being directed by the satnav up a small residential road, and I could feel my heart thumping in my chest. Trying to stay calm I peered through the darkening evening gloom at the house numbers, searching for the one I wanted. Finally I saw it.

"There – number seventeen," I tried to say, but my voice was too squeaky. I swallowed and tried again, but Grace had seen and stopped the car a few doors up.

"Hmm, no lights on. Let's hope she's out the back." She turned to look at me. "Ready?"

I gulped. "Ready," I agreed, rather unsteadily.

"Do you want me to come with you to the door?"

"No, I think it'll be best if I try her alone, at first anyway. You just keep an eye from a distance."

"Sure? We know that she's got a really violent streak."

"I know but I think it's best to face her alone, honestly."

"OK," Grace agreed dubiously. "But I'll be watching."

I stepped out of the car and looked up the street. It was a residential road with a line of nearly identical little chalet-style houses. Some were obviously homes and had beautifully tended gardens, but others were clearly holiday lets with telltale low-maintenance gravel and inoffensive decor. It was a warm summer's evening and several barbecues were well under way. The smell suddenly made my mouth water, despite the fact that I couldn't have swallowed a bite. Music wafted from open windows and every now and then I caught a glimpse into living rooms framed by undrawn curtains.

Number seventeen was silent and dark. I walked up the paved path rather than risk crunching across the gravel to the front door, then stopped, squaring my shoulders before pressing the bell. It buzzed unexpectedly loudly and the noise made me flinch.

There was no response. Not wanting to give up I tried again but still there was no sign of movement through the frosted-glass windows. I bent down to the letter box and pressed it gently. Squeaking in protest it opened and I peered into the hall. It was fairly dark inside, but there was some illumination from the picture window at the rear. I let my eyes adjust to the light. The hall and room behind were tidy but bland, with no sign of occupation, no suitcases stacked by the door. We were too late.

I couldn't believe it. After all the effort of tracking her down and getting to Cornwall, we had missed her. I had no clue where to start looking next, and I could feel the tears of frustration suddenly pricking my eyes. I peered through the letter box again; not really in any expectation that something might have changed, I just didn't know what else to do. The hall remained dark and empty. I was just straightening up when I heard Grace behind me, her voice strangely harsh.

"I'd drop that if I was you, or I might be forced to hurt you."

I spun round. Grace was standing at the end of the path, her fists clenched tight. Standing between us was Catherine, a long wooden post in her hands, making ready to swing it at my head.

Showdown

"So you brought reinforcements this time," Catherine said, feigning boredom as she lowered the weapon slightly. "Didn't feel you could manage me on your own then?"

"You do have form for not playing fair," I said, pointing at the post. "Would you mind?"

Catherine tossed the post to the side of the path. "Suit yourself." She crossed her arms and stood looking down her nose at me. Neither Grace nor I said a word as we all wondered who would crack first. The uneasy stand-off lasted for a couple of long minutes and I realised it was going to have to be me. It was me who was going to be asking the favour, so however much I hated the idea I had to speak.

"Rob told us where you were."

"So?"

"But he has no idea who you are. All his memory of you has been wiped."

"So?" she repeated.

"So your little plan of making a lot of money by outing the Dirges to the papers failed. He's forgotten everything."

She gave the smallest of twitches of the head. "Huh. And how did that happen, I wonder?"

"Lucas took his memories of you, and your evil plan, and left him for dead."

The bored look was back and she kept silent.

"Look, Catherine, I know you can't stand me, even if I don't know why. But I need to ask you for a favour. You're the only one who can help the Dirges."

Her laugh was sudden and brutal, and I could see Grace readying herself to wade in if Catherine suddenly turned on me again. "*You* want a favour from *me*? That's rich!"

"It's not for me, it's for them; your old friends and family. Don't you want to help them?"

"You are a triumph of hope over experience, you know that? What makes you think I care about any of them?"

"Because Callum is your brother, and in some life you might have loved him!"

"Ah, sweetie, you've read me all wrong again. I hate Callum nearly as much as I hate you. You make a perfect pair."

"But there's no point in behaving like this, Catherine. You have absolutely nothing to gain by refusing to help and they have everything to lose." I could feel my voice rising in anger.

"I don't need to gain anything: I'm just not going to do it."

"Why would you condemn them to an eternity of misery when you could bring them back to life? Why?" I took a step closer, the words coming fast and furious, my hands curled into tight fists.

"Oh, that's easy." She paused, infuriating me even more.

"And. . . ?" I hissed.

"Because neither you nor Callum deserve to be happy, that's why. The rest I couldn't care less about anyway."

"But—"

"Alex." Grace's firm voice interrupted me. "Alex, I don't think you're going to get anywhere like this. Let's back off a little."

"Oh, the strong silent one actually speaks," said Catherine

in a voice dripping with sarcasm. "And speaks a bit of sense too."

"Look, Catherine, I know that you don't know me, and that you have no reason to listen to me, but can't we at least discuss this like adults?" Grace was trying to keep her voice even.

"Actually, I know everything about you, Grace. I know that it was you who shut the kitten's tail in the door and who spilled nail varnish on Issy's bedroom carpet. Your favourite cuddly toy is called Whiskers and you once faked an injury so you wouldn't have to compete in a gymnastics competition that your mum wanted you to enter. Shall I continue?"

Grace was staring at her, open-mouthed.

"The kitten and the nail varnish were accidents," I pointed out. "You know that too."

"True," said Catherine with a snide grin. "But it sounds better like that."

"How . . . how do you know all that?" Grace had recovered her voice and looked as if she was about to take up her fighting stance again.

"She has all my memories, remember?" I explained. "Everything I know about you, every detail, it's all in her head too."

"Unfortunately true. And such childish drivel, all of it. Mind you," Catherine paused for a second whilst she looked Grace up and down, her eyebrow raised, "you're a bit feistier than I was expecting. Alex seems to think you're a complete wimp."

I couldn't help the sharp intake of breath in indignation, but before I could speak Grace cut in. "If you think that I'm going to believe that then you've learned nothing from Alex's memories. Nothing."

"Really? Don't you want to hear about what Alex thinks of the lovely Jack? I was thinking about dropping you a little note so that you got a clearer picture. I wouldn't leave the two of them alone if I were you. She really can't be trusted. She's been lusting after Jack for years, and can't wait to make a play for him." Catherine's smug smile was evident in the dim orange glow of the streetlamps, which had just come on. I could feel the rage building in me. How dare she try and turn my best friend against me! I was just about to launch into a tirade when Grace snorted with laughter.

"Oh, Catherine, that's brilliant! I didn't realise you were a comedian." She shook her head, smiling to herself.

For the first time Catherine looked nonplussed and didn't have an instant, sarcastic retort. Grace took the opportunity to continue. "You see, you might have Alex's memories, but you don't – evidently – have her emotional understanding." I looked at Grace in surprise as she continued. "You don't seem to grasp that best friends – real, proper best friends – would never even think of doing that."

"Really." Catherine's sarcastic retort wasn't a question.

"Yes, *really*. You can't have had a best friend, you see, Catherine, because you'd know that some things would never even cross our minds. Alex would no more hurt me than I would hurt her." She turned to me and smiled. "Isn't that right, hon?"

I smiled back. "Absolutely."

Catherine's face was tight with anger and the red cloud of her aura became even more obvious in the gloom. "Well, I hope the two of you are very happy together." She turned back to me. "You're going to need a friend like that as things get bad with Callum. She'll help to keep you sane."

"Why would things get bad with Callum?"

"Oh, come on! You'll get fed up with him soon enough. He's only in the mirror! What good is that to you? I know what you want, remember. I've got your memories. Are you really going to go through university with a secret ghostly boyfriend? Are you going to abandon all thoughts of one day having a proper relationship with someone? Getting married? Having kids?"

"Steady on! I'm only seventeen; I've no intention of getting married."

"And you never will, not with Callum. He'll always be there in the background, making you feel guilty. Eventually you'll start to resent him. You'll meet some fantastic bloke and think, you know, time to dump Callum and get on with life. But you won't be able to. He'll be there, watching, forever. Every single thing you ever do, he'll be there. Even if you did try to live without him, and manage to get rid of the amulet without one of the others killing you, every day you'll wonder if he's standing broken-hearted in the corner of the room, watching your every move."

As she spoke, the cold hard truth of what she was saying wrapped around my heart like icy fingers. There was absolutely no way I could hurt Callum like that, and that made my mission even more vital.

"That's why I need your help," I said quietly, looking her in the eyes. "I'll beg if I need to. You know how to bring them over, to make them alive again. Help me, Catherine, please."

She looked at me for a long moment, then glanced towards Grace. "Is she having a laugh?"

"I'm not joking, honestly. I want your help. You're the only person who can bring them back to life."

Catherine stood back, arms folded. "Why do you think I can do that?"

"Veronica told me."

"Ahh, of course. Good old geriatric Veronica. She found me

pretty sharpish. I guess it's no surprise that she found you too."

"So you know, you understand. It has to be you."

"No, it doesn't. She can do it too."

I swallowed hard before I continued. "She doesn't have the energy any more. She can only release them so that they all die. Only you can help them to live again."

Her laughter rang out into the still evening. "Perfect! You've made my day. So you have to choose between killing my beloved brother or leaving him to pine after you for all eternity. I couldn't have organised that better myself!"

"Or you can let them live," I added quietly.

"Have you not been listening to a single word I've said? I've no intention of doing that. You're on your own, sweetie."

Grace couldn't stand by any longer. "Look, I'm sure it's not that hard. We'll do all we can to help you."

"It's like talking to Tweedledum and Tweedledee," Catherine muttered under her breath before turning towards Grace and stabbing a red-tipped finger at her face. "Listen, stupid. I'm not going to do it. I know that I *can*, I just don't *want* to. They can all rot over there forever as far as I'm concerned."

The hate and anger was seeping out of her and I still didn't know why. It was time to find out, and to see if that gave me the leverage to change her mind. I stepped towards her, my hands up in front of me to try and calm her down.

"OK, you've made your feelings crystal clear. But I do have another question to ask. That night in the alley behind the pub, you said that there were two things you wanted to tell me. One was how the Dirges could escape, the other was why you hated me so much."

"And then your little friend Olivia stole my memories from

me," she snarled.

"Exactly. And I can understand why you are so cross. But then when we were at the train station, when I was chasing Rob and you were coming down here, you said that you had written down everything, that it wasn't lost after all." I tried not to see the loathing in her eyes and pressed on. I had to try. "So tell me, why do you hate me so? What did I ever do to you?"

A small smile suddenly played around her lips, and for a second she looked the beauty that she could be and not a bitter and twisted lonely woman. "Do you know, I might show you the notes I wrote to myself. It could be quite entertaining. You'd better come in."

Grace and I exchanged uncomprehending looks. What was going on? "Sure," I said quickly, motioning Grace to stay close as I stepped towards the door. Catherine went to a little grey box on the wall of the house and punched in a code. With a click the lid of the box popped open and she took out the key that was inside, then used it to get into the house. She walked straight in, ignoring us. With another glance Grace and I followed behind, shutting the door as we went. Catherine walked directly into the kitchen and flicked on the lights. All three of us flinched in the sudden glare of the halogen spotlights. It had got pretty dark while we had been arguing outside.

With a single sweeping movement Catherine scooped up a small wheelie bag. It obviously contained just as little stuff as it had when I had seen her on North Sheen station. Flipping it on to the kitchen table she deftly unzipped it and pulled out a small over-the-shoulder bag. There was little else in the suitcase: a few items of clothing, what looked like a small sponge bag and a sunglasses case.

She undid the clasp on the bag and pulled out a wad of folded paper. I felt my palms go sweaty as I watched. Part of me wanted to run away, to never find out what was written on that harmless-looking page, but I knew that I needed to know. I suddenly felt quite sick and wished we were back outside in the fresh seaside air.

Catherine obviously sensed my discomfort. "Are you sure you want to know?" she asked in a taunting voice. "I mean, this was something I knew would bring your cosy little world crashing around your ears." She dangled the piece of paper from her long scarlet fingernails.

I was rooted to the spot. Faced with knowing what it was, did I really want to? But in the fraction of a second I stood there, Grace took control. She whisked the paper out of Catherine's fingers and scanned it quickly, a frown forming as she read.

"She's playing with us," she finally said, dismissively. "This can't hurt you." She held out the paper towards me and I forced myself to move, hoping as I took it that the shaking of my hand wasn't too obvious to Catherine. Grace caught my eye. "It's fine, honestly," she said in an undertone.

It was a single sheet of A4 paper, white and lined, and it looked as if it had been torn out of a spiral-bound notebook. There was a title on the top of the page, which was underlined three times, and underneath, in surprisingly childish writing, was a shopping list.

I looked up, momentarily speechless. "What on earth is this?" I managed finally. "Where's the real list?"

"You didn't think I was telling the truth at the station, did you?" She paused to look at my gobsmacked face. "Ahh, you did! Shame."

Above Catherine's head a small bright-yellow light danced. "Oh, it was worthwhile having to talk to you two losers for so long just to see the fear on your face! So now you know what I know – nothing. Everything got sucked up by Olivia. And actually, I don't care. All I need to know is that you did something and that I hate you for it. Simple, really."

I felt my knees begin to buckle, and quickly sank into the nearest chair, burying my head in my hands. None of this was any good at all; none of it was getting me any closer to my goal of persuading Catherine to help, to rescuing Callum from a life of misery. There had to be some way of making her cooperate, some nerve I could touch. I squeezed my eyes tightly shut and waited for inspiration. What leverage could I possibly use? What did I have that she wanted? I knew that she wanted the amulet, but she also knew I would never, ever, give it up, so it was pointless to try for that. There had to be something else. And finally it came to me.

"Money. You don't have enough money, no identity and nowhere to go. How much will it cost to get you to help us?"

The smile was back on Catherine's face. "Now you're talking sense," she said, pulling up a chair on the other side of the table and resting her chin on her clasped hands. "Time to negotiate."

Catherine had stolen the contents of my bank account a few weeks previously but the bank had quickly replaced the money, so I still had something to do a deal with. It wasn't a fortune and I hoped it would be enough to buy her off. It was mentally draining thrashing out a deal; negotiating was hard when she knew exactly what I had in the bank and I could see instantly if she was getting what she wanted. She also knew that I couldn't afford to lose, that eventually I'd give in and agree, just to make sure I could get Callum over. We were getting nowhere until Grace offered to stump up some of her savings, and finally we were done. Grace and I were exhausted, the long drive and emotion of the evening taking its toll. Grace then pulled a masterstroke and persuaded Catherine to agree to let us camp down in one of the bedrooms for the night, and I sank thankfully on to the bed. There was only a scratchy blanket each but we were beyond caring, and as I shut my eyes I had a sudden vision of seeing Callum properly; of pulling him out of the river and into my arms; of holding him tight. It was going to be all right.

I woke with a start in the morning, and for a moment was completely confused about where I was. Grace was still motionless under the blanket on the other bed, so I picked up my shoes and crept out of the room, leaving her to sleep.

Downstairs the house was deserted, but the kettle was warm and the back door was open. In the twilight the night before I hadn't really noticed how close the sea was to the little row of houses. At the end of every garden was a small gate, then a small, gorse-covered slope. I could hear the crashing of waves coming from somewhere beyond it. Shutting the kitchen door carefully behind me I walked down the garden and on to the dewy heath-land beyond. Within minutes my Converse were drenched, but the sun was already beginning to warm everything. They would dry soon enough.

I followed a narrow path through the gorse up to the top of the slope, and gasped in wonder at the panorama that opened up in front of me. The small rise I was standing on sloped away sharply towards a gravel path, beyond which were rocks and a faint haze of sea spray. The sea was a dark blue, with several big ships on the far horizon. To the left I could just see the land on the other side of the estuary by Padstow, but on the right the ground rose slightly so I couldn't see the town or beaches of Polzeath. On the highest point a figure was standing alone, looking out across the water, and even from that distance I could see the cloak of purple mist that enveloped Catherine. I had never seen anything like it before. She had been miserable before, of course, but nothing on that scale. A shiver ran down my back as I realised that she was standing on a cliff edge. Was that the aura of someone about to jump? My walk turned into a sprint as I raced towards her. I couldn't let her die, not after what she had promised.

She was probably about two minutes away at my fastest pace. There was no point in shouting; I didn't want to startle her, so I put my head down and ran faster, leaping over the smaller gorse bushes and ferns where the path ambled away from a direct line. Sharp thorns pulled at my clothes and caught my skin but I didn't slow down. Finally the gorse gave way to the close-cropped grass, and as I crashed through the last line of ferns I startled a small herd of sheep. Bleating loudly they scattered. Catherine turned automatically to see what was causing the disturbance, the purple mist shimmering around her like a cloak. I thought about not mentioning it, just greeting her like a friend, but I instantly knew that would be a mistake. I pulled up quickly, not wanting to frighten her into making any sudden moves.

She was standing on the very edge of the cliff; one stride forward and she would be over the edge. From where I was I couldn't see how far the drop was, but I could hear the angry crashing of the waves on to the rocks below. The noise was loud enough for me to have to raise my voice to speak to her.

"It's a bit wild up here," I called, walking slowly forward and trying to catch my breath.

Catherine ignored me, her gaze following the sheep that were still galloping along the cliff path. The purple cloud that surrounded her pulsed as if it were alive. As I got to within an arm's length or so, she turned to glare at me. "I'm not going to jump, you know."

"I wasn't suggesting you were." I shrugged. "I just wanted to make sure you were OK." I hoped that she couldn't hear the pounding of my heart after my sprint up the hill.

"I just love your sudden concern. The minute you know that I'm prepared to help you, you're all over me like a rash."

I raised my eyebrows. "I prefer to think of it as protecting my investment. Let's be clear, Catherine. We're never going to like each other, and this little truce is only until we both get what we want out of the deal. Agreed?"

She inclined her head in a short nod.

"And in the meantime, I can't be bothered with your constant sarcasm. We have a long drive ahead of us and it'll go much quicker if we're civil."

The purple cloud suddenly pulsed with an angry red, but I stood my ground. "Truce?" I asked, holding out my hand, still keen to get her away from the edge. It would be like her to jump just to spite me.

Catherine thrust her hands deep into the pockets of the shapeless cardigan she was wearing, but turned and took a step towards me. Finally she looked at me. "Don't push it!" she snarled, walking past. "The best you'll get is if I ignore you completely," she called over her shoulder as she stalked back towards the house. Heaving a sigh of relief I turned to follow her.

Passenger

Catherine was as good as her word. She sat motionless in the kitchen while Grace and I tidied up from our impromptu sleepover. I was keen to make sure that when Rob's family appeared there was no sign that we had ever been there. It didn't take long, but by the time we were finished I was starving. There was nothing to eat in the house at all.

"I'll talk to her," whispered Grace as we dumped the bags in the hall ready to leave. "She must have been eating somewhere. You load the car while I ask."

I heard the murmur of voices as I opened the door, and before I had stashed the bags in the boot both Grace and Catherine were coming out of the house. Catherine locked up and punched the code into the little security box, leaving the key inside. She then marched to the car and got into the back without a word.

"Apparently Catherine has been eating at the hotel, but we might find something rather cheaper down at the beach." I could see the gleaming art deco façade of the hotel further along the main road, and even from this distance it was clear that it wasn't going to be a budget option.

"Beach, I think. It would be nice to see it before we leave anyway."

"Good call," said Grace, crashing the gears as we made our way out of the little close.

The road down to the beach was steep and winding, and surprisingly busy given how early it was. As we rounded the corner we saw why: a vast expanse of sand stretched away to the left, and in the distance lines of surfers were bobbing on the water waiting to catch the next wave. There was a large car park and Grace nipped in quickly to grab one of the few remaining spaces. Coffee bars and surf shops were doing a roaring trade, and dozens of people were walking past in wetsuits carrying surfboards.

"I think you might get your mochaccino after all," I said. We chose the closest café and ordered cooked breakfasts. Catherine didn't say a word throughout, just nodding when we asked her if she would like the same as us. It was really awkward at first, but Grace and I soon pretended she wasn't there. We instinctively knew which topics of conversation to avoid, and spent quite a lot of time discussing the various people we saw walking down the beach with their boards.

"If they do it on the Gower, I'm going to try surfing next week with Jack," said Grace as she finished off the last of her fried egg by wiping a piece of buttered bread around the plate.

"You'll have to watch out if the sea air there has the same affect on your appetite as it does here. I don't think I've ever seen you eat quite such a huge breakfast."

"I know." Grace laughed, sitting back. "I'll be enormous if I eat that every day!" She stretched and reached for the last of her coffee. "Are you ready to go, Catherine?"

Catherine had avoided eye contact the entire time we were sitting at the table, and she didn't even speak then; she just pushed her plate away from her and got up.

"I guess that's a 'yes' then," Grace muttered as we gathered our bags and returned to the car. Yet again Catherine positioned herself in the back, and immediately slumped down in the seat, folded her arms and closed her eyes.

It was still reasonably early so the traffic wasn't too heavy, and within an hour we were on the main road. I was trying hard not to get overexcited but I could hardly wait to speak to Callum. With Catherine's help I was going to be able to set not only him free but all of the other Dirges too. I started to make a list in my head of all the things I needed to do to make the process work properly. There was a lot to cover, and I fished around in my bag for a piece of paper.

"What are you writing?" asked Grace as I started to compose my list.

"Oh, just a few things I'm going to need to do."

"It's OK, I reckon Catherine's asleep. I've been keeping an eye on her for the last half an hour and she's barely moved."

"I don't think it would matter if she did hear what I need to plan. She has to be part of it, after all."

"True. So what's at the top of your list then?"

"I need to phone Veronica and tell her we're on our way. She's the only one who knows what exactly it is we have to do, where we need to go, and stuff."

"OK, that's pretty straightforward. What next?"

"Depending on when we do it, I have to get the lifeboat guys on high alert. If hundreds of people are suddenly going to appear in the Thames they'll need to be ready."

"That's going to be a bit tricky, isn't it? How on earth are you going to get them to believe you?"

"I don't know," I admitted. "Perhaps I can ring the emergency services and say that I'm worried that my friend is about to commit suicide by jumping off a bridge into the Thames. Do you think that would work?"

Grace pursed her lips as she considered the plan. "It might work. But whose name would you give them?"

"I could make one up, or. . ." I gestured at the sleeping Catherine behind me with a nod of the head.

"Yes, I quite like that idea. OK, what else is on that list?"

"I need to talk to Callum. Just as soon as I get close enough to London. He needs to tell them all what we are going to try and do."

"Will they all agree?"

"I think so. They all seemed happy enough to let me kill them, or so Callum said, so I can't imagine that they will object to being given their lives back."

"You might be surprised."

The leaden voice from the back of the car made us both jump, and the car swerved across the carriageway. "Oh, hi, Catherine. Did we wake you?" said Grace as cheerily as possible as she straightened the steering wheel.

I jumped straight in. "What do you mean? Do you think they don't want to be alive?"

"They'll be like me. No memory, no money and no place to go. It's not exactly ideal."

"But with that many of them appearing at the same time in the Thames, people will have to believe that something odd has gone on, and they'll be able to help."

"By locking them into psychiatric hospitals like Veronica? Yeah, that does sound appealing. I reckon they'll find being alive again worse than being a Dirge." She made a short huffing noise. "Anyway, not my problem."

I glanced round: the purple mist was thick again, settling

around her. "So what do you think we should do?"

She didn't respond, just folded her arms tighter and continued to pretend to be asleep. Grace and I exchanged a quick look, and Grace shrugged helplessly. We fell into silence as she continued to drive, the list of things to do lying unfinished in my lap. I stared out of the window, not noticing the wild countryside we were driving past. Catherine was absolutely right. The practicalities of the life that the resurrected Dirges would face were hugely problematic. The authorities were going to be deeply suspicious of all these people, none of whom had any sort of identity. True, there were going to be rather a lot of them, all saying the same thing, but at the end of the day they were going to need to find homes, jobs, friends. It was a huge task.

I needed to talk to Callum about it. He would know the best thing to do. He could get Matthew to speak to all the Dirges and they could decide. Perhaps I could do it twice, once with Catherine and then again with Veronica, and give everyone what they wanted. The important thing was that I would be able to bring Callum over and we could be together forever.

I made inane conversation with Grace to keep her alert as we worked our way up the M4 towards Swindon. The traffic had thinned out after Bristol so the journey was reasonably straightforward, but because of Grace's driving it continued to be slow. As we approached the next services Grace pointed at the sign.

"I'm going to have to pull in. I shouldn't have drunk all that coffee earlier. Will she mind, do you think?"

She nodded towards the back of the car, where Catherine still appeared to be asleep.

"Oh, don't worry about her," I said as Grace manoeuvred into the right lane. "I could do with stretching my legs too."

The car park was packed with families all stopping for lunch, and it took us a while to find somewhere to park. Catherine pretended to be asleep until the engine was actually switched off, then opened her eyes and looked disdainfully about her.

"I can't believe how stiff I am," said Grace, opening her door and easing herself out. She stretched out her arms and neck, and even in the noise of the car park I heard her joints cracking.

"Oh, that doesn't sound good." I winced on her behalf. "I wish I could do a stint of driving for you, but I can't."

"I know, it's OK. You just carry on keeping me awake. I'll get some more coffee while I'm in there if you want. Come on, Catherine, let's move!"

"I'm not moving. I don't need the loo and I don't want to eat anything they make in there." She didn't budge.

"OK, suit yourself. We'll be ten minutes. Don't leave the car."

Grace motioned me to go with her. "Are you sure that's sensible?" I asked. "She might disappear." I looked back over my shoulder as we walked towards the building's entrance.

"I didn't leave the keys in there and we're in a service station. There's nowhere to go except along the motorway. Relax, it'll be fine."

"I'm not convinced. I'll stay here and keep an eye on the car. I need to phone Veronica anyway."

I positioned myself so that I could see the front of the car, and tried to keep out of the sun. It had begun to get oppressively hot and I thought wistfully of the gentle sea breeze I had been standing in earlier. I pulled my phone out and scrolled down to Veronica's number. She answered immediately.

"Hi, it's Alex. I've got some good news for you."

She sounded much more tired than she had before. "Really?

Where are you? Did you find Catherine?"

"Yes, we tracked her down last night. She took some persuading but she's agreed to come back to London with us."

There was a brief silence. "Did you hear me, Veronica – Catherine's going to help. They'll all be able to live!"

The voice that answered me was wary. "Can she overhear you?"

"She can't hear a word. What's the problem? I thought you'd be pleased she said yes."

"Why is she doing it? What did you promise her?"

"Money, actually. Everything that Grace and I could scrape together."

There was another moment's silence as Veronica digested the information. "Don't trust her, not for a minute," she said eventually.

"Why? It seems reasonable to me. She needs money."

"She'll be bluffing you. I don't believe for a second that she's actually going to go through with it."

"I don't think she has any other option. She has no friends, she's terribly depressed and I think maybe it's given her something positive to do."

"Well, I guess we should be grateful then," Veronica said slowly, but I could hear the doubt in her voice. "I was worried about her motivation, but if greed is what drives her, then we should be OK. Just keep on your guard though. There's something not quite right about that girl."

"Don't worry, I will. So come on, what do we need to organise? We can actually do it now, can't we? Save everyone, I mean. So what's the plan?"

I could almost hear her pull herself together at the end of

the phone. "We need to get all of the Dirges gathered together in one place, in a long line with you at one end and Catherine at the other. But we need to talk to them first, make sure they understand what's going on."

"That should be pretty easy; they'll all be delighted. Catherine was bleating on about most of them wanting to die, but that's just nonsense," I said confidently. But there was another silence in return.

"She's right, you know," Veronica said quietly. "Many of them may prefer to take the other option, you have to remember that." She paused to let her words sink in. "We have to give them the choice. I was going to talk to you about this earlier but you shot off before I could speak to you. Personally, I think most of them will choose to die, and you will be doing them a great disservice if you don't offer them the choice."

"Well, if that's what some of them want then I guess that's OK. The important thing is that I can save those who want to be saved. I can rescue Callum!" I was determined not to let her pour cold water on my plans. I hurried on. "So I need to talk to all the Dirges together, to give them a little while to think about it. My plan is to bring Catherine straight into London this afternoon, talk to them, and then get on with it. I don't want to wait too long as I'm not sure how quickly Catherine will lose interest in helping, and I can't hold her prisoner." I paused for breath, my mind racing on to the possibilities of the evening ahead. Within a few short hours I could be sitting by Callum while they checked him out in hospital, holding his hand, kissing his lips. . . I brushed aside thoughts of where he was going to live and how he was going to get money, all those mundane trivialities. None of that was important in comparison to him being with me.

"When can you speak with Callum and tell him what your plans are?" asked Veronica. "How close to London do you have to be?"

"I can't call him just yet; it'll take him too long to get out here and back. I'll call before Catherine and I get on the train in Twickenham."

"I'll go to the cathedral and wait. I think today might be overambitious though."

"Well, that's what I'm aiming for, even if we just rescue the ones who want rescuing first. You said that you and I could help the others without Catherine."

"I know what I said. I just need to think things through."

"All right, keep your phone on and I'll call you just as soon as I can." I clicked the phone off and looked around towards the service-station entrance. I really wanted Grace to hurry up, but everywhere was packed with people. She could be queuing for some time.

Abandoning my little square of shade I walked slowly back to the car. I didn't want to get in with Catherine until I really had to, but it was better to keep a close eye on her. I couldn't fathom why Veronica was quite so dubious about Catherine's involvement. Money seemed a perfectly good motivation for her, especially given the rate she seemed to be able to get through it, and I wasn't going to let Veronica dampen my excitement. I was going to rescue Callum! It was real; the plan was coming together.

My thoughts ran on to what was going to happen later, and when the phone rang I answered it automatically, assuming it was Veronica with more instructions. "Hi, that was quick," I started, before realising that it wasn't her calling.

"Well, I did tell you that I was on a mission..." Max's voice dripped out of the phone like honey. "I wondered when you were coming back to London. I've got tickets for the big concert in Hyde Park and was hoping you'd like to come." He hesitated for a moment and then ruined his cool by adding, "Please?"

I couldn't help laughing. "Nice try, Max! But as I keep telling you, I've already got a boyfriend."

"But he can't take you to the concert next weekend, can he? Why not come with me? I know you like the bands."

My good mood made me reckless. "Actually it looks like he might be here by then."

He sounded as if I had winded him. "Oh. So he's flying in? Sod it!"

"I'm so sorry, Max, but I know you understand. Our timing has just been appalling. Maybe in another life. . ."

"Yeah, right. Well, let me know if he doesn't make the flight and you fancy using the ticket."

"I'm sorry," I repeated softly. "I really am."

I clicked off the phone and tried not to think about what I had just done. I really didn't want to hurt him, but there was no alternative. Looking up I realised that I could no longer see the car as it was blocked from view by a large people-carrier and the family deep in discussion on the pavement next to it. It was a huge vehicle, more of a van than anything else, and it completely dwarfed the cars on either side. Mumbling "Excuse me", I edged around them, anxious to get close to our car so that we could leave as soon as Grace was back. I leaned on the bonnet for a moment but it was too muggy to be in the sunshine; inside the car I'd at least be in the shade. I opened the door and automatically checked the back seat. It was completely empty.

Suffering

I wrenched open the back door, hoping that I was wrong, that Catherine was just slumped down out of sight. Then I saw the page torn from a map, with *Thanks for the lift, losers!* scribbled over it in the same childish hand.

I couldn't believe that she had tricked us so easily. I stood up on the edge of the door to see if it gave me a better view around the car park but it didn't. There were people and cars everywhere, and all Catherine needed was a lift into town or down the motorway in either direction, and she would be gone forever. I couldn't let that happen; she was still my only chance, the only way I was ever going to be able to get Callum over to me.

I scanned the heads of the people but couldn't see her distinctive, long blonde hair anywhere. I ran round the car and rudely interrupted the people on the pavement. "Sorry, but my friend, the one who was in the car, did you see where she went?"

"Oh no, sorry, love," said the rather matronly mother in a gentle Irish lilt. "I didn't see a thing."

"It's really important. She's not well and shouldn't have got out of the car. Did none of you see anything?"

"Maybe the girls in the back of the van saw something. Just a sec." I thought she was going to go to the van door and ask them, but instead she bellowed, "Girls! Get out here now." Nothing much happened and she gave me a look. She put her hands on her hips and took a deep breath. "Rosie, Megan and Amy, get out here this minute!" All around the car park heads were turning, and finally the rear door of the people carrier slid back to reveal three young teenage girls. I turned quickly down between the cars to get to them.

"Please, the girl in the car – who was in *this* car," I tapped it on the roof, "did you see where she went? It's really important. I need to find her now."

The three of them looked at each other, and seemed about to burst into giggles. "Please! It's really important," I urged.

The oldest one finally looked me in the eye. "She left just after we arrived, maybe about five minutes ago. I didn't see where she went."

Five minutes. Enough time to get into someone else's car and be away, or she could be hiding somewhere in the car park. I ran, shouting my thanks as I scanned up and down the rows of vehicles, hoping that Catherine was still trying to persuade someone to give her a lift. But cars were coming and going all the time; it was an impossible task. I stopped at the end of the row, gasping for breath, my hands on my knees. But after a few seconds I realised that I didn't have the time to waste on trying to recover. I had to keep going or lose my only chance – *Callum's* only chance. I would be better off at the exit, looking at all the cars that were leaving. They all had to go out the same way so if she wasn't already gone I might be able to stop her. Fishing out my mobile as I ran, I called Grace.

"Hi," she answered breezily. "Won't be long, I'm nearly at the front of the queue now."

"She's gone," I gasped, not wanting to stop running to speak.

"Gone?"

"Left a note. Gone. I'm going to the exit to check cars that are leaving." I sucked in another lungful of air. "You check in there, OK?"

"Crap! The lying little—"

"No time. Go and search."

"On it. I'll call you back." Grace had turned brisk and efficient, and I knew that she would have the place thoroughly checked in no time at all. I had made it through the coach and lorry park and in front of me was the petrol station. On the forecourt was a man in a uniform, picking up the litter. I ran towards him and he looked up, startled, as I approached.

"I'm looking for a girl, maybe twenty, long dark-blonde hair, wearing jeans and a baggy top. Have you seen her come through here?"

He looked at me uncomprehendingly. "I'm sorry?" he said in heavily accented English. "I no understand."

I was too impatient to try and explain. "Never mind," I shouted over my shoulder as I went on. Within a few minutes I was at the side of the exit road, peering into all the cars as they passed. But there were hundreds, and lorries and coaches too. It wouldn't have taken much to sneak on to a coach. She could be miles down the road already. I realised that she wouldn't have gone into the service area where Grace might have seen her, and I knew it was hopeless. I slumped down on the kerb and dropped my head into my hands. I couldn't believe it. How had I gone so quickly from being delighted at the thought of being with Callum forever to total despair at the side of the road? If I hadn't got distracted talking to Max I would have noticed her trying to leave. A huge wail of guilt and frustration escaped me and the tears streamed down my face. Slamming my fists into the kerb, I wept.

I wasn't there long before a car drew up beside me. Peering up through my hair I saw the blue flashing lights on the top.

"Not again," I muttered to myself thickly through the tears, reaching for a tissue and trying to control my breathing enough to speak.

"Now then, miss, what's up?" said the officer in a kind tone, crouching down beside me.

"I've . . . I've lost someone," I tried to say, but it came out as incomprehensible noise. I blew my nose loudly and tried again. "Lost someone. Was taking them to London but they've run off."

"I see. And just how old is this person?"

"About twenty."

"Is anything missing? Did they steal anything from you?"

I shook my head. I really didn't want to get the police involved, and unless they were able to stop all the traffic on the motorway they weren't going to be able to help anyway.

"Seems she just wanted a lift this far, then ditched us."

"Well, if she's scarpered there's not much I can do, I'm afraid." He looked me up and down for a second. "Are you hurt?" he asked finally. I shook my head again, not wanting to speak. "I'm going to have to take you back to your car, miss. You can't stay here."

It was easier to give in, and I slid into the back of the patrol car. The smell of air freshener was overpowering, and if it hadn't been cool from the air conditioning I would have felt quite sick. Muttering my thanks I got out as quickly as possible and walked into the service station. My phone buzzed as I crossed the food hall.

"Did you find her?" demanded Grace. "She's not in here. I've checked pretty much everywhere."

"She's gone."

"Are you sure? It's a big place."

"She'll be on a bus going somewhere. There were dozens of them in the coach park. Where are you now?"

"Actually, I'm right here." She tapped me on the shoulder as she said it.

I hugged her tightly, squeezing my eyes closed so that I didn't cry. "I can't believe she did that. We had a deal!"

"She has absolutely no morals, you know that. Just be grateful that she didn't run off after she had taken all your money." We stood together, a small island of still in the constant stream of people getting food, buying drinks, or heading for the loos, and Grace stroked my back rhythmically, as if I were a child who needed comforting. But a cold pit of despair had opened in my heart, and all the stroking in the world wasn't going to be able to help.

Back in the car Grace looked at the note that Catherine had left. "Cheeky mare! She's torn a page out of my new *A to Z*."

"I'll get you another one, don't worry."

"I'm not worried, just cross. Do you think the fact that she's written on the Thames is some kind of clue?" asked Grace, examining it from all angles.

"It's the only clear bit of space on that page, so I doubt it. It wouldn't be like her to give us any kind of help, anyway." I tossed the book on to the rear seat as we set off.

"I do wish that you didn't need her so badly. Is she really your only hope? Are you sure there isn't anything else you can do?"

I shook my head, then realised she couldn't see that as she was driving towards the slip road back on to the motorway. "No, there's nothing. That's what Veronica told me. It's Catherine or death for the Dirges," I said, peering around desperately, just in case Catherine was about to appear between the parked coaches, but there was no sign. I slumped back into my seat, defeated.

Grace reached over and gave my hand a sympathetic squeeze. "We can't avoid talking about this any more, Alex. I know that you didn't want to before, not when there was hope of bringing the Dirges back to life, but without Catherine you're going to have to think about letting them die."

I couldn't speak, but just sat, staring out of the window across the countryside in front of us, not really taking in the gathering clouds.

"You should do it, Alex."

"I can't," I whispered. "I just can't bear it. I love Callum so much, the thought of not being to be able to be together is just awful. We've been through so much already, and we were so close to being together..." My voice was scratchy but I was beyond tears. The idea of losing Callum again, and permanently, turned my heart into a gaping void. It was all I could do to breathe.

Grace was silent for a moment, and when I glanced at her she was frowning hard and chewing her lip. "What is it?" I asked after a few moments.

"How many Dirges are there?"

"I don't know, maybe a couple of hundred?"

"And their lives are made up of unrelenting misery with no way out?"

"Uh-huh."

"So that's two hundred desperate souls, and you are their only hope of release?" I nodded miserably as she stole a quick glance at me. "Then you don't have a choice; you must help them."

"But what if I can find Catherine in the future? There might still be some hope!"

"You said that the power she has at the moment will wear off, as it has for Veronica. Do you know how long you have before that happens?"

"No," I said miserably.

"And you can't guarantee that when – or if – you find her you'll be able to persuade her to help anyway."

"I know."

She was silent again for a minute while she negotiated her way past a large lorry that was grinding along in the slow lane. "Damn it, it's going to rain," she muttered under her breath. "I hate driving in the rain."

"Do you really think I should do it then, kill them all?"

"Do you remember what you told me about your work experience week? With the little dog?"

Of course I remembered. I remembered his soft eyes, his licking tongue, his appalling injuries. And I remembered with perfect clarity what the vet had said to me that day. "We can stop the suffering, and sometimes it's kinder to do just that. Existence is not the same as life for these little guys, and we need to know when to exercise that judgement." And remembering that, I knew what I had to do, and I knew that waiting any longer was cruel.

It was time to let Callum go.

Truth

The trip back to London dragged on. I was desperate to talk to Callum, to share a few more moments now that I'd made my decision. I knew it was the right decision, but I still wanted to have another hour at the top of the dome, a last opportunity to hold him close before. . .

Every time I thought of what I would have to do next I could feel panic rising in my chest. I watched the wipers flick back and forth as the rain pelted down, unaware of anything but my pain. Grace kept silent; she knew I was in no state to talk, and she had to concentrate on driving.

As we finally approached the end of the motorway she asked, "Are you going straight into town now to tell them your decision?"

I nodded. "Yes, I think I have to. You're right; it's cruel to wait. I have to let them know that I'll help, and we have to work out how and where we're going to do it."

"Will you talk to Veronica?"

"I'll call her later. I want to tell Callum first, and he can then tell the others. Most of them will remember her well, it seems. Callum and Catherine are the only ones who became Dirges after she'd escaped."

"So you're not going to do it today?" Grace let the question hang in the air.

I shook my head, the tears welling up instantly again. "Not today. I need a little more time."

"OK, well, I'll drive you to the station in Kew, then you can jump on the Tube."

"Are you sure that's all right?"

"Not a problem, and definitely not now that it's stopped raining." She flashed a quick smile at me. We had driven through the weather front and the scenery around us looked washed clean as the sun started breaking through the clouds. She carefully negotiated the huge roundabout at the junction of the motorway and set off towards Kew. It was still well before the afternoon rush hour, so the roads were moderately quiet, and before long she was pulling on to the station forecourt.

"Thank you so much, Grace," I started with a catch in my voice. "I don't know how I would have managed this without you."

"Any time." She gave me a quick squeeze. "Call me later, yes? Give me an update? I'm going to be at home packing for tomorrow so you can reach me any time."

"OK." I held her tight for a moment, then quickly got out of the car before she could see the tears on my cheeks.

I walked into the station looking around for somewhere quiet where I could sit and call Callum. I had to tell him my decision, but putting it into words would make the whole thing real, irreversible, an admission of defeat. So as a Tube train pulled in I got on it immediately, telling myself that I'd have more time with Callum later. But I knew it was a cowardly decision, and I knew that I had to be strong. I nipped back off the train just as the doors were closing and made my way to the quietest bench on the platform.

Taking a deep breath I called his name as I groped around

in my bag for my earphones. Within moments the welcome tingle was there in my wrist, a tingle that I wasn't going to feel many more times, I realised.

"You're back. I've missed you." His voice was warm and welcoming, and so full of love that I couldn't speak. His touch was gentle on my hair. "Did it not go to plan?"

I shook my head as I tried to set up the little mirror. "I'm so sorry, Callum, for a while I thought it was going to be OK, that I was going to be able to make you all alive again, but it all went horribly wrong."

"Shh, calm down. Take a deep breath and try to explain that again. It didn't make much sense to me."

Quickly, I told him everything. In a few short sentences I destroyed all our hopes.

Callum was silent, staring unseeing down the tracks. "I'm so sorry," I continued. "I wanted to save you all, but I can't."

He gave a slightly crooked smile that didn't quite reach the deep pools of his eyes. "You *can* save us, Alex. You can let us all die."

"I know." I looked at his trusting face and I knew what was right. "And I will."

I felt the almost imperceptible touch of his arms tighten around me. "Thank you," he whispered as he gently kissed my hair, the look of love in his eyes almost overwhelming in its intensity. I tried hard but the tears brimmed over, dripping hot and wet on to my hands as they lay in my lap. "I can feel that," said Callum. "You're crying on me. I've never felt that before." He paused for a second then continued. "You've given me everything, Alex; don't be sad. This is a happy ending, it's just not the one we'd hoped for." I could tell he was trying to make me feel better, but I knew that nothing was ever going to feel the same again. I had just agreed to the mercy killing of someone I loved with all my heart.

Another Tube train arrived and left as I sat slumped on the bench, defeated. Catherine had won; she had got what she wanted and ruined my life. Callum stayed with me, gently stroking my hair, murmuring things that he thought might comfort me. I registered nothing; I was numb, knowing what I was going to have to do. Finally, as another train approached, Callum made me listen. "Come on, Alex, get on the train and come up to St Paul's. I need to hold you properly. I can't bear to see you like this."

I looked into the mirror, taking the opportunity to drink him in while I could. "OK," I said eventually. "We need to talk to the others anyway, to let them know what the plan is. Do you want to go ahead and talk to Matthew first? Then when I get there I can talk to everyone. There may be some who need a bit of persuasion."

He snorted. "I don't think so! They'll all be delighted."

"You should find Olivia then, and talk to her. I know that she's really worried about all the rumours flying around." I had to raise my voice to be heard as the Tube train screeched to a halt alongside me. I snapped the mirror shut and stood up.

Callum sighed. "Come on, get on the train. I'll go and talk to her and Matthew before you get to the cathedral. I'll see you in an hour or so, OK? I love you."

He had walked with me as I got on to the train, and as I replied the tingle abruptly went from my wrist as the train lurched forward. "I love you too," I whispered into the silence.

I hunched down in one of the seats, ignoring all the other passengers and trying not to cry. I couldn't be crying as I talked to the Dirges; I really had to get a grip. It was also going to be one of the last times I saw Callum at the top of the dome. I couldn't bring myself to believe that it was *the* last time I would hold him, but there weren't going to be many more. I rubbed my hands over my face and pulled my bag into my lap. Luckily I still had a pack of wet wipes in there from my dog-walking duties, so I wiped my face clean of the salty streaks that the tears had left, then rummaged to see what make-up I had with me. It was a pretty poor selection: just an old mascara and the stub of a lipstick. My face in the mirror was tired and drawn. I had to do better than that.

I looked at the time and then at the Tube map up on the wall of the carriage. I could get off slightly earlier and buy some concealer, and still make it there before the last entry time. I was on the District Line, so getting off at Blackfriars would be perfect. There was bound to be a chemist's or something near there. It was then only a five-minute walk up the hill to St Paul's.

With my plan settled I sat back and tried not to think. Thinking wasn't helpful; I just had to work on instinct. I tried to distract myself with watching the scenery but within minutes the train had plunged underground. I started thinking about how I was going to be feeling on that trip back, when everything was over, when the one I loved was gone. Before I realised it I was imagining Max comforting me; having him hold me tight while I mourned for Callum. It was only for a second but I was horrified with myself. How could I be that callous? Was it because I secretly wanted Max? Was my subconscious telling me what I needed to do? I put my head in my hands and gazed unseeingly at the worn floor while I tried to examine my motives.

No, I decided, sitting up straight. I was positive I was going to release the Dirges for the right reasons, not to make my life more convenient. It was a momentary daydream, nothing more.

I picked up a discarded newspaper to try and get the images out of my head by reading about the latest celebrities, but it was a waste of time. The news stories weren't much help either. Reading about various disasters around the world was also hopeless. I couldn't help comparing the disasters with the one I was about to create, when two or three hundred people appeared dead in the Thames. What would the headlines be on the papers after that? Or would they cover it all up? No one would be able to explain what had happened so it might be easier to pretend that it hadn't.

I was so wrapped up in that train of thought I nearly missed the announcement that came over the intercom.

"Due to a passenger under a train further up the line this train will be terminating at Temple. All change at Temple."

There was an immediate wave of irritation from the other passengers; lots of tutting and heavy sighs, and every aura turned red or purple. I looked up at the map: Temple was only one stop short of Blackfriars and I knew that I would be able to walk along the Embankment really easily. I would just have to walk quickly.

As the train pulled in I made sure I was at the door ready to beat the rush up the steps and into the daylight, and thankfully the stairs were right next to the carriage I had been in. I was outside in a matter of minutes, walking quickly along the busy road that followed the north bank of the Thames. The rain here had only recently stopped so the pavements were still slick and I could see that the river was at high tide. The grey seawater was rolling and swirling as it fought its way upstream against all the rainwater coming in the opposite direction. I shivered at the thought of being thrown into it, even on a summer's day.

I was trying not to think about being in the river when I nearly walked into a couple coming out of an ornate gateway. Glancing through the railings next to it I could see a beautiful garden, which was lovely but not very helpful in my search for a shop that sold make-up. I tried to edge past the pair, who were having a fairly animated discussion while walking slowly – too slowly. I needed to go faster as I couldn't afford to miss the cut-off time for getting up to the top of the dome. I was so wrapped up in my problems it took a few minutes to place the voice.

"Look, if that's what they say is the deal, then that's what you're going to have to live with. Dad always said that there's no point in trying to argue with lawyers."

I was so surprised I stopped dead, then had to run a couple of steps to catch them up again. I didn't understand how it could be possible. He was talking again as I got back in earshot.

"Well, you haven't exactly helped yourself, have you? This can't be a surprise." His red aura matched his exasperated tone.

"You would say that," spat the young woman, her deep-red aura suddenly morphing into a livid purple shade. "None of you care what's happening to me!"

"Catherine, that's not true, and you know it." A phone suddenly went off and he pulled a handset from his pocket. "Crap. I've got to take this – I won't be a second. There are some benches over there. Hi, yes, we've just finished. . ." Callum turned around, phone pressed to his ear, and glanced past me. My mouth fell open as I watched him ignore me completely and move away to continue his conversation. I couldn't believe it. Veronica must have persuaded Catherine after all and the two of them had come up with some sort of magnificent rescue plan while I had been travelling back from Cornwall. The shock and surprise was being overtaken by joy. I couldn't wait to speak to him.

"Callum?" I ventured carefully, touching him on the arm in wonder. A real arm, attached to a real, living, breathing person.

He turned around, a small frown of irritation on his

forehead. "Hang on a sec, someone wants me," he said into the phone. "Can I help you?" His stunning blue eyes met mine without a hint of recognition.

"Callum?" I repeated, unable to keep the grin off my face or my hands off his arm. "You made it! How on earth—"

He stepped back ever so slightly, forcing me to let go. "I'm sorry, do I know you?" His face had a look of polite bewilderment; he had no idea who I was.

"I . . . I'm sorry, I think we have met, but maybe you don't remember."

"OK, well, it's good to see you but I'm on the phone right now. Some other time?" He lifted the receiver away from his ear to make his point, flashed a brief smile and turned away to continue his conversation. "Hi, sorry about that, OK, so what we agreed was. . ."

I backed away, a feeling of cold dread seeping through my body. Whatever Veronica and Catherine had done, however they had managed this, he had absolutely no memory of me whatsoever. For a moment I stood and watched him, taking in the strength of his shoulders, the sunlight on his hair, the way he used his free hand to punctuate whatever it was he was talking about on the phone, and the feeling of loss was almost overwhelming. Here was everything I wanted, everything I had hoped for, but he had forgotten all about me.

I turned away blindly, not knowing what to do next. I didn't want to leave him, but to him I was a passing stranger. As I looked up I saw a familiar figure on the other side of the road. Catherine had crossed over and was walking slowly up towards the bridge. She would have the answers.

Dodging the traffic I made it to the far side, but by then she

216

was some way ahead. She wasn't hard to spot, though; the purple mist that she wore like a cloak was as obvious to me as a flashing light on her head. I had never seen anyone so depressed. When I finally caught up with her she was about to go up the steps on to the bridge itself.

"Catherine, hang on, talk to me!"

She turned around slowly, and her green eyes settled on me like a laser. Her aura pulsed with red but she stayed silent.

I held on to the railings, getting my breath back. "You do walk fast when you want to," I said with a smile, determined to be friendly. Whatever she had done before, she had come back and helped to save Callum. "How did you get here so quickly?"

She looked down her nose at me, obviously annoyed. "What?" she snapped. "What are you talking about?"

"Look, there's no need to be like that, truly." I smiled again, but more hesitantly. "It was a great thing you did for Callum. Thank you."

"Callum!" she exploded. "Has he put you up to this?"

"No, hang on, no one has put me up to anything. I just wanted to say thank you. I wish it had made you a little happier."

"What do you mean?"

"I mean that we can help you. There's no need to be so depressed." The look she gave me was one of pure hatred, and the purple mist became alarmingly dark. I tried again. "Look, it's obvious to me how you feel. I do want to help, whatever you think. You've been given another chance and you need to learn how to be happy. Please don't think about jumping again."

"What's he been telling you?" Her voice was low, ominous. "What's he been telling you, a perfect stranger, about me? He thinks I'm suicidal, does he? Do you? I'll make you regret interfering!"

She was suddenly yelling and I stepped back in alarm.

I looked around wildly. Callum was walking towards us having finished his call and I saw him suddenly break into a run. I turned back towards Catherine. She had run halfway up the steps and was in the process of climbing over the railings. I was paralysed with fear. The water below her was churning and angry. As I tried to move I found myself shoved to one side as Callum raced past but he was too late. Catherine had made it over the railings and had leapt into the Thames.

"Get help, now!" he yelled at me as he ripped off his jacket and vaulted over the railings. I ran to the side and could see him fighting the currents, trying to see where she had gone. She had disappeared completely and he dived again and again to try and find her. The tide had turned and the currents were whipping back under the bridge. His head came up again after the longest time and I could see him being swept along towards a torrent of water that was pouring out of a gulley in the river wall. Suddenly everything seemed to go into slow motion: Callum's head slipped under the surface again but I saw his hand reach a ladder at the side of the gushing outflow. The long fingers had a good grip on the rusty ironwork and I could see the tendons straining in his wrist. And then in the blink of an eye, his hand was gone.

I realised I was screaming, the sound echoing off the underside of Blackfriars Bridge, screaming at the water that was the River Fleet. I fell to my knees as people ran to help, summoning the lifeboat, but I knew it was pointless; they couldn't save them and there would be no bodies to find. I knew now that Catherine had been right. It *was* all my fault. I had made her jump so, thanks to me, Callum and Catherine were worse than dead. They were Dirges.

Consequences

I was still kneeling on the pavement, my hands gripping the bars of the railings, when someone in the crowd stepped forward to try and comfort me. Their hands were firm on my shoulders. "It's OK, lassie, the lifeboat's nearly here. Try and quieten down a touch." As he spoke I became conscious of a heart-rending keening noise and realised that it was me. I couldn't stop though; I didn't deserve to stop. It was no wonder Catherine hated me so badly: if she had got that memory back, if she replayed that little scene in her head time and time again she would have to come to the conclusion that I was to blame. And I *was* to blame.

Strong fingers prised mine from the railings and I felt myself being lifted up, taken away from the water's edge. I could see the lifeboat sweeping the area under the bridge, puzzled looks on the faces of the crew. I fought to continue watching, even though I knew it was hopeless, but the man who had picked me up just held me tighter.

"Put me down!" I finally gasped. "Please, I need to go, to help…"

"Shhh. The experts are here now; they'll find them. They just might get washed a bit downstream that's all. Plenty of people are fished out of the water after an hour or more and are perfectly OK. The water's not that cold at this time of the year, not really. I'm sure they'll be fine."

I felt numb, horrified. Finally I stopped struggling, allowing myself to be helped to one of the bench seats. I kept replaying the hideous scene again and again, watching Callum jump into the water, seeing his hand suddenly vanish from the ladder as the hideous world of the Dirges claimed them both. How could it be? How could drowning in the Fleet have taken him back in time? He wasn't old after all, not like Lucas had been. He was still a teenager. The world of the Dirges hadn't held off the ageing process for him; it had done something quite different.

The guy still had a firm hand on my shoulder, stopping me from moving as the pointless sweep of the water continued. I could hear the powerful engines of a second lifeboat coming to join the search, and wondered how long they would look for; when they would give up and assume the worst. Were they the ones who had watched Lucas burn? They would definitely be the ones plucking the bodies out of the water when I finally released them all. Yet again my eyes welled up thinking how close I had got to saving them all: if only Catherine had been persuaded to help us, the lifeboat crews would have been rescuing everyone, setting them free regardless of how long they had been captured in their torment. Would those who had been Dirges longest die first? I wondered.

That thought continued to echo around my head as I watched the police helicopter sweep downstream. A full, fruitless rescue effort was in process, and looked like it was going to carry on for some time. As the helicopter returned up the southern bank my subconscious suddenly broke through: Callum had actually only been a Dirge for a matter of minutes so far. Maybe he wouldn't be consumed by fire, and given that there was already a search-and-rescue operation going on, if they all appeared in the river immediately, there would be a much better chance of saving him. My head snapped round towards the man who had lifted me away from the edge, and I grabbed him by the arm.

"Please, what's going on? Why do they need a helicopter?" I asked in a voice that came out scratchy and rasping, tugging his sleeve again. "Could you find out for me?"

"You just carry on sitting there for a moment," he said kindly, "and I'll go and get an update for you." The minute his back was turned I leapt up from the chair and sprinted across the road. Ignoring all the shouts I ran as fast as I could up away from the river and towards St Paul's, reaching for my phone as I went.

Veronica picked up on the first ring. "Alex! Where have you got to? Are you still coming into London today?"

"There's no time to talk," I gasped. "I need you at the cathedral – now. Where are you?"

"Well, I'm here, but the place is shut. Whatever's happened?"

"Shut!" I exploded. "It can't be shut! It's a church."

"They are getting ready for an event tomorrow, setting out the chairs in the nave. It's nearly done now though. Why do you need to be here?"

"I need to do it now," I gasped as I negotiated my way around a crowd of people waiting for the lights to change. "I need to release all the Dirges NOW!"

"Now?" Veronica's voice was an uncharacteristic squeak. "Why the sudden rush?"

"I'll explain everything when I see you, but you need to help me. Callum is getting them all together at the moment, but they only think I want to talk to them. They don't know I have to kill them all now."

I could sense Veronica trying to calm herself – and me –

down. "OK, Alex, whatever you say. Come to the cathedral. The café entrance will be the best. Wait there and I'll come and let you in."

"OK, five minutes," I blurted out as I shut the phone off.

I carried on running, trying and failing to obliterate the picture in my head. I had spoken to Callum, a real, living, breathing human Callum. I had even touched him, and then I had been responsible for him having to jump. If I hadn't spoken with Catherine, if I hadn't said what I did, then she wouldn't have leapt into the water and none of this would have happened. They wouldn't have been Dirges and their lives would have carried on. But if I *hadn't* done that, then I wouldn't have been there either. The whole impossibility of it threatened to overwhelm me. I knew that time worked in a strange way for the Dirges, that Lucas thought he had been there for much less than fifty years, but I would never have guessed that Callum and Catherine had been dragged in from their own future.

What I was positive about, what was absolutely clear, was that I had to try and fix things. I had to make things right, and I had to do it quickly. Perhaps there was a chance, a tiny chance, that by releasing Callum immediately he would be OK, that he wouldn't explode in a hideous fireball. I had to try.

As usual in late afternoon Ludgate Circus was packed with office workers starting to make their way home. I was about to turn up towards the cathedral when I realised that I had to talk to Callum in private; I had to confess what I had done.

I didn't want to go too close to the cathedral as all the Dirges would be there. Standing on the traffic island in the middle of the road I looked around desperately, earning some strange looks from the people standing nearby. I pressed my phone to my ear. "Callum?

Can you join me for a moment? There's something we need to talk about." I was never sure how many of the others could hear what I said when I called him, so I didn't want to give too much away. The tingle in my wrist was almost immediate.

"Alex? What's the problem? I was busy getting all the others together so that you can talk to them. They're all on the steps at the moment as the cathedral is shut for some reason so you can't come in."

"We need to talk – urgently. Somewhere no one will be listening."

"Umm, OK," I could almost hear him thinking. "St Bride's Churchyard – none of us ever go there."

"Back up Fleet Street, yeah?" I started to walk.

"It'll only take a minute." He paused for a second. "Do you not want to do it after all?" I glimpsed his face in a passing window, and there was nothing but kindness and understanding there. I couldn't believe that I was going to have to tell him what I knew. I could imagine the look on his face changing from one of love to one of loathing.

"It's not that, it's something else but we need to hurry." I was running up Fleet Street, looking for the little side alley we had been down a few weeks before. I felt him nearly lose contact as I turned down the little lane, the church glistening white in front of us.

I ran up the worn steps and into the deserted churchyard, sinking down on to the nearest bench. Pulling out my little mirror I sat up tall and tried to feel strong. "Thanks. I need to talk to you on your own, somewhere quiet where we won't be overheard."

"Well, this is perfect," he said with an encouraging smile. "This churchyard always gives me the creeps and I've never seen any of the others here either. Ironically, I think it's something to do with all the dead people." He smiled again. "So what's up?"

"I have to tell you something difficult, Callum. Please believe that I love you completely and always will." I finally found the courage to look him in the eyes. His happy smile was being replaced by a slightly bewildered confusion.

"OK, I believe you. I love you too, you know that, whatever you have to do." He gently kissed the top of my head and I nearly lost my nerve. I could do what Veronica wanted and let them all go and he might never need to know my part in it all. If he died, he could die happy. And if he lived, well, he would have no memory of our love anyway, and it wouldn't matter what I said.

But I couldn't be that dishonest. He deserved to know my part in his tragedy. "I did something terrible and you'll hate me for it."

"Have a bit more faith in me!" Callum kissed me quickly. "I love you, remember?"

Would that be the last time he ever uttered those words to me? The butterflies in my stomach were making me feel sick and my palms were clammy with sweat. I tried to settle my breathing.

"Alex?" Callum's voice was getting concerned. "Are you OK? You look like you've seen a ghost."

"I did, in some ways. I found out why Catherine hates me so much. Not half an hour ago I was walking along the Embankment coming to meet you here when I saw you and Catherine on the street."

"What? What do you mean?"

"You were walking along in front of me, arguing. You were real, alive. You stopped to answer the phone and Catherine walked on. I tried to talk to you but you had no idea who I was. I . . ."

I wrongly assumed that Catherine had changed her mind about helping so went to thank her. She was standing by the steps leading up to Blackfriars Bridge." Callum looked at me sharply but still didn't say anything so I carried on. "She was so miserable, I could see that from her aura, and I had to say something. This morning she had told me she was considering jumping off a cliff, you see. I told her that she shouldn't think about hurting herself and she went mad, accusing you of telling me, a stranger, all her problems. Then she jumped. You tried to save her. You both disappeared as you were swept under the bridge and into the water from the Fleet."

He was silent for a moment, his eyes guarded. "And this was when?"

"Twenty, maybe thirty minutes ago. It's only just happened. That's why we need to do the transfer now. It might not be too late for you." His gaze remained steady and unreadable. "Really, I mean it. I reckon that there's a possibility that if we can get you back in the water immediately then perhaps it will be OK, you won't have been a Dirge long enough to count; perhaps you'll be able to live. And I'm so, so sorry. If I hadn't spoken with her, if I hadn't bumped into you at all, none of this would have happened. You would have spent your life as you should have done, and never had to suffer like this." I hung my head in shame. "Please, come with me to the cathedral. You might hate me now but if you let me I can try to fix it; I just want to make things right for you." I kept my gaze on my dirty Converse, not daring to look him in the eye any more.

When a slow finger traced a path down my cheek I flinched in surprise. I quickly glanced up at his face in my little mirror, prepared to see a look of loathing and blame on the features I loved so well. But he was smiling a sad, gentle smile. "I could never hate you, Alex, don't you know that yet? Whatever happened to bring us here, whatever strange set of random circumstances, it doesn't alter the fact that we *are* here." He paused for a second until I looked up again, his eyes melting into mine. "Or that I love you."

"Still?" I had to ask, not really believing what he was saying. "Even knowing that I'm to blame for everything?"

"I would happily die now, as we expected, knowing that I loved you, and that you loved me."

"Oh, Callum, I don't deserve you!" I rested my cheek against his as he leaned in to see me better in the mirror. "Come on then, there's no time to waste. We must hurry." I jumped up, turning towards the gate. "Let's talk to the Dirges now. If I release you immediately you might have a chance. Maybe the fire that consumed Lucas was so big because he had been there for so long. You might just get a bit hurt, just a scorch – the point is we don't know! And all the rescue teams are out searching the river now – isn't it worth a go?" I could feel the tingle come and go as he struggled to keep pace with me as I dived back on to the pavement of Fleet Street.

"I think you're deluding yourself. Once we took that fatal last lungful of Fleet water, we were doomed. There's no way back."

"Can't we try? Please? I mean, if you're going to die anyway, what have you got to lose?" I was getting more and more breathless as I ran, dodging the tourists who stopped mid-pavement to take photos of any old statue and carving.

"I was hoping for one last visit to the top of the dome, I guess. One last chance for us to be together."

My thoughts flicked instantly to the Golden Gallery, the thought of being up there with him, time we would never get to spend together again, and I was torn. Holding him tight, kissing

226

him, feeling his strong arms wrapped around me, keeping me safe... But I had to stop myself indulging in that particular fantasy; there was no time. "I would love that too, but I'd rather take the chance that you might be saved. If we get that right you can be with me forever."

"OK, we'll do it your way." There was a wistful tone to his voice though, and I felt bad for denying both of us the opportunity. But I was sure it was worth the risk.

"Why don't you get all of the Dirges up into the Whispering Gallery? If the cathedral is shut it will be easier for me to talk to them there and they will all be in a line ready for the . . . the end." My voice wavered as I realised what I was saying.

"I'll get them organised. I'll have a quick word with Olivia first though; make sure she's ready."

"Thank you," I said, feeling guilty for not giving Olivia a thought in days. "We have to make sure that she's OK."

Ludgate Hill was heaving with people so I dodged on to the road and started jogging up that, ignoring the beeps from the angry drivers. I was nearly there when I realised that the tingle had gone. Stopping by the statue in front of the cathedral I called out impatiently. "Come on, Veronica will be wondering where I've got to."

The tingle was back. "Wait, please? Just for a second?"

I lifted the mirror so that I could see his face, raising an eyebrow in a question. He was right behind, his arms wrapped around me, his eyes full of emotion.

"This may well be our last moment alone together," he said gruffly, not quite meeting my gaze. "I want you to know that I wouldn't have changed a second of the past, none of it, if that would have meant not meeting you. Whatever happens now, I can go content that we had this time together. And you'll remember me, so I'll always be with you." He nuzzled closer, his lips brushing my ear. "I love you, Alex. I love you more than life itself."

I couldn't speak, the lump in my throat was too huge. I reached up and stroked his face, feeling the gossamer lightness of it under my fingers. We stood together for a few long seconds, drinking each other in for one last time. I thought my heart would burst with love for this strange, beautiful ghost, and I knew that whatever I might feel for Max was a poor substitute. Callum was my life too. As I watched he suddenly smiled.

"I thought you were in a hurry! Come on, we need to go."

I nodded briefly and ran my hands over my face, wiping away the tears. He was right; there was no more time to waste. I had to kill him as quickly as possible.

Love

Callum ran on ahead to the cathedral to organise the Dirges and I jogged as quickly as I could up the hill. The rush hour was well under way, so the pavements were packed with people all pleased to be going home. Their yellow auras were bright even in the watery sunshine. I tried not to think about what I was going to do, I just wanted to get it done quickly. There had to be a chance that it would work, that they would find his body in the water and revive him.

As I ran past the cathedral steps on my way to the crypt entrance I glanced around using the mirror, but there was no sign of any of the Dirges. Callum must have already got them inside. Veronica was waiting at the door, her face etched with worry. "Where have you been?" she asked as she ushered me inside. "I was beginning to think that something terrible had happened."

"I'm sorry. I had to tell Callum in private what we were going to do, and that took a few minutes."

"So why the rush? What's changed your mind?"

I took her arm and started walking her down the corridor towards the café, anxious not to lose any more time. "It's a long story. Catherine has run away, refusing to help, then on the way here I bumped into her and Callum, but real and alive, and—"

"What!" she interrupted, pulling me to a halt. "How? How did that happen?"

"We're in a hurry," I reminded her, taking her arm again. "I saw them just before they drowned. Catherine jumped in the Thames because of something I said; Callum tried to save her. It's all my fault that they were Dirges in the first place, and that's why Catherine hates me."

I glanced at Veronica quickly as we worked our way through the ticket barrier; her mouth was hanging slackly open. "So I reckon that, given they have only just gone in the water, if I can return them to the water quickly, maybe he won't die. Maybe his fire will only be a little one as he's only been a Dirge such a short time; maybe he'll be rescued and survive." The more I carried on talking, the lamer the possibility seemed. As we got to the lift I turned and looked at her. "Am I wasting my time, Veronica? Please – what do you think?"

She seemed to shake herself out of a daze, and started scrabbling under her cassock for something. Pulling out a keycard she activated the button to summon the lift. "I don't know," she said annoyingly slowly. "I can see why you think that might work, but I really don't know." She shook her head. "They were alive earlier this afternoon? Truly?"

"Honestly and truly."

"So that would mean that for the last few weeks there have been two Catherines walking around. Am I right?" There was a hint of wonder about her voice.

"Umm, yes, I guess so."

Veronica stared unseeing at the lift door. "She had a doppelgänger. Catherine came back as her own doppelgänger," she whispered.

"What? What's that?"

"It's an old folk tale – if you see your doppelgänger, someone who is an exact copy of you, then it's an omen for your own death. Some cultures see them as being evil."

"Does that mean that you're one too?"

"I suppose I might have been, but it's all so long ago now that the original Veronica – the original me – is long dead."

The arrival of the lift was announced by a bell that was shockingly loud in the empty crypt. We stepped inside and she used the card again to make the buttons inside work and we started rising rapidly towards the Whispering Gallery.

Veronica became suddenly brisk. "Just so I'm clear on what we're doing: you're prepared to release all the Dirges now, in case there's a chance that you might be quick enough to save Callum?"

"If there's any chance that I can put things right, send him back to the life where he belongs, then I have to try. I owe him that much." I could still feel the echo of his gentle touch on my cheek as he had said goodbye outside. In just a few minutes I could be up at the top of the dome and holding him in my arms, as he wanted. I clenched my hands into fists and pushed the thought away. I had to take the chance, and I had to do it immediately. I turned to face Veronica in the small lift, her face looking even older than usual in the harsh neon glare of the overhead lights. "So what do I have to do? What do you want me to tell them about you?"

"I'll tell you what to say and do as we start. That will be best, and quickest." The doors slid open on to a dark and gloomy landing. "Damn it!" she exclaimed. "They've turned out all the lights already. Hold my hand and I'll guide you through."

Veronica's hand was cool and almost leathery, but her grip was surprisingly strong. I hesitated a couple of times as we moved further away from the little window in the stairwell, which let in a glimmer of light, and she promptly dragged me along again. It was easier to trust her, obeying instructions when she announced the steps. It was terribly claustrophobic, touching the walls close on either side but being able to see nothing. All I could feel was the cool stone under my feet, worn smooth by countless others over the centuries. Finally the door on to the gallery swung open and I blinked at the comparative brightness across the vastness of the dome.

Looking around I could see that the gallery was packed. Hardly a seat was free; cloaked, translucent figures filled every one, and every hood was turned towards us. "Are they all here?" whispered Veronica, suddenly and uncharacteristically nervous.

"It looks like a full house," I whispered back. "Do you want to see?"

Her old eyes were watery as she turned towards me and nodded. As much as I trusted her I couldn't help keeping tight hold of one side of the amulet as she slid her finger under the other side. I heard her gasp. "I can hardly believe it; I never thought I'd see any of them again."

As she spoke I felt the telltale tingle in my wrist and looked to my right. I could see Callum standing there, looking more like a ghost than usual. "Hello, Veronica," he said. "There's a lot of people here who'll be very surprised to see you."

"Oh . . . hello, yes. I guess so. Is Matthew here?" She sounded distracted, scanning the hooded figures that she could suddenly see as if she didn't quite believe that it was actually happening.

"He's just coming." Callum turned to face me, looking concerned. "Alex, I told them that you want to talk to them all, but not exactly what you are planning. I wanted to be sure that you were absolutely positive, that you hadn't changed your mind."

"I'm not changing my mind; I want to give you the chance

to live. Look, we don't have very long. Have you spoken to Olivia?"

"I couldn't find her earlier but I think she's here now. Let me get her while Veronica speaks with Matthew."

"OK. Get them to hurry up though, will you? It could make all the difference."

"I will, I promise." He bent down to brush my cheek with his lips as he went. The tingle in my arm was immediately replaced by the slightly different one, which I recognised as Matthew's. His shadowy figure wasn't as distinct to me as Callum's, but I could see he was smiling.

"Alex, it's good to see you. I hope that you're here because of what Callum told me that you could do. You are our only possibility of escape; you know that, don't you?"

"I do, Matthew, but before I help you there's someone here you need to talk with, someone you obviously don't recognise." I looked at Veronica. "Can you hear him OK?"

She nodded briefly and I saw Matthew turn towards her, his forehead creased in an even bigger frown than usual. "It's been a long time, Matthew."

There was a moment of stunned silence. "I recognise that voice," he said eventually. "It can't be . . . not Veronica, surely?"

She nodded again and I could see the tears in her eyes. "I'm so sorry that it's taken me so long to try and help you."

"I don't think any of us were expecting you to," he said gruffly. The Dirges closest to us had obviously heard what he was saying, and they were starting to lean in to listen. I could see the news spread in a ripple around either side of the enormous round gallery. "How long has it been? Sixty years? Seventy?"

"About forty-five, I think. It's hard to know as I spent a long time in a psychiatric hospital when I first came over, and there was no one like Alex to help me then."

"Seems much longer," he grunted.

"I did come back, as soon as I could, but I had no way of contacting you. I don't know if any of you recognised me? I've been working here in the cathedral for the last few years."

"You don't look much like you did back then," said Matthew.

"I know. It's been a tough few decades." Matthew made to interrupt her so she carried on quickly. "But not as tough as yours, I know."

"So are you here to help us now?"

"Of course, it's what I've been waiting for. When you become human again you get given the knowledge of how to save everyone, but not the means, not until someone else finds the amulet. I've been waiting to do this for decades."

"And what exactly are you going to do?" Matthew was trying hard, I could tell, but he couldn't keep the edge of suspicion from his voice.

"I'm going to help you to die, properly this time. Alex has agreed to do her bit so that all of you can go together."

"Is this true, Alex? I'm sorry if I sound a bit ungrateful, but Veronica was always bit of a loose cannon. Caused no end of trouble when she was here."

"It's true, Matthew," I said. "I've been talking to her for a while, and she genuinely wants to help. I *can* release you all individually, but it would be horrible to have to do it. Together we can help you all at once."

"Do you trust her?" His eyebrows knitted further together as he asked, and made him look even more like a thug than usual.

"I do, I think. She seems sincere."

"I know I was a bit of rebel, Matthew," interrupted Veronica.

"But I'm much older now, and appalled at what I did. Please, let me have this chance to make things right."

"And can we do it quickly?" I pleaded. I lowered my voice as I leaned in close to Matthew. "I think there is a tiny chance that I can save Callum, but only if we are quick. Please?"

His eyes twinkled as he looked away from Veronica and towards me. "Anything for you, Alex. None of us wants to be here a second longer than necessary anyway." He quickly looked over his shoulder at the hundreds of Dirges around the gallery. Most of them were on their feet and leaning towards us, desperate to understand what was going on. He glanced back at Veronica. "If this is one of your tricks, lady, you will regret this for the rest of your days, I guarantee it."

Veronica held herself as straight as she could, lifting her chin as she answered him. "I deserve that, I know, but I'm here to do what's right, whatever the cost."

Matthew nodded once, briefly, then turned back to me. "I'll tell them all what's happening. What do you need us to do?"

It was Veronica who answered. "I need everyone in a big circle, each Dirge holding the amulet of the one next to them. Alex will hold one end of the chain and start the process, and I'll be standing next to her at the other end where it will finish."

"I'll go last then," he said. "Next to you. Alex, you put Callum first in line, make sure he gets to where he needs to go." I couldn't be entirely sure but I think he winked at me.

I was scanning around the crowd of featureless black hoods as I spoke. "And Olivia must be next to him, because she'll be frightened. We'll need to help her."

"Of course," agreed Matthew. "Where is she?"

"Callum's gone to talk to her." Even on my tiptoes I couldn't pick out either of them. "Can you see them anywhere?"

He scanned around the assembled crowd before visibly relaxing. "Callum's right behind you, love, with Olivia. Right now, let me talk to everyone." At that the tingle left my arm and I gently extracted Veronica's finger from under the amulet.

"OK?" I asked her as she suddenly looked dazed and vacant.

"I can't believe that I could see them all." She looked at the amulet almost greedily.

"And they're all still there, listening to everything we both say," I reminded her gently. "Are you ready to do what you need to?"

She stood to attention, smoothing the skirt of her cassock. "I'm ready. Let me know when we're going to begin."

"I think Matthew is about to start telling the Dirges what's going to happen, and I need a quick word with Callum."

She got my drift and nodded sharply, turning away and leaning on the railings, looking down into the body of the cathedral. Far below, the mosaic floor and central gold star gleamed in the slanting sunlight, dust motes highlighting the shards that pierced the gathering gloom. It was getting darker; we had to hurry or the search of the river that was currently going on outside would end, and I had no idea how long it would take for the Dirges to drift in their pools of sparks from the cathedral to the Thames.

I turned towards the door which we had come through earlier, and saw Callum and Olivia waiting. Callum looked tense and Olivia had obviously been crying. She was making her usual strange repetitive movements with her hands. I raised my eyebrows at him and mouthed the words, "Shall I talk to her?" He nodded and whispered in her ear. She slowly raised her tear-streaked face towards me and I lifted my amulet towards hers.

"Olivia, I know this is difficult, but really, it is for the best."

Olivia sniffed loudly. "Callum's explained everything, but I don't understand why we have to do it so quickly."

"Because I believe that if we get you all in the river right now, as quickly as possible, that Callum might live. I don't know for sure, and I don't know about the rest of you, but I know it's the best chance we're going to get. If it does work, well, we'll all be together, I promise you. If it doesn't you'll be at peace at last." I struggled to keep my voice even but I felt the tears pricking my eyes. "No more gathering to do, ever."

She turned her trusting little face towards me. "Will it hurt?"

I couldn't lie to her, but neither could I risk her staying behind on her own. "Maybe just a little bit, but it will be very, very quick and you won't really notice."

I should have lied. "Noooo!" she wailed, her voice reverberating around my head. "I don't want it to hurt. I won't do it."

"The thing is," I said quickly, trying to keep her quiet and not upset the others, "we don't actually know. The key is, though, that you won't be *here*, you'll be able to escape this horrible life of continuous misery. I mean, isn't that worth it?"

She sniffed again and gave the smallest of nods. "I s'pose so."

"You know it is." I tried to give her insubstantial hand a reassuring squeeze. "Now, I want you to stand right next to Callum. He'll go first and you'll be the next one over. He'll look after you, as usual. Isn't that right, Callum?"

He smiled and nodded at Olivia, saying something that I couldn't hear. Olivia listened to him and then turned back to me. "OK, if you say so. You'd better be right though."

"I'm sure I am," I said, mentally crossing my fingers. "We'll be finished in no time."

Olivia stepped forward to take her place in the chain of Dirges that snaked around the gallery.

I couldn't wait any longer. "Callum, I have to do this now. I couldn't bear it if we were too late."

He gave me a heart-rending smile and stepped towards the line. But before he took his place he held out his arms and I fell towards him for one final time. This high up he was tantalisingly real but still without quite enough substance for me to hold him. I could see him though, and I drank in his features one last time; his unruly hair, his strong jaw and his perfect, perfect eyes. I knew that whatever happened I would remember the touch of that first kiss, the warmth and strength of his body close to mine. "I love you, Callum, more than you will ever know."

"Oh, I know, I promise you. And whatever happens I'll always love you." He tried to smile as he stepped away from my arms. "See you on the other side!"

Brushing the tears from my eyes I took my place, with Veronica on my left and Callum on my right. Beyond him was Olivia, rigid with fear. Matthew had evidently finished talking to the other Dirges and all the hoods were facing towards us. I took a deep breath: it was time. "OK, Veronica, what do we need to do?"

"Can you all hear me?" she asked in a clear, carrying tone. All the hoods nodded.

"They can hear you," I muttered, translating for her, realising that from her perspective she was talking to an empty gallery.

"Please stand up and place your hands on the railings."

As I watched, the hundreds of Dirges, most of who were already standing, stepped forward as if pulled by a string, and gripped the brass rail. I could see hundreds of pale, bony fingers all holding on tight.

"Now place your right hand on top of your neighbour's left hand so that your wrist is pressed up against their amulet." There was some quick shuffling and a few heads turned back and forth in confusion, but they seemed to get the hang of what she was asking. Callum had Olivia's fingers laced between his own to get a good contact with her amulet. Her head was bowed and I could see the tears dripping off her cheeks. Callum leaned in to kiss her on the forehead and whispered something to her. She smiled weakly and lifted her shoulder to wipe her cheek without loosening her grip.

"Is she going to be OK?" I asked as he turned back towards me. He shook his head almost imperceptibly, then leaned towards me as I raised my eyebrows in a silent question.

"She's losing it; we need to get a move on."

"OK then, Veronica," I said urgently. "What's next?"

"It's ready. You need to hold my hand and push like you did before." She raised her voice again. "We're about to start. Whatever you do, don't break the chain, OK?"

The hoods nodded, and the air of anticipation was almost unbearable. I stole one last glimpse at Callum to find him looking at me. "I love you," I whispered.

"I know," he smiled back. "Go for it!"

I grasped Veronica's hand on the railing, linking my fingers through hers. She squeezed them slightly, and whispered, "Goodbye, Alex, and thank you," before shouting across the gallery. "It's time to go, Dirges. It's finally over. Good luck on your journeys."

I turned towards Callum, my heart pounding in my chest and my breath shallow and erratic. Cold fingers of fear walked up my back. I shut my eyes briefly, then, before I could change my mind, I started. Remembering how it felt attacking Lucas was easy, and I let that feeling flow through me, pushing it harder and harder. The power was like a living thing, much, much stronger in the cathedral than it had been on the little square with Rob, and it leapt from my wrist the second I had the thought. My amulet glowed fiercely and I watched Callum to see the sparks engulf him, but nothing happened. My amulet was pulsing though, and I saw Callum's eyes open wide with shock at something on the other side of me. I whipped around. My other hand and Veronica's were a ball of sparks and as I watched the light erupted out of Veronica's left hand, the one holding Matthew. His face was a picture of wonder as the wave of glittering gold swept up his arm.

"It's going the wrong way!" I gasped to Veronica, but she didn't respond. Her eyes were vacant, glassy, and she was swaying slightly.

"Matthew – good luck!" I called over to him as the golden sparks raced up his arm and across his chest, then streaked down his legs. As it made its way down his arm towards the next Dirge in line his face and head were suddenly just a cage of lights, as if he had disappeared from within. The sparks started to fall as a glimmering rain down on to the floor where his feet had been. The glittering wave moved on. A Dirge I had never spoken with and would now never know looked at me in gratitude as the sparks took hold of his body. He gave me a brief smile and mouthed the words "Thank you" before he was consumed by the light. As my arm flexed of its own accord I felt the amulet getting warm, then in an echo in my head I heard the Dirge cry out as he disappeared.

The wave moved on relentlessly.

One by one the Dirges to my left were consumed, and as each one imploded in the network of lights I heard their final cries in my head. I couldn't believe that I wasn't hurting them, that I wasn't inflicting huge pain and suffering, but they stayed in line.

Veronica was now attached to a thin line of lights that snaked round the railing. She seemed incapable of speech. Next to her, in the space where Matthew had been, the puddle of glistening light moved as if it were some strange alien creature, and finding the edge of the balcony it started to drip over. One by one the puddles started to do the same, and the glittering sparks fell to the cathedral floor below. The late afternoon sunshine was being replaced by their soft glow, which cast a hauntingly beautiful light on the old stonework.

I carried on willing the amulet to do its work, to keep going until the wave reached all the way back to me, but it seemed so slow. It was only about a quarter of the way around the gallery and I was conscious that my wrist was becoming extremely warm. I dragged my eyes away from the progress of the sparks to look at the amulet. There was a glow deep within it that swirled and writhed just under the surface, and I realised it was the same movement that I had seen all those weeks ago in the pub when I had just dug it out of the mud. Then it had been calling Callum; now it was taking the Dirges home.

As I watched, the surface of the amulet suddenly juddered and a small crack appeared on one edge. The fear, which I had been getting under control, suddenly leapt up and claimed me again. If the amulet broke during the process, if it shattered now, everything would stop and no more of the Dirges would be rescued. It would leave Callum and Olivia behind, and I would have no way of talking with them. I would have failed completely.

I looked at Callum quickly to see if he had noticed the damage, but even though his amulet was in the same space as mine, his attention was elsewhere. He was watching Olivia.

I leaned slightly forward to get a better view of her. Her

241

hood had fallen back and her face was rigid with fear. Watching the creeping progress of the glittering wave was freaking her out, and as each Dirge cried out, she flinched. Callum's hand was tight on hers, stopping her from shaking, but the Dirge on the other side hadn't got such a good grip. Although I couldn't hear her I could see her thrashing about, shaking her head.

"Olivia, please. It'll be fine." Callum was trying to calm her down. "We'll be together, you and me. I'll keep on looking after you, I promise. Try and take a deep breath and wait for your turn. It won't be long now."

The sparks had progressed to nearly the halfway point; still far too slowly for my liking. I tried to gently increase the pressure on the amulet, but the fire in it was becoming too hot. "Make sure she stays in line, Callum, please!" I hissed under my breath.

"I'm doing my best," he mouthed back.

Half the gallery was now a curtain of sparks, falling like never-ending rain. The effect was stunning but I was too worried to appreciate the beauty of it. The crack in the amulet was fractionally bigger, and I was trying to measure its progress against that of the wave. Which was going to end first?

I was so caught up in the drama of the process that it took me a few moments to register that someone was calling me.

"What *are* you doing up there? You look remarkably silly!"

I leaned forward and peered over the railing, not quite believing what I heard. A familiar face was peering up at me from the middle of the star on the floor.

"Catherine? *Catherine!* You came after all!"

"Oh, did you start without me? That's a shame. How far have you got? Are they all dead?"

"There's still time. Come up here quickly and take Veronica's place. We're only about halfway; you can still help!" I couldn't believe that she was actually in the cathedral, that she had turned up after everything she said. If only I hadn't insisted on starting the process so quickly I might have been able to save them all. But it was too late now; I couldn't slow it down. All I could do was get her up to the gallery as quickly as possible. "Come on, Catherine, please. You know where the stairs are."

"It's an awfully long way up there though. It'll take me ages."

"You can use the lift. Let me throw down Veronica's pass."

Veronica was still standing in a trance-like state. I moved my right hand next to hers, forcing Callum to stretch, and, making sure I didn't lose contact with her, slowly moved my free hand to the pocket of her cassock. Grabbing the keycard I flicked it over the side before clasping Veronica's hand again. I leaned over the edge and watched Catherine retrieve the small piece of plastic from the floor. "Hurry, Catherine, please!"

From wanting the wave to speed up I was now desperate to slow it down, to make sure that she arrived before it was too late for all of them, before they all died.

"Did you say Catherine's down there?" whispered Callum incredulously. "What the hell does she want? Has she come to crow?"

"I think she's come to help. Maybe her conscience got the better of her."

Callum's answering snort told me everything I needed to know about his opinion of his sister.

I strained my ears, trying to listen for the sounds of the lift arriving, but the walls were too thick. Any second, though, she would walk through the little wooden door. Any second. . .

I was so focused on waiting for Catherine that the

commotion beside me took a few seconds to register. Olivia was trying to break free from the line. The sparks were well past halfway round and the tension had become unbearable. But she didn't realise that with Catherine in the line she was guaranteed a very different outcome. I could see her sobbing, head thrashing back and forth, her shoulders heaving. And suddenly she was free. The Dirge on her far side was no longer able to hold her and she pulled hard against Callum, catching him off guard. He looked around in a panic as she disappeared. The shimmering line of sparks suddenly faltered as the line broke, so Callum quickly grabbed the hand of the Dirge on the other side, pulling her towards me. I could hear him shouting.

"Quick, Jessie, shuffle round and grab Alex's hand. You'll be fine, I have to go and get Olivia."

Before I could object he had put the other Dirge's hand in mine. It felt horribly insubstantial after Callum's. "Don't worry, I'll get her back, and you can always do the two of us afterwards."

"No, don't go, I don't think. . ." But it was too late; he had shot through the wall after Olivia. I stole another glance at the amulet, which was almost unbearably hot against my skin. The crack was continuing to creep across its surface. I had no idea where they had gone and no way of chasing them, even if I could have got out of the line. "Callum!" I hollered at the top of my voice, causing the remaining Dirges to momentarily stop watching the progress of the wave and peer round at me. They were soon drawn back to it though; that miraculous force, which was going to set them free.

The voice behind me made me jump.

"Oh dear, have you lost him? Such inconvenient timing!" I whipped round as far as I could without letting go of either the

Dirge or Veronica. Catherine was standing behind me, leaning casually on the door frame. "Thanks for the card. Much easier than having to take that very dull walk up the stairs." She flicked it carelessly into the void in front of us and it skittered down to the floor. I opened my mouth to object when she laughed. "Well, *she's* not going to need it again, is she?" Catherine pointed at Veronica, who had been entirely unresponsive since the process started.

"What . . . what do you mean?"

"Didn't she tell you? No wonder you've been so enthusiastic about this whole circus."

"Didn't tell me what?"

"This is a one-way trip for her, sweetie."

"No!" I cried. "That can't be true."

"Get real. You have to sacrifice yourself. It's the only way to get the power that the amulet needs. It's why I really wasn't keen to volunteer. And that's not all. It takes two, you know. She didn't tell you that, did she?"

"What? I don't understand. Do you mean. . ." But as I thought about the conversations I had had with Veronica, I knew with a chilling certainty that Catherine was right. It all suddenly made sense: Veronica had to die and so did I. The amulet was demanding its final sacrifice.

Veronica knew that and was prepared to give up everything, but was I? Just how much did I love Callum? Was it enough? Could I let him live and die myself? My blood ran cold and for a moment I hesitated. As I did so the light circling the gallery suddenly dimmed. I had to decide, and decide quickly.

My mind raced through the last few months, reliving the moment when I first saw Callum, falling in love with him and thinking he was lost to me forever when the amulet was smashed.

And overlying all those memories was the one that Callum had given to me as a gift, of the moment when he realised that I loved him too, and my decision was made. I knew how much he loved me: he had sacrificed everything to keep me safe and now it was my turn to do the same for him. I could save Callum's life at the price of my own, and it was right that I should. Everything else was irrelevant. As I had that thought the gallery suddenly brightened, and the wave continued its all-consuming path. But, I realised, there was no point in keeping it going unless Callum was actually saved, and right now he was nowhere to be seen. I looked around wildly but there was no sign.

"That doesn't look too healthy either," Catherine said, stepping forward and peering at the amulet. "'I'm not sure it's going to last the course. How far have you got?" She waved her arm around. I had momentarily forgotten that she couldn't see the spectacle that was unfolding in front of me. The shining gold curtain was nearly three-quarters of the way around the gallery, the number of Dirges reducing every moment.

"There's only about a quarter of them left to go," I gasped. "Please, now you're here, get in the line and let's help the last of them. Some of them could still live!" I turned away quickly. "CALLUM!" I bellowed again into the empty space, the noise reverberating off the far wall.

"Is he still not back? Dear dear, that is going to make life difficult."

"Catherine, please, if you're going to get into the line, now would be a really good time to do it!"

She gave me one of her more enigmatic smiles. "Ah, I'm not disappointed. Optimistic to the last, eh, Alex?"

"What? What are you talking about?" The pain in my wrist

was becoming harder to ignore, but I didn't want her to know that.

"My reasons for being here are surprisingly similar to yours," she said, stepping towards the railing on the other side of Veronica, out of my reach.

"What do you mean?" My voice rose in horror as she nimbly lifted herself up so that she was sitting on the railing, balanced precariously over the vast drop. "What are you doing?"

"I'm not living like this, and I can't think of a more poetic place to die, can you? Especially when I could have done you such a lot of good. You lose, Alex. You lose!" She gave me one last smile and suddenly leaned back, falling into the void below.

Death

Everything became a blur. I tried to move, to react, but Veronica's grip was suddenly vice-like. Her other hand had shot out towards Catherine at the same time as Callum and Olivia had run back on to the balcony. I couldn't be sure what was going on. Veronica had grabbed one of Catherine's feet as she tumbled backwards over the balcony, and was holding her there, with her knee hooked over the railing. Catherine was hanging head down over the two-hundred-foot drop, cursing wildly. "Let me go, you stupid old woman; *let me go!*" She punctuated each word with a kick of her free leg, but she couldn't get the angle right. Veronica showed no emotion, just gripped her tighter. But Catherine was working out what she needed to do. She grabbed hold of the metalwork of the railing and started to haul herself round. Any moment she was going to be able to kick Veronica in the face, and I didn't think she'd be able to ignore that.

My wrist was now alive with pain. I could smell the singeing of my skin beneath the red-hot amulet, but I couldn't let go. The wave was nearly round to me; the circle of sparks falling like a curtain was nearly complete.

I could see Callum grappling with Olivia behind Veronica. "Please!" I shouted as loudly as I could manage. "Get into the line. I'm not sure how much longer the amulet is going to last!"

Callum's head snapped up and he looked at me in horror.

But the second he was distracted Olivia made another break for it. This time she didn't go for the door; she went for Catherine. As Catherine pulled her foot back to take the final kick at Veronica, Olivia fell upon her. Callum also leapt forward just as the wave of sparks started to consume Jessie, the Dirge on my right.

"Now!" I screamed. "Now, or it'll be too late!"

Whatever Olivia was doing to Catherine was working: she suddenly went limp. But that made her heavy, and Veronica began to sway under the strain. She still hadn't acknowledged what was going on, but she was definitely weakening. Catherine began to slip through her hand. The other was still pinning me in place. The Dirge next to me imploded under the net of sparks and joined the puddle on the floor. As she disappeared the sparks leapt up my hand, towards the amulet. Callum was still fighting Olivia, trying to get her back to the balcony. As the sparks began to consume me I slid my hand along the railing and touched Veronica's rigid fingers. The sparks leapt to her too.

"Callum, I'm sorry, I tried. I love you." I wanted to say it in a calm and collected way, but panic was overtaking me and it came out in a screech. He looked towards me again, his face a picture of dismay as he took in the rising tide of sparks that were racing up my arms. There was one last chance, one final opportunity to free Callum and Olivia. I pushed with my mind as hard as I could, directing the wave of energy from the amulet towards them. It leapt like an animal from me, but the amulet made a hideous groaning noise and the pain shot up my arm like a knife. The sparks no longer rolled as if they were a wave; they shot like lightning through me to Veronica and on to Olivia and Catherine, who were still locked together, and finally Callum. Almost in one movement the sparks consumed them all and I was left with an image of

Callum's face, the face I loved, writhing in agony as the sparks became an incandescent wall. The shape that had been Veronica fell backwards, and the sparkling figure of Catherine plummeted towards the floor far below, trailing Olivia in her wake. Callum seemed to stretch out towards me before he too was nothing but light. As he disappeared his cloak fell to the ground with a noisy whump in the suddenly silent church.

"Callum! No! Please don't go!" I screamed into the soft light being cast by the endless sparks. My hands were still aflame, my wrist in agony. I tried to take a step towards where he had been, to find his sparks, but as I moved my legs collapsed beneath me. As I fell I reached forward as far as I could, catching some of his pool of light in my hand. For a second I held it as it rolled around in my palm as if it were mercury. All around me the glittering sparks fell silently into the empty cathedral, the circle finally complete. It was as if someone had hung thousands of strings of fairy lights, each twinkling and glittering as they twisted in slow motion to the floor below. It was shockingly silent, and the gentle falling of the lights was the only movement to be seen. Suddenly the brightness was overwhelming but I didn't want to let go of the last trace of Callum; I wanted some small part of him to stay with me while I died but the light in my hand was trying to get me, to drag me down. However hard I tried I couldn't contain it; it slipped through my fingers and joined the shimmering puddle on the floor. As the last drip fell everything suddenly pulsed and a wave of energy shot around the gallery. The amulet made a hideous noise, as if metal was being torn, and the beautiful stone was ripped in two. For the briefest second the glittering sparks turned blue and green before everything burned too brightly to watch. I didn't see, only felt, the sudden explosion. Everything went from pure light to pitch-black in an instant and I realised I was howling with pain as a very different wave engulfed me.

I woke on the darkened, deserted balcony with no idea of how much time had passed. No evidence of the glittering tide of sparks remained, no Dirges, no cloaks. The pain in my arm was excruciating and I barely dared to look. I might have been alive but the amulet was gone, leaving a hideous burn around my wrist, and I knew that without it I wouldn't be able to see any of the Dirges, even if there were some left behind.

I gingerly tested my legs and, apart from the pain in my wrist, I seemed unhurt. Taking a deep breath I hauled myself upright using my left arm and peered over the edge of the balcony. I distinctly remembered Catherine falling into the void but there was no sign of her: no broken body lying on the mosaic floor. I looked around quickly. There was no sign of Veronica either. Perhaps she had already recovered and gone downstairs? It didn't seem likely though. There would be no point in moving the body; there were going to be questions and inquests and more questions, all of which would be far, far worse if we moved her.

Weak evening sunshine was still piercing the gloom, and the dust motes swam lazily in the air. It looked as if nothing at all had happened. I felt like falling back on the seat and weeping with the injustice of it all. I couldn't believe that Catherine had chosen to die without helping the others to live. The ultimate act of selfishness. Tears pricked my eyes again as the picture of Callum's final moments sprang into my mind. I knew it was a memory that was seared on to my brain and it would never, ever leave me.

I sat for a few moments before I realised that I had to go: I had to get down to the river to see how much of my plan had worked, although I knew in the deepest recesses of my heart that I was deluding myself, that he was gone. I had watched him die in agony. But there was nothing to wait for in the cathedral, and the least I could do was help to get them out of the water and send them on their way.

I worked my way down the long spiral staircase to the cathedral floor, where it was eerily quiet. I couldn't see any sign of Catherine's fall: no overturned chairs, no blood, nothing. Staying in the shadows I slipped across to the stairs to the crypt. Down there it was really dark, but I had a good idea of the layout and was soon able to make my way over to the far side and the entrance by the café where Veronica had let me in. It was shut but unlocked, and I guessed that was how Catherine had been able to make her unexpected appearance. I slid through it with a lump in my throat, knowing that I would never be coming back to visit the Dirges.

Outside, the early evening light reflected pinkly on the old stonework. The commuter crowds were thinning out and the bars were filling up. It was a lovely summer's evening. I walked down towards Blackfriars Bridge without thinking, just putting one foot in front of the other. No one took the slightest bit of notice of me and I suddenly stopped dead as I had a hideous thought. What if I wasn't alive but transported into some other amulet-induced nightmare existence? Was that my punishment for releasing them all – to be the only Dirge left? I could feel the panic rising and I started to run blindly, tears obscuring my view.

"Hey, look where you're going, will you?" admonished a man in a grey suit as I ran straight into him.

"I'm sorry," I said, holding on to his arm for a moment. He took one look at my tear-streaked face and backed away.

"Just be a bit more careful, yeah?"

I nodded as I turned away, relieved that, whatever else had happened, I was still in the real world. Catherine had lied about that too. I carried on towards the river, but as I got closer I was conscious of something going on, of an edge to the air. I rounded the last corner and finally got a view of the water: the Embankment was heaving with people. Traffic had stopped and blue lights were flashing everywhere. People were lining the bank, hanging on to the railings, shouting and pointing. I had to see, and found myself walking more and more quickly before breaking into a run.

I ran up on to Blackfriars Bridge, where I would have the best view. The lifeboats were scudding about, joined by a flotilla of other small boats. They were hauling bundles of rags up out of the water and racing to the shore before coming back for more. There were plenty of bodies to keep them busy. The police helicopter had been joined by a news helicopter, which was swooping as low as possible to get the best pictures of this inexplicable event. The lifeboats were taking the bodies to the nearest available landing place, the Millennium Pier riverboat landing stage. I could see them lining up on the deck and suddenly realised that I had to go and see. I had to say goodbye to the Dirges in person and I wasn't going to get a better chance.

Pushing people aside as I ran down the steps I ran along the Embankment until I got to the walkway down to the pier. There was only one small entrance, which was nominally being guarded by a woman in uniform, and in the disorder and panic it wasn't difficult to slip past her. Heart pounding, I quickly made my way down to the pontoon. It was complete chaos and no one tried to stop me as I made my way to where they were laying out the dead. There were far more bodies than blankets and as I started to walk up the line I could see their faces, at peace at last.

I walked blankly from one to the next, wincing as I looked at each face in case it was someone I knew, and it was only a matter of time before the familiar features stopped me in my tracks. Matthew was finally serene, his tired face uncreased and uncaring, his responsibilities over. I quickly looked around but no one was paying any attention to me at all. Kneeling down beside him I found his hand: where his amulet had been there was a charred ring of skin with strange black lines that disappeared up his arm under his shirtsleeve. "It's good to finally see you, Matthew," I whispered, lifting his hand. "Thank you for all your help. I know Callum appreciated it." I realised as I said it that I was already thinking of Callum as dead, and a knife speared my heart. "I hope that you are at rest now, wherever you are. Look after Callum and Olivia for me, won't you?" The last words became an indistinct sob and the tears in my eyes made it impossible to focus. I lay his hand gently across his chest and stood up. It didn't seem right to leave without standing for a moment, but then I had to move on, I had to keep searching until I was thrown out.

The long line of bodies continued, with more being added all the time. Not one of them had made it over alive, it seemed, and a new, pure hatred for Catherine started building in me. Every one of these Dirges could have had another life, some payback for all the decades of pain and misery they had endured. But thanks to her they were all lying motionless, body after body.

I continued picking my way down the landing stage, the fury taking over from the sorrow when I saw another familiar shape. "Olivia!" I wailed, dropping to my knees by her head. "Olivia, I'm so, so sorry. I know that you didn't want this. It's so unfair, so mean. . ." This time it was harder to restrain myself and the tears flowed thickly as I finally held her delicate hand in mine. The burn looked particularly vicious on her pale wrist, and the same strange black lines laced up her arm. Although still wet, her chestnut hair framed her face in perfect waves, and she looked for all the world as if she were asleep, as if she might suddenly open those pretty eyes and laugh at something Beesley was doing. I reached up to stroke a stray strand away from her forehead and realised that she was unexpectedly warm. Puzzled, I cupped her cheek with my hand; that too was warm, not the cold, clammy skin I was expecting.

"Olivia!" I called excitedly. "Are you OK? Please talk to me!" I gently stroked her face, hoping that there would be some movement. She couldn't be dead, not at that temperature. My mind raced: maybe something I had done at the end gave her and Callum a different outcome? Maybe that final push had saved, not killed them. I tried to remember how to do CPR but I couldn't figure out how to start. Instead I shook her gently, calling her name. But there was no response, no other sign of life.

I looked around wildly. I wanted to carry on searching for Callum but I couldn't leave her, not when she clearly needed medical attention. I had to find someone who could help. I leaned over and gently kissed her forehead. "I'll be back in a second, Olivia. I'm just going to get some help. Hang in there." Her skin was so hot as to be feverish. I glimpsed a woman with a stethoscope further down the pier and, folding Olivia's arm carefully over her chest so I could find her quickly in the long line of bodies, leapt to my feet.

The medic was young and teetering on the brink of being overwhelmed. Her fear made her officious. "What do you want? Are you a doctor? If not, you have to leave." She brushed her lank hair away from her face as her eyes skittered from body to body.

"Please, I need your help. I think a girl down here might still be alive."

"Alive! Show me now!"

I ran back down the row towards Olivia, trying to glance at as many of the others to see if I could spot Callum. There was no sign of him. Olivia was exactly as I had left her and I quickly pointed her out to the doctor. "It's her. She feels really warm, as if she has a fever or something."

The doctor shot me a look of fear, which I didn't understand, at the same time quickly touching Olivia's face. She then turned to the next Dirge and felt her face too, and the one on the other side. She jumped to her feet and grabbed me by the arm. "You have to leave. Go now, immediately." She pushed me away.

"But what about the girl? She's not dead! Please, I want to help her!" But I was talking to her back. She was running down the platform, slowing every couple of metres to touch another of the Dirges. I quickly felt the foreheads of the Dirges next to Olivia: they were equally warm. In fact, they were almost burning to my touch. Suddenly there was a shout. Further down the line there was a flurry of activity, people jumping backwards and pointing. It was hard to see in the gloom of the dusk, but it looked as if a curl of smoke was rising from one of the bodies.

The shouting got louder and I whipped around: one of the Dirges near to me also had a strange question mark of smoke rising over him. I didn't understand, how could this be happening? They were all soaking wet from the river – how could two of them be burning? As it hit me I froze for a second before leaping into action, racing down the row, desperate to check to see if I could find Callum before it was too late. But I had missed my chance. Like Lucas, the Dirges were about to spontaneously combust. The little pillars of smoke were appearing everywhere, and then the first one burst into flames. The fire burned intensely, with hints of blue and gold in the flame, and almost as quickly it was gone, leaving nothing but a charred pile of rags. But then another started, and another, each burning with slightly different hues, but each having those same flashes of gold. I tried to get down the line, desperate to see Callum, but strong arms hauled me away and I was conscious of a loud bell ringing.

"Emergency evacuation procedure!" bellowed the man holding my arms. "Everyone off the landing stage *NOW!*" He propelled me towards the exit, where I was dragged along by the tide of people leaving, past more bodies that had been lined up on the walkway. Glancing over my shoulder I could see the individual fires burning on the quayside, all evidence of who they were being reduced to dust. The bodies we were passing were also starting to give off the telltale smoke, spurring the crowd into a small stampede. I only just managed to keep to my feet as the press of bodies carried me back up on to the Embankment.

Once I was up on the pavement again I ran back towards Blackfriars Bridge, determined to get a better view. On the water it was utter mayhem as bodies in the process of being rescued suddenly burst into flames. Some of the boat crews were frantically trying to extinguish the fires, while others were just dropping the Dirges back into the river where they continued to burn. I could see dozens of little pyres floating along in the water as the Dirges finally made it home.

As I looked around I knew my plan had failed: there was no way Callum was going to be rescued from that level of carnage. He had even less chance than if he had ended up in the water on his own. I couldn't believe that I had forgotten that Lucas's body had burned. If I had remembered earlier I could maybe have done something different, but it was too late.

I leaned on the stone wall and watched through dry eyes; I had cried so much nothing else was left; no emotion, no pain. I was numb, not knowing what to do next. I fixed my eyes on a random body in the water, one that was in mid-blaze. The flames licked high into the dusk, flecked with blue and green and gold, colours I knew and loved; the colours of Callum's eyes.

"Goodbye, Callum," I whispered. "I'm so sorry. I hope you are somewhere peaceful now. I'll never forget you, I promise."

There was no answering tingle in my wrist, no voice like honey dripping into my head, no gossamer stroke of my cheek. Callum was gone forever. My head dropped and I realised quite how exhausted I was. I was trying to summon up the energy to move away when the woman next to me started screaming.

I looked up in alarm to find that she was backing away from me, pointing at my wrist. "You're going to go up in smoke too! Get away from us! Get away now!" It was the medic I had spoken to earlier, all trace of professional behaviour stripped away by the horror of the unfolding events. I looked down at my arm: the burn that the amulet had left was exactly the same as the one every Dirge had, but without the black lines radiating out of it.

"It's not the same," I muttered dully, but there was no one near enough to hear. Everyone in the vicinity had backed away from me, and most had their hands over their mouths in horror. "It's not the same!" I said again, louder this time. "It's just a burn, that's all." I tried to show a few people but they backed away as if I had the plague. I didn't know what to do: all I wanted was to leave, to go somewhere quiet where I could mourn, and now even that wasn't an option. The impossibility of everything overwhelmed me and for the second time in less than an hour I passed out.

Memory

I came to in the back of an ambulance. A paramedic smiled at me as I looked around. We weren't going anywhere and the back doors were wide open. I couldn't help noticing that he had a small fire extinguisher in easy reach.

"I'm not going to burst into flames, you know," I said pointedly, looking at the extinguisher. "I wasn't in the water."

"I know, love, but I'm just taking precautions." He edged the extinguisher behind him as if my not being able to see it would make all the difference. "So, how are you feeling now?"

I shrugged briefly, not wanting to get drawn into conversation. There was no point in trying to explain the grief and loss: I just didn't have the words.

"How did you get that then?" he asked in a conversational tone. He gestured to my wrist, which was now covered in a huge bandage. "It looks really similar to all the others."

I looked at him mutely, not wanting to say anything that would lead to trouble later. A completely inexplicable event was going on outside and I didn't want to be implicated in any of it; it would all be far too hard to lie my way out of.

"I . . . umm. . . It was a kettle. I spilled boiling water over my wrist when I was making a cup of coffee. No big deal."

"That's a bit of a coincidence, don't you think?"

I shrugged, unwilling to say any more. He waited a moment

before sighing and continuing.

"It's a very nasty burn, deep. You need to go to the A&E department and get them to treat it properly, otherwise it'll scar badly."

I swung my legs over the edge of the trolley and sat up. "Thanks for the advice, and thanks for patching me up. I can see that you're all busy here so I'll get to my local hospital."

"Hold hard, love," he said, putting his hand on my good arm. "If you want to wait a bit we'll take you."

"Thanks for the offer, but you must be needed here. Perhaps some of the people in the river will be alive," I added forlornly.

"I don't reckon there's much chance of that. It's a bad day, that's for sure. Every single one since we were called out was already dead," he said gloomily. "Hundreds of them. Only those first two were different."

I had been edging my way sideways along the trolley towards the door but his words made me freeze. I suddenly found that I couldn't speak. Swallowing quickly I tried again. "First two? What happened to them?"

"A couple fell off the bridge earlier and were being rescued just as the dead guys started bobbing up out of the water. I don't think they were anything to do with this." He waved his arm around to indicate the continuing mayhem on the riverbank.

"And then what?" It took all my self control not to leap up and try and wrestle the information out of him. "Where were they taken?"

"Guy's Hospital, I think."

I took a deep breath. "Do you happen to know anything about the couple? Were they male? Female? Ages? That sort of thing."

"Sorry, love, not a clue. All I know is that the lifeboat pulled them out, and as long as they didn't manage to torch the ambulance on the way, they'll be in Guy's Hospital. Why – are you missing someone?" He looked at me shrewdly.

"Oh, no. Nothing like that." I cast around quickly for something that sounded convincing and wouldn't bring the police back to my door, but failed miserably. "I . . . I just don't want to think that everyone here today died," I said, making my lip quiver. The ambulance paramedic looked at me suspiciously, but obviously decided that, whatever I was up to, I wasn't a danger to anyone.

"If you don't want to wait for a lift, Guy's is in that direction." He pointed over the bridge. "Just get that arm looked at soon, OK?"

I smiled briefly at him as I jumped out of the back of the ambulance. The scene outside was still one of chaos, with people lining the riverbank, shouting and pointing. The sun had almost gone and a deep-pink sky was lighting up all the buildings with a rosy glow. But to the east it was almost dark: the lights were on in all the buildings and the river twinkled with the reflections. All the fires had gone out but the flotilla of little boats was still sweeping up- and downstream, using spotlights to find the smoking piles of rags. I no longer wanted to watch. If Callum had been among them then he was gone, I knew that. I had to rest my hopes on him being one of the two people rescued. I could barely contain my excitement. There was no time to lose. I ran back up to Blackfriars Bridge, where the traffic was still moving, and hailed a cab heading south.

"Where to, darlin'?" asked the cabbie, straining to see past me to the scene down on the river.

"Guy's Hospital A&E department, please."

"What's going on down there then? I heard on the radio

261

about some sort of boating accident."

"I don't really know. It all seems to be a bit chaotic, whatever it is." I settled back in the seat and let him ramble on about his theory as to what had happened and how the government were to blame. Luckily it didn't take long to get to the hospital and I had enough money to cover the fare. Once I was alone I stood for a moment outside the entrance, trying to decide on a plan. My heart was racing and my palms clammy. I was also conscious that my wrist was in agony, but I didn't have time to worry about that. I stepped inside.

The A&E department was bright and surprisingly empty, and I realised that I wasn't going to be able to mingle with the crowd. The woman behind the desk looked at me sharply, taking in my dishevelled appearance and bandaged arm. "I'm sorry but we're closed to non-emergency admissions because of a major incident. The next nearest casualty departments are—"

"I don't need a doctor; I'm here to see someone." She opened her mouth to object but I carried on quickly. "Someone who was pulled out of the river earlier? I know some survivors have been brought here. I've lost my friend and I wondered if it might be him." It was no time for elaborate lies. I just wanted to see if it was Callum, to see if he was OK.

"Wait here a moment and I'll see. What's your friend's name?"

"Callum." She looked at me expectantly, hands poised over her keyboard. My stomach was a tight knot of tension. What if it was him? What if it wasn't? "I'm afraid I don't know his surname," I admitted.

She raised an eyebrow ever so slightly and tapped away for a minute. "I'm sorry," she said, looking up slowly as I practically broke my fingers gripping the edge of the counter. "If you don't have a name I can't confirm anything about the patients who came in earlier." She looked around behind me. "I'd talk to the police officers if I were you. They're pretty keen to speak with anyone who knows anything."

I whipped around, not ready to face the police yet again. As the receptionist peered round me we could both see that the room was almost deserted. "Hmm, they must have gone off to get something to eat. I'll get them paged for you."

"No! I mean, please don't worry about it. I'll just sit here and speak to them when they come back. Thanks."

She shrugged and went back to her typing. I sat on one of the cold, hard chairs and tried to think. I needed to get behind the closed doors of the treatment area, but she would see me do that. I couldn't stand waiting any longer though. After drumming my fingers for a few moments I went back to the desk. "Excuse me, where's the ladies'?"

The woman looked up briefly and then pointed through a different set of doors. I slid through quickly and found myself in another corridor. Ignoring the loos I marched along as purposefully as I could manage, turning sharply through more doors when I saw the police officers coming towards me.

I worked my way through the maze of corridors, trying to get to the other exit from A&E, the route that patients would be taken if they were being admitted. I eventually made it and could see through the glass doors to the curtained cubicles. Slipping inside, I wondered if I was finally in the same room as Callum.

It was warm and bright in the ward, with none of the expected hum of conversation. Only about a quarter of the cubicles were occupied, the others being emptied ready for the influx of casualties who were never going to come. I dodged in beside the first closed curtain, listening hard. There were no sounds from within so I gingerly drew it back far enough to sneak in.

I couldn't believe what I was seeing: the familiar dark-blonde hair framing the face I knew so well, sleeping peacefully. But it wasn't the face I loved; it was a face I would detest forever. Rage overtook me and I moved towards the bed.

"How dare you!" I hissed. "How dare you play with all those innocent lives?"

Catherine's eyes snapped open and her hands flew to her mouth. "And I don't understand why you're not lying in a mangled heap in St Paul's," I continued hotly. "That at least was what you deserved!"

There was something strangely familiar, yet out of place about the fear in her eyes as I spoke. "I'm s-s-sorry," she stuttered eventually. "But I don't know what you're talking about."

"Don't give me that! This is all your fault. All the others are out there in the river, dead. Dead! And you could have saved them. You make me sick!"

Tears suddenly sprang into her eyes, wobbling on her lower lids. "I really, really don't know what you're on about. Who are you? What am I doing here? Why are you and that other woman giving me a hard time?"

"I've had enough of your games," I said harshly, leaning over and making her recoil in fear. "I guess you and Veronica are the two who reappeared then, the ones who were human already." The crashing disappointment that was coursing through me made furious. "I can't believe I ever thought you might be helpful. You must be the most evil person on the planet!"

The tears brimmed over and streamed down Catherine's

cheeks. "But I don't know anything," she wailed. "I don't know who I am or who you are or how I ended up here. I just want someone to help me."

"Nice act," I sneered. "I'm sure you'll have the staff here eating out of your hand in no time." I stepped away from the bed, fuming and not trusting myself to stay within slapping distance. "So where's Veronica? I need to talk to someone with some sense, someone who can tell me something useful."

Catherine sat up, clenching her hands together and looking at me piteously. "I don't know anything," she whispered. "Everything is blank." She started to rock gently backwards and forwards, fidgeting with her hands, making chain links with her forefingers and thumbs, which she pulled against each other in time with the rocking. As I watched her, a strange creeping sensation worked its way down my back. I had only ever seen one person do that before, but she was dead. I'd even seen the body.

"I need to find Veronica," I muttered, tearing aside the curtain. "I need to know what's going on."

There were only three other occupied cubicles. I peeked into the first one to see an old man with an oxygen mask on. The next was a child, covered in bandages. As I stood next to the final curtain I took a deep breath. I knew it was going to be Veronica, but until I saw her there was a small, microscopic chance that it might be him. Once I pulled back that curtain, that chance was gone. I wiped my sweaty palms down my jeans, took a firm grip and pulled.

The cubicle was brightly lit, a body motionless on the raised bed. Next to it a figure in a white coat was adjusting the settings on a machine that beeped constantly. I crept closer, unable to wait any longer to know the truth. Clutching the bar at the side of the bed, I finally came to the attention of the doctor.

"Excuse me, what are you doing in here?"

But I couldn't speak. Whatever else she said was lost in a roaring in my ears as I saw the face lying there, strapped to a dozen machines and covered in tubes, a face I knew I would love until the end of time. Callum.

"I asked you what you're doing in here?" demanded the doctor again.

"I wanted to see if he was safe. Is he OK?"

"Are you family?"

"No, no, I'm a . . . a friend. Very close friend."

"I'm sorry, I can't talk to anyone but family at the moment. You'll have to wait outside." She looked at me with scorn for a moment. "Honestly, you journalists. How do you get here so quickly? We only found out who he was about half an hour ago."

"I'm not a journalist," I protested, puzzled. "I'm a friend. We've been close over the last few months."

"Well, in that case you'll understand that we need to keep on our guard. Will you please go and wait in reception?"

"Please, just tell me, is he OK?" I couldn't tear my eyes away from his face, and my fingers reached down to touch his. "Will he be all right?"

Before I could touch him the medic wheeled me around and firmly escorted me out of the cubicle. "Don't make me call security, there's a good girl. Wait outside and I'll come and find you when there's any news."

Without ceremony I was ejected through the door and into the waiting room, which was still mostly empty. Exhausted, I slumped down in one of the plastic chairs. Behind me a TV was fixed to the wall and I tried to ignore the inane chatter of the nation's favourite soap opera. I had succeeded – Callum was over with me. But was he going to make it? Had I spent too long before getting him into the water? He hadn't looked burned but he was clearly very ill. Part of me was elated but mostly I didn't feel I could celebrate until I knew for sure that he was OK.

The sound of the main evening news coming on broke through my thoughts and I swivelled round in my chair to see what they had to say about the events on the Thames. Unsurprisingly it was the headline item, and they had stacks of footage of the bodies lined up and then bursting into flames. On the TV the chaos looked even worse than when I was there, and the reports were interspersed with interviews from the police and fire brigade, all of whom were utterly clueless. In a breaking-news update, though, they interviewed the head of the lifeguards.

"So, Commander Maguire, from what you were just saying, this isn't the first time this has happened?" The interviewer was almost breathless, realising the potential of what he was about to reveal.

"No, that's right. About a month ago we were called to a shout in the exact same stretch of the river. We pulled out a young white male who we managed to revive briefly, but then sadly lost. As we were loading his body on to the ambulance it burst into flames and within minutes it had gone."

"And why wasn't this widely reported at the time?"

"We filed all our usual reports and were quite surprised when there wasn't more about it on the news."

The reporter nodded sagely. "And what was it you discovered when it was reported?"

"Well, that was very curious," continued Commander

Maguire. "The remains were sent as usual for a post-mortem, and were identified by both dental records and a tattoo that one of my team had seen before he caught fire. The man we pulled out of the river was no more than twenty-five, but the records put him at seventy-six."

"So just over fifty years older than he appeared?"

"Indeed."

"Any other similarities with the current tragedy?"

"The original victim had exactly the same injuries as all the people who appeared tonight, and burned in the same intense way. We have no idea what's going on."

I smiled to myself. As long as they had no idea then no one would come asking me questions I couldn't answer. And they wouldn't be asking Callum, either. I was starting to relax when the news moved on.

"In a bizarre twist it has been reported that the only two people to be pulled alive out of the Thames under Blackfriars Bridge have been informally identified as Catherine and Callum Bailey. They have been taken to hospital where they are suffering from minor burns, but it is not yet confirmed if they have similar injuries to the bodies in the river. Eyewitness reports from the scene suggest that Ms Bailey jumped into the Thames and her brother attempted to save her. No links have as yet been found between the Bailey family, who live in Kent, and the subsequent events on the river."

The news carried on while I sat there, agog. Callum was on the TV – I knew his name, and that he lived in Kent! I hugged the tiny snippets to me as I waited for news. In the long hours as I sat there the receptionist turned away about a dozen journalists and photographers, all desperate to see the ones in the river who didn't burn up completely. I listened to a couple who were gossiping in the chairs behind me, waiting for their chance.

"Of course, she's a psycho, you know that, right?"

"Yeah, I heard about the traffic accident. Parents killed in dodgy circumstances. She must have done it, it's a no brainer. God knows how she managed to get off the murder charges."

"Different rules for them types, ain't it?"

"You reckon both of 'em are involved?"

"Nah, just her. All the rumours say she's been weird for years. Apparently as a kid she was done for fraud."

"Did you hear the other rumour? Barry at the news desk says that she found out earlier today from the family lawyers that her parents had cut her out of their wills. She's getting nothing."

"No wonder she tried to top herself!"

"Yeah. Her parents must've seen right through her. Didn't do them any good though, eh?"

"Nah. Should've made sure she knew about the will, eh? Then they might still be alive."

The other man laughed. "They won't be making that mistake again!" He paused as he took a noisy slurp of his vending-machine drink. "So, worthwhile hanging about here, you reckon?"

"I'm going to have another crack at the receptionist but if that doesn't work I think we should get back to the river. Do you know, Mike was saying that. . ." The voices faded as they walked away.

My mind was swirling with all the sudden information about Callum and Catherine. She had obviously been a nasty piece of work for years, and that made me even more angry that she should be a survivor. Even Veronica, who had deceived me, had done it with the best of intentions. But something about

Catherine's behaviour when I saw her in the ward didn't add up, and I couldn't work out what it was. She looked like Catherine, but her mannerisms were definitely Olivia's.

I was still puzzling over it all when the doctor I had seen earlier appeared at the door. As soon as she caught my eye she beckoned me over.

"Look, you seem like you're on the level. No family have turned up yet, so why don't you sit with him for a bit? Any nonsense, though, and you're out, OK?"

"Thanks, doctor, I appreciate it. How is he?" But she'd disappeared behind another curtain. I walked down the room to the right cubicle and slipped through the gap in the curtains.

The scene that met my eyes left me breathless. Most of the machines had been disconnected and Callum was sitting up in the hospital bed, examining the bandages on his wrist. His thick, tousled hair seemed to glow in the bright light, his long, strong fingers picking at the fastening of his dressing. As he lifted his head I saw a shy smile just touching his eyes, eyes that still shone blue and green in a face that was young and carefree. I stepped forwards without thinking, a huge grin forming on my face, ready to leap on to his lap and kiss him until I was thrown out.

"Hello?" he said, and his look of polite enquiry stopped me in my tracks.

"Callum? Don't you know me?"

A puzzled frown flitted across his achingly familiar features. "I don't think so. I'm sure I would have remembered you." He smiled briefly but then his frown deepened. "Hang on; weren't you at the riverbank earlier? Were you the girl talking to Catherine?" He looked at me intently. "How do you know my name?"

Disappointment flooded over me, mingled with joy that he

was OK. My plan *had* worked but it had been as I had originally feared. He had no knowledge of being a Dirge, or of me. Everything had been put back as it was before I interfered. Everything we had shared over the last few months was lost; every look, every touch, was all gone.

Tears pricked my eyes as I started to back out of the cubicle. "Oh, it's nothing. I'm sorry for disturbing you."

"Wait a second, I'm sure it was you! What on earth did you say to my sister to make her jump?"

What could I possible say that wasn't going to sound completely mad? "I'm sorry, I thought she was someone else. I didn't mean for it to happen, believe me." There was so much to apologise for, so much pain that I had caused, but also so much joy that I was now never going to have. I risked a glance at his beautiful, distant face: a face I would never hold in my hands and kiss again. This *was* vastly better than him being dead, but it was just as painful. A huge sob erupted out of me before I could stop it and he looked at me in alarm as I swayed, lost in my grief.

"Here, sit down quickly before you fall over," he said, edging sideways on the small bed and patting the space he had made.

I did as I was told, conscious of the warmth of his body so close to mine, the smell of his skin, the light touching his hair. I couldn't stop sobbing, and howled afresh when he tentatively patted me on the back to calm me down.

"I think you need a tissue," he suggested, nodding towards the box on the treatment table beside the bed.

I tried to nod, but hiccuped instead. I blindly groped for the tissues at the same time as he reached for the box. I felt my bandaged wrist brush against the identical bandage on his arm, then froze. Our wrists were as close together as they could be in the same world. Where my amulet had been suddenly felt warm, and for a brief second the wave of power from it flooded through me again. Almost as quickly as it appeared it left, and I'm sure I saw the wrappings around his hand glisten with fleeting sparks. He froze too, his eyes widening in shock as he stared unseeing into the distance. Our wrists were locked together by some invisible force and I was powerless to move, to stop whatever it was that was happening.

After several long minutes his head dropped to his chest and he groaned. His wrist fell away from mine, clattering on to the treatment table and knocking several things to the ground. I finally remembered to breathe as I watched, not knowing what trick the amulet might be playing on us now. The waiting became too much. "Callum?" I asked gently. "Are you OK?"

He finally moved, raising his eyes to mine. I could have sworn I saw a gold fleck dancing in one, but then it was gone. My heart was pounding so hard I could barely hear myself think, and the fear made me feel quite sick. I saw him prepare to speak, those soft lips parting while he worked out what to say. I couldn't tear my eyes away from him, even though part of me wanted to run, to hide, to never know that I was still a stranger to him. But I was pinned to the spot, utterly unable to move, waiting for his words.

"Alex?" he whispered. "Is it really you?"

The relief was like a wave, washing away the fear and horror that had been circling me. I put a tentative hand towards him before pulling it back. He might not be happy about what he had just learned.

"Callum? Do you remember?"

He nodded briefly, then pressed the heels of his hands into his eyes. When he finally straightened up he looked older, more tired, and he sounded exhausted. "I remember everything; every last minute of it."

"I'm so, so sorry, all of it was my fault. And now I've made you remember everything as well." I hung my head, desperately ashamed of all the suffering I was continuing to cause.

The gentle stroking of my hair made me jump. "Don't say that, Alex. Thanks to you, all those unhappy people are now free. That was the bravest thing that anyone could have done."

I turned my tear-streaked face to his. "I just wish I had been able to persuade Catherine to help, then some of them might be alive."

"Are they all . . . gone?"

I nodded miserably. "They're all appearing in the water, dead, and then going up in flames. It's causing quite a stir outside."

"Catherine made it, didn't she?" His strong hand reached for me, curling his fingers through mine, and although my head was still reeling from the horror I was describing, my heart was soaring as I felt his warm skin against mine.

"She's over there." I nodded towards her cubicle. "But something's not quite right. What do you remember about those final moments in St Paul's? What happened?"

Callum sat back on his pillows, pulling me with him so that I was curled up on his lap, safe in his arms at last. "It was the strangest thing," he murmured into my hair. "I had just managed to chase Olivia back to the Whispering Gallery when I realised that something was wrong. Veronica was hanging on for grim death to something, and I saw it was Catherine. Then you shouted, and I knew that we had trouble, that if we didn't get into the line Olivia and I would be stuck as Dirges forever. I think she realised something at the same time, and that was when she dived for

Catherine. She started destroying Catherine's mind, desperate to make her stop. I guess she was trying to make up for the mistakes she caused before.

"I was trying to hold on to Catherine, to stop her plummeting before Olivia had a chance to get into the sparks, but of course that was hopeless. Then, as the Dirge next to you disappeared, you unleashed that huge pulse of power." There was a distinct air of respect in his tone. "I saw the bolt approach, taking out Veronica and then the girls before it got to me."

"But how come Veronica disappeared? I mean, she was a human, she should have been OK."

"Watching them, there was no difference between the way the sparks reacted to Veronica or Catherine than to the rest of us. You were the only one they had no effect on. I guess they both disappeared because they had been Dirges before, but you hadn't. And as you predicted, because it was so quick, Catherine and I managed to get back to our real bodies in time." He paused for a second, pulling me even closer to him and wrapping his long arms tightly around me. "What – what happened to Olivia?"

"I saw her body on the quayside, along with all the others—" I started.

"I suppose that figures," he answered before I could finish. "But I had hoped that she might have—"

"But I think she may have done!" It was my turn to interrupt. "Something isn't right with Catherine. She doesn't seem to remember anything, is acting like a small girl, and is doing this with her hands!" I sat up to show him what I meant, linking my fingers in a chain. "I've only ever seen Olivia do that."

"Really? How can that be?" Callum sat up, frowning in concentration, his eyes glazed as he remembered the scene. "I think," he started slowly, "I think Olivia succeeded in wiping Catherine's mind. Maybe the wave came along and pushed Olivia's personality into Catherine just before we got transported back to our bodies."

"Do you think that could happen?" I tried to keep the incredulity out of my voice.

"Olivia certainly managed to do *something* to her before they fell."

"But how come they didn't smash on to the floor?"

"The sparks consumed them both before they got there, I guess."

I replayed the scene in my mind; maybe he was right, but we would never really know. What was more important was what was going to happen next. "And what about you? What do you remember now?"

Callum held me by the shoulders and gently turned me around to face him. "I remember everything, from being a Dirge to the life before."

"All of it? Everything about who you really are?"

"Every minute, the good and the bad," he sighed. "If Catherine really has gone that would probably be for the best. She did some terrible things."

"I heard," I said softly, squeezing his hand. "Let's hope that Olivia managed to wipe her out completely."

"Olivia certainly deserves a second chance, much more than Catherine anyway," Callum agreed, holding me close again. "I can't believe that you did it, Alex. You gave me back my life." He leaned down to kiss me but I ducked, burying my face against his chest, determined to remember the smell and feel of him before I finally asked the question which I could no longer avoid.

"And I guess there's a girlfriend in that life, someone who's racing towards the hospital right now, coming to check that you're OK?"

His fingers were soft on my chin as he lifted my face towards his. He leaned in and kissed me very softly, very sweetly. "There is only one love, Alex, only one love in both my lives." And just for a second, for the very last time, I caught the flicker of a bright, happy aura before he kissed me again.

Betrayal

London, 1665

She always knew she was different, gifted somehow. Things she wanted usually came her way, things she decided tended to happen. But she said nothing to anyone about this special talent; it wasn't safe. Here in the city most of the people were sophisticated, but just outside the city walls the mob would still hang or drown anyone they determined was a witch.

So her life was good, easy. There was plenty of money in the family, no one went hungry and she always had the nicest dresses to wear. When he came into her life she decided that she wanted him. He was tall, with glorious thick hair, a perfect smile and looks that could have captured the heart of the ladies at court. Luckily he hadn't been summoned so far, and neither had she, but there was little time. At seventeen she knew that she should be betrothed soon, and it was him she wanted. He was from a good family; there would be no problem from either of their fathers. Without even trying she wove her magic round both their hearts, sealing them together.

Spring was a glorious time. They walked and rode, mostly outside the city to avoid the problems with the sickness and the poor people who would follow them about, begging for any crumb they could provide. They made their plans to marry and a date was set for Midsummer Day. Her father was away travelling to the north but would return by then. So they waited impatiently, keen to start their married life, to be together forever.

As the spring wore on the sickness in the city worsened. Most of the noblemen and women left to go to the country where the air was cleaner, but she knew she was safe, safe with her love, ready to be joined as one.

When her father returned he bought a fabulous selection of gifts for her dowry, and news that they had been granted permission to marry in the best church in the area. "St Paul's!" he exclaimed, chortling. "My daughter is to be married in St Paul's! It will be a beautiful day." He scooped her up and laughed with her, the daughter he loved so much. "I have something else for you both, something very special." Opening a small suede pouch he lifted out two identical bracelets, beautifully wrought in silver and each with a mysterious, mesmerising stone. He placed one on the wrist of his daughter, the other on that of the man who would be his son-in-law. "They come from far away," he said, dropping his voice. "And they are the only pair in the world. They symbolise love – love that will never be broken, never forgotten. Each is inscribed with the same words – *Amor memoriae* – Love of memory – so that when you wear them you will remember this love that you have for each other and never forget."

She looked at her new bracelet and was filled with joy; her marriage was set for the next week, her father was home and she was wearing the most beautiful piece of jewellery she had ever, ever seen. Everything was perfect.

It was the sickness that ruined everything: the sickness that was running rife through the poorer sections of town, where the people lived close together and wallowed in filth. Her world was far apart from that, she thought. But she was wrong.

She had seen her love that morning; they had met and walked together. He had tried to urge her to run away with him, to abandon the plans for the wedding in St Paul's, to be together that night. But she had laughed, telling him that it was too close to the date, that they must wait. He had kissed her with an unusual passion before leaving.

She was returning home after stopping at St Paul's when she saw one of her servants, a good man, running down the street. She stopped him and he looked at her with eyes wide with horror, not wanting to tell his young mistress what he had seen. But she insisted. "It – it is the plague, mistress. The mark of the plague is on their door."

"What are you talking about? Whose door?"

"The door of your intended; your man." He hung his head, not wanting to watch her world crumble. "I saw him being escorted inside myself."

She stepped back in dismay, waving at the servant to leave. "No, there must be some mistake. He is well, I know he is! He will be at the wedding."

"They sealed the door yesterday. He must have slipped out before they caught him and brought him back. No one can leave now."

"You must be wrong. I will see for myself. Give me your cloak."

The servant did as she commanded and left quickly, not wanting to disagree with her. She wrapped the cloak around herself and made her way towards his neighbourhood. He had not talked of it that morning when she had been with him, so the servant must have got his facts wrong. He must have!

She walked up Fleet Street towards his family's home, praying that her gift would not desert her; that what she wanted most would come true. But the servant hadn't lied. The door was sealed, the mark of the plague freshly inscribed on the wood. Still refusing to believe the evidence of her own eyes she slipped down a little alley to the side of the house, where she had sometimes stolen secret kisses with her love. There was a small window leading to one of the maid's rooms. Perhaps she could get the girl to open the window and talk with her. Quickly checking that no one was watching she bent down to peer inside.

There was no mistaking what she saw. The servant girl was lying in her bed, pale and exhausted, looking as if she was close to death. Someone was leaning over her, tending to her with utmost kindness, kissing her feverish brow, holding her close, declaring his love. And as she watched this tragic farewell she suddenly realised who it was who was holding the maid so tenderly. The same hands that had caressed her face not an hour earlier, the same lips that had declared their undying love to her, the same blue bracelet flashing on his wrist: the man she would marry.

She realised that she had been deceived, that his reason for wanting to run away with her was to escape from the plague. And having been refused, he had been about to escape alone when he had been caught and returned home. Back to the girl who had probably given him the sickness, locked in where they could die together.

She thought that she would die of the pain in her heart: how could this have happened? How could the man she loved with her very life have done this to her? She stumbled away from the scene at the window, running without thinking, desperate to be far away.

She ran until she got to the wharf, and stopped, gasping for breath, looking into the murky water.

A cold dread ran through her veins as she considered her limited choices. She couldn't yet tell if he had given her the plague, but by the time she was sure, she could have given it to her entire family: her beloved parents, her little sisters. That wasn't a choice. She couldn't risk anyone knowing that she might have it, as they would automatically lock up her family, so she couldn't go for help.

She looked up at the familiar façade of St Paul's, where she would not now be married, and realised that there was only one real alternative.

Ripping the bracelet off her arm she searched on the rough ground for a suitable stone, then scratched and scratched at the inscription until she had made the change she wanted. The Latin wasn't perfect, but it was enough for her. Placing the bracelet back on her wrist she stood and looked around at her familiar world, silently bidding it goodbye. Wrapping the heavy wool cloak tightly around herself she stepped off the edge of the wharf. As the cold waters of the River Fleet met over her head she made one last wish; that he should continue to suffer until someone was willing to sacrifice everything for him.

Two days later the cart carrying bodies delivered another load to the hastily dug plague pit in the grounds of St Bride's Church. With cloths over their mouths the men worked quickly, tipping in the rich and poor together, not bothering to check for any signs of life. They were all doomed anyway. As they started to cover the bodies with quicklime the sun caught the fire in the bracelet on one man's wrist for the last time before disappearing forever. The little stream rising through the festering soil swirled around him and as he took his final breath the water scorched a track through his lungs. In the dark of the pit and the murky recesses of the River Fleet the two amulets set her last wish in motion on a far grander scale than she had intended. They had their first sacrifice, the first to search incessantly for what was now inscribed on her amulet. She had removed just one letter, and added a very faint one of her own, but that was enough. *mors memoriae* it said now – death of memory, not love. That would be Arthur's punishment until someone's love was strong enough to set him and those who followed free. The waiting had begun.

Acknowledgements

Scattering Like Light was mostly written after the publication of *Small Blue Thing*, so for the first time I had the feedback of real readers to guide me. In fact, I've been overwhelmed by the support I've been shown by readers: on the website, by fan mail, and during school visits. You have all been fantastic and spurred me on to bring Alex and Callum's story to its conclusion.

I'd also like to thank Mike Evans, who bid an unfeasibly large amount to have his daughter's name in the book and to support the Authors for Japan fund (for the 2011 earthquake), Alice Jacobs for Latin advice and translation, and all the other writers I've met along the way who have been so positive and shared my (occasional) pain.

As usual the staff at the ever-expanding Nosy Crow have been magnificent, but the biggest thanks must go to my family: the newest member, Bailey (I was outvoted on Beesley), who brings new meaning to the old excuse *the dog ate my manuscript*; Ellie, who read the draft copy first and made some vital changes; Jake, who hasn't read a word but gives silent encouragement in his own recognisable way; and Pete, who is constantly supportive, constructive in his criticism, and always there for me. This final volume is dedicated to him, as without him there would have been no book, and Alex and Callum would never have left West Wittering beach.

Find out more about Alex and Callum at
www.smallbluething.com